Book Description

Owen, an introspective student of literature, finds himself dislodged from society, searching for meaning and purpose in his life. His own failed relationships mixed with his objective analyses of his generation leaves him disillusioned and seemingly lost in the flow of an utter meaningless existence. As Owen achingly desires to understand the world and humanity, he begins to dissect himself and his beliefs to make sense of the culture that produced him. Through interactions with Owen's iconoclastic best friend, Sam; the poised intellect, Lilly, who wriggles her way into Owen's solipsistic existence; and the most unorthodox and mundane of everyday life, Owen starts to deconstruct his skewed, kaleidoscopic view of the world, finding patterns and meaning in chaos. This story, through its idiosyncratic character and voice, strikes a chord that reverberates throughout the ubiquitous chambers of those hearts that aren't afraid to ask the big questions.

Author's Note

There is such an overwhelming mixture of sadness and love that fills my heart and soul. I am thankful for all these events in some capacity or another; I am certainly thankful to be finished with this novel. But is anything truly finished? I feel that perhaps I had written this novel for a multitude of reasons. Perhaps, I did write it to purge myself of all those thoughts and ideas and feelings that I had, a metaphoric snake-skin I had to shed of my former self to become the person I am today. Perhaps, I wrote it to reach out and touch the souls of people I love or people that long and deserve to feel loved but instead feel lost, longing to understand themselves and the world around them. Perhaps, which seems relevant on a lot of levels, I wrote it for my current self: a testament of my own personal strength, to remind, in the hardest times, to remain both a strong character and human being, and not to lose faith in such beautiful components of this world.

This is a novel that deliberately attempts to skew the line between reality and fiction, blending semi-memoir with imagination. This story is above all else about thought, emotion, and exploration of the self in an attempt to understand, if only a fragment, of humanity. Including influences from a vast array of literature and philosophical, psychological, and scientific ideas, such as Synchronicity, Chaos Theory, Relativity.

So. Yes. My first novel is largely about myself. Not so much as story goes, but ideas. Is that narcissistic? Maybe. But I don't think so. I would feel too arrogant to write about another individual, another character, another human being first, pretending to know them so intimately. How can we pretend we understand humanity if we do not understand ourselves? If we do not put ourselves out there? But is this me? I don't know. Neither do you. Are there similarities? Probably. Perhaps, it's more of a potential schizophrenic projection, in order to create a framework for a 'story' or a philosophy. Because philosophies are ingrained within every creation, every story ever told, every human being who has ever lived. I believe that that must be analyzed and assessed before we can move forward and pretend like we know others, before we can empathize, before we can attempt to understand the human condition.

Pittsburgh, 2012

Then Stirs the Feeling Infinite

A Novel

Joseph Ripple

"Then stirs the feeling infinite, so felt
In solitude, where we are *least* alone;
A truth which through our being then doth melt,
And purifies from self: it is a tone,
The soul and source of music, which makes known
Eternal harmony, and sheds a charm
Like to the fabled Cytherea's zone,
Binding all things with beauty; —'twould disarm
The spectre Death, had he substantial power to harm."

-Lord Byron, *Childe Harold's Pilgrimage*

"Those who have experienced love with any intensity will not be content with a philosophy that supposes their highest good to be independent of that of the person loved."

-Bertrand Russell, *The Conquest of Happiness*

X

•

It was October. Halloween night. Sam and I lay in the back of Vernon's shitty pickup truck, while Vernon drove down the winding roads, covered with autumn leaves, and Emily rode shotgun, flipping through Vern's collection of music. The two of us lay there shivering: winter had arrived early. The snow had already begun to form in the clouds, and the cold seemed to descend from some unknown source down upon the world and shroud us in its misery.

There was a thin tarp that covered our bodies in a futile attempt to warm us. I gazed up as Sam occasionally would burst into conversation, either out of boredom or in some defense mechanism to keep from freezing. The pickup sped down the s-turned back roads, hoping to reach the destination faster, and I lay there, thinking about, almost romanticizing, the images of passing trees overhead that arched across the road, analyzing their intricate but obvious patterns of foliage.

"Liz's going to have beer and booze tonight, if you want to get completely annihilated." The words came from Sam's mouth with steam, and I thought whether that was intentional, perhaps stressing the importance and philosophical statements that flowed from Sam's mouth. But then I reconsidered. I knew that he had not stumbled upon any divine truth. Instead, he just wanted to get really drunk, because sometimes life will make you want to do that.

More trees passed overhead and then all faded into darkness, and as my eyes adapted and adjusted better, I watched all the stars illuminate the sky. I saw some that burned brighter than others, and I believed that the stars weren't much different than people after all, and maybe the old astronomers were not completely ignorant and led astray by mystical thinking. The truck swerved and bumped down the road, and I stared in admiration at the stars, tracing some of them into shapes in my mind: pagan symbols, fertility creatures, lurking through the heavens. Then I looked over at Sam and said, "Maybe we will have too, just maybe."

"I was thinking about eating some shrooms before we watch *The Labyrinth*."

My sense of reality returned as I laughed outwardly at Sam and said, "I am pretty sure that either of those separately could potentially lead to a schizophrenic breakdown. Combining them makes it an unavoidable certainty."

We both began laughing, and Sam said, "Why do you always have to be so serious and philosophical? Now I have to come out of the experience sane but enlightened just to prove you wrong."

"I am just saying. That movie is completely fucked as it is...but Bowie is the man."

We continued laughing, and the truck raced into the dark: turning, speeding up, slowing down, until we eventually reached our destination.

~~~

     This was my first Halloween party in almost ten years. Sam told me that I didn't have to wear a costume, because no one else would be. "Everyone is just going to get sloppy," he said. But when I hopped out of the pickup's bed, jogged up the steps blowing hot air into my hands, and opened the door, I felt like a complete asshole when Liz swung open the door saying, "Where's your fucking costume, dickhead?"

     "Sam told me we were all here to drink. No costumes."

     "I don't know why you listen to him. He is always just stoned anyways," she said.

     "You got that right. He wants to go on some fantastic voyage tonight for the big movie premiere. Anyways, enough with that asshole. You look beautiful as always," I said.

     Liz's face lit up a little. Diamonds in the night. A face I used to know. She kissed me on the cheek and told me to come in and shut the door behind me, giving Sam the finger, while he was still standing outside talking to Vern and smoking cigarettes, Emma sitting in the truck, smiling.

     I had been in Liz's house probably a dozen times before, but for some unknown reason I would still always examine all the family portraits that lined the mantle-piece and the end-tables adjacent to both sides of the couch. I didn't look at her family in the photos. No, I didn't stare at their awkward, overtly enthusiastic fake smiles. I just stared at Liz and her big beautiful eyes, her long hair, and I would think about how her smile looked genuine. I had seen it so many times that I believed in it. But now there were a lot of newer pictures scattered about the room, and the people in them looked older and less believable.

     "Everyone is downstairs already. Naturally you and asshole were the last to show," Liz said with her beautiful smile and her musical laugh.

We passed through the kitchen and turned to go through the basement door and down the stairs. The wood-paneling began on the walls about half-way down the stairs, and then we were in the basement. The basement was mostly an entertainment room with puffy, leather couches gathered around the television. Liz's parents had recently put in a bar in the back left corner of the room, but the last time I was over it wasn't finished. Now it was, but Liz's parents were in Chicago for the weekend, and all of her friends were scattered about the room, drinking vodka and whiskey and beer, talking and laughing loudly. Everyone was dressed up. Not like children get dressed up for Halloween but like adults, I guess. Girls dressed like whores or vampires or vampire-whores. Guys dressed like pimps or business executives or zombies, built to fuck vampire-whores. Fuck, I was glad I didn't dress up.

I felt out of place immediately, so I poured myself a large glass of whiskey and downed it. Then I poured another and repeated this mechanical process. I instantly got a little bit of a buzz, and I felt better, so I opened up a can of beer and went to sit down on the couch and wait for Sam to finish his cigarette and conversation and get his ass inside with Vernon and Emma.

The whiskey was beginning to work its way slowly through my blood, and I could feel my chest and arms getting warmer and my head getting lighter, slightly lighter, but things were becoming clearer and more vivid. I thought of how many times I had been in that basement before. In all kinds of different circumstances. Tonight Liz was wearing a short black skirt, a black wife-beater shirt that she colored a white spot in the center of, and two ears on top of her head, whiskers drawn on her cheeks: she was a black cat. Cunning, but fucking cute. I remembered being in that basement before, Liz sitting on my lap, my tongue in her mouth, and our bodies close to one another's. Back then I felt like a fool, because I would get turned on and try to hide it, but if it were now I would let it be obvious, and I would take off her shirt, continuing to kiss her.

But that seemed like so long ago. A faded photograph in my mind from the distant past. Now even the paint was a different shade. It's funny how things change with time.

I watched Liz pour herself a mixed drink of something over at the bar, say something to one of the guys standing there waiting to pour a drink, then she made eye contact with me and began to walk in my direction smiling.

"Hey, good looking, how's everything going?" she said, as she sat down on the couch next to me.

"Oh it's going," I said, unable to help myself from smiling, which was mostly a typical reaction from the two glasses of whiskey I had just swallowed.

"So, what's new in Liz's world?" I said, as I put my arm around her but kept my eyes focused and darting across the room at all the different people I didn't know. It's interesting how rapidly and drastically peoples' lives change. I hadn't really hung out with Liz since a couple years before she graduated the year before me, and I hadn't even seen her since then, except maybe once or twice I had run into her out somewhere. But in those couple years, she had completely changed and the people that now filled her house and life were people I had never even seen before. I didn't know any of them, and I didn't even really know why Liz had invited Sam, Vernon, Em and me.

"There's not much new going on with me. I will be graduating after this semester is finished, and then I am going to be moving to Seattle for work. I had an internship this past summer, and they decided to offer me a position, so I am really excited."

"That's awesome, congratulations. I think Seattle would be an awesome place to live."

"Yeah, I can't wait. So what's been going on with you?"

"Oh, you know. Just kind of drifting through life. Being a bum."

Liz laughed, and I could see that she turned and was looking at me, but I was still scanning the room. There was a brief silence between us, and I could feel her still looking at me.

"Well I hope you are at least behaving yourself. Are there any new women in your life?"

"There has been a few, but nothing too serious. There's plenty of other things to pretend to be serious about right now."

"That's unfortunate for all those women out there then."

"I wouldn't go that far. There's really not much that they are missing."

"Oh, you know that's not true, honey."

Then Liz leaned over and kissed the side of my face, hesitating briefly as if she wanted to whisper something in my ear, but then I guess she changed her mind and stood up.

"Well...I've got to mingle. Got to be a good host. But I'm really glad you're here."

I just nodded, then took a sip from my drink, and my eyes followed her as she walked across the room over to a group of girls, who after a couple minutes started laughing, and one or two of them glanced over in my direction.

Just then I heard the basement door closing, the creaking of the stairs, and I looked over to see Vern and Em descending the stairs into the basement. They both acknowledged me then turned and headed over towards the bar to get some drinks. Liz excused herself from the girls she was talking to then went up and greeted Emily and Vern. They stood there, talking for a while, and then Vern exited through the basement door that led out to the driveway as Em came over and sat down next to me.

"Who the fuck are all these people?"

"I have no idea, Em."

"Do they realize how absurd they look in those ridiculous fucking costumes?"

"I don't think so. Perhaps, you should let them know."

I took a sip from my drink.

"Have you talked to any of them?"

"Do you know who I am?"

"Good point. Owen: the gregarious sycophant."

"Absolutely."

Em and I sat there, drinking our drinks without saying anything, silently judging Liz's new breed of friends, not because we felt superior to them. We just felt less absurd. Then Em started to talk to me again.

"So how's everything with you and Liz? Have you guys talked yet?"

"Yeah, we just talked a little. Everything's fine. Not awkward or anything."

"That's good. She said she's moving to Seattle after she graduates."

"I know. She told me. It sounds awesome. I'm proud of and happy for her."

"And you're sure you're okay?"

"Yeah, I'm golden. Couldn't be better."

I had originally been hesitant about coming to Liz's party at all, because I was afraid that it would've been difficult to see her and talk to her. But it wasn't at all. I thought that me going there would evoke some emotion that used to exist years ago. But there was nothing. A drought had fallen on that field, and it had no intentions of yielding any crops ever again, and I was glad. Just like when a climate change comes and leaves a field completely barren and unable to produce anything, it makes more sense to just move on, move somewhere new, instead of sticking around only to slowly, painfully suffer for no obvious reason except pure idiocy and masochism. Liz had changed so much, and not in a bad way. She had just changed. And, in many ways, I had too.

Sam stumbled in through the basement door, laughing. He was clearly stoned already, and no one was really all that phased. To everyone at the party, Sam, Vern, Emma and I were the ousted assholes, but Liz apparently found something amiable about our personalities throughout high school. I finished my beer and stood up to walk over to him with a smile on my face. He slammed the door and marched over to the bar, and then he started to pour himself a tall drink of vodka, still just chuckling to himself. I met him there and asked him how he was doing and grabbed another beer for myself and opened it and took a long sip before he said anything.

"That was some good shit. It's already hit me," Sam said.

"What is? Did you take the shrooms?" I asked him, sure that it was probably the shrooms, but with Sam you can never really know.

"Vern and I smoked some of this weed he had. Holy…fucking…mother of shit. It changed my life. I'm saving the shrooms for later. You gotta hit some of it. Real good headies."

"And why in the fuck didn't you invite me?"

"You were too busy talking to lovely fucking eyed Liz and romanticizing your dead love."

"Fuck you, smart ass. She invited us all to the party. I am not here to live the past anymore. I'm over her, you know that. What's dead is dead, and it stays that way. And I'm glad. Just like you if you don't slow your shit down soon," I said.

"Sorry, mommy. Next time I'll invite you to smoke. I still have some for later anyways, so don't shed any tears," Sam said, barely able to talk, because he was laughing so hard. And I started laughing too.

The lights slowly started to dim, and the room was beginning to get dark. Liz was turning the lights down, because it was about time for the ritual party movie. *The Labyrinth*. What a fucking weird movie. I figured Sam would be going into the bathroom soon to perform his ritual, but instead he was chatting up a storm with this girl named Ella. She had short, dirty-blonde hair. Her lip was pierced, and the black mascara she applied to her eyes was a little thick, but I guess that's the style. She didn't look bad by any means; in fact, she was pretty fucking cute. And the thick black mascara and the surf green eye shadow really made her eyes stand out nicely.

I had resumed my seat on the sofa in the corner next to Em.

But I decided to make a decision. So I stood up and walked towards the bar, towards the basement door. On my way towards the door, I reached into Sam's back pocket and pulled out a baggie with several joints inside of it and stepped outside, gently clenching the bag in my fist. Sam was so stoned he didn't notice, and he wouldn't care anyways. I removed one of the thicker joints and lit it up, watching the paper slowly catch fire and start to burn from my encouraging little puffs on the other end. I blew out the flame, so the joint wouldn't start to burn unevenly or too quickly. I took some deep hits, and the smoke felt dense inside my lungs, then it began to burn, and finally I let it all blow out, up into the starry night. I sat down against the side of the house with my back against the cold bricks in the driveway and crossed my legs. I could hear the music perfectly outside. I took another big hit and held it in longer this time. As the smoke was coming out of my mouth, I was starting to feel the out of body, spacey feeling that is both desired and expected. I was an astronaut, sitting in Liz's driveway, leaning up against the bricks, smoking an incredible joint. The world around me was slowly changing and starting to make more sense. I had a mystical feeling inside of me. I felt like Whitman leaving the lecture hall and lying down on the grass, just staring straight up into the sky. I took one more hit then died it out to save the rest for Sam. I stood up and could hear the music fading down as one song ended, and as I pulled the basement door open, the new song began. The room was now completely dark except the beam of light from the television. I felt like I was moving slowly through space and time, and the melody from "No Surprises" by Radiohead rose into the air, and my stoned mind immediately began to dissect the notes, and they started to float around in the infinite space of my brain, ringing and echoing some hidden meaning. The door closed behind me, and I was lost in the room of strangers. I was lost in the music.

●

I came out the doors of my building, walked down the steps and onto 5th Ave. I crossed the block, across onto Forbes, down the street and through the doors, up the stairs three flights, then into my apartment. Sam was half unconscious on the couch with the television on. I went to the refrigerator for a drink and slammed the door, so I could wake Sam up.

"Holy fuck," Sam said, rising suddenly from his sleep.

"You have class in thirty minutes. Get your ass ready, dude," I said.

Sam stared idiotically for a while, then yawned and rubbed the sleep out of his eyes. He turned off the television and slowly started to stand up. I walked down the hall and entered my room to the right, shutting the door behind me. Once I was in my room, I tossed my messenger bag onto the ground, unpacked my laptop, kicked off my shoes, and lay down on my bed.

I opened up my laptop and put on some music. "Dark Matter" by Andrew Bird started playing, and I lay there with my eyes closed for a little. It had been a long day. Tuesdays and Thursdays were the worst, because I had five classes back-to-back. Rhetoric. Philosophy. British Lit. Creative Writing. Psychology.

With my eyes still closed, I reached to the top of my bookshelf next to the bed and fumbled until I finally managed to grab the bottle of migraine pills. I took two, then put the bottle back, rubbed my temples and opened my eyes as if it were for the first time. I sat up a little and leaned over the side of the bed to examine the bookshelf that was overflowing with books, and after about fifteen seconds of contemplation, I slid a book out from between the others and leaned back against my pillow on the wall. I flipped the pages, reading intently, trying to relax, as the music filled my ears and slowly I began fall asleep, contemplating what chapters I had to read from my philosophy book.

~~~

When I awoke it was almost 5 p.m., so I knew that Sam would be done with classes soon, and then we would be able to go to the coffee shop to study and bullshit. I wiped the droll from my mouth and sat up, trying desperately to remember what I had dreamt: nothing. I couldn't remember anything for the life of me. I have always been fascinated with dreams, Freud and him injecting cocaine into his blood system not so much, but dreams, yes. I always thought they were organic and a window into thought, but I could never remember any of my own dreams, regardless of how hard I would try. I would awake, hoping that I would remember some incredibly lucid dream that would open the door into my own subconscious, but that day has yet to arrive at my cognitive door knocking.

I heard the front door slam, and I knew that Sam was back. I frequently slept with my clothes on, because I thought it was more convenient, so when I got up I didn't have to dress again, and I walked out of my room to greet Sam. By the time I got out to the living room, his body was sprawled across the sofa again, the television on but muted, and he was reading a book with a smile taking over his face and a lit cigarette dangling from his mouth.

"What are you all giddy for?" I said, a little afraid of the answer but interested enough to ask the question.

"I left class early."

"What do you mean? It's only a little after five now, where have you been all this time then?"

"I got this great idea, so I left class to walk around and brainstorm," Sam said.

"Uh, okay. What is your great idea now?" I said, this time even more frightened by his possible response.

"Tomorrow is Friday, and tomorrow we are going to the Science Center baked as hell to watch the Pink Floyd Laser Show," Sam spoke these words, smiling still.

"Well I got a lot of shit to read, so if we go to the coffee shop tonight, I should be able to get most of it done. And I'm definitely not going to object if you're giving me pot," I said, thinking that my arguments were valid and clear.

"No shit man, let's get rolling now, so you can get all your serious shit done," said Sam, getting up and laughing, then walking over to me to pat me on the back.

Sam passed me and walked down the hallway into his room on the left, leaving the door open. I could hear him rummaging through some things, and I decided to walk back to my room to pack up my bags. As I walked passed his room, I looked in and saw him, the cigarette still dangling from his mouth, and he was sliding books off his desk into his bag. I entered my room, and my bag was mostly packed, but I decided to grab a couple extra, leisurely books. Putting my bag on my shoulders, I looked back to double-check I had all my shit, then I turned off the light, shut the door, walked into the living room where Sam was standing. He nodded confirmation that he was ready to go, and we left through the front door, down the stairs and outside into the unknown streets of the city.

•

My favorite coffee shop was on Forbes Ave, across from the museum: Kiva Han. For some reason unknown to me, I had always been drawn to coffee shops. In fact, I preferred them over libraries and bars and most other places too. I hadn't been able to truly figure it out. There were clearly persistent coffee shop goers. I knew that it was something far beyond my addiction to coffee, because I could just as easily brew my own coffee at my place. Maybe I enjoyed getting out of our shitty apartment; perhaps, I simply appreciated the vibe I got from the atmosphere. I thought that maybe Hemingway was onto something when he wrote about "A Clean, Well-Lighted Place."

    I ordered the bold roast, black. A bold, bitter person needs their coffee to complement their character. I sat at a table near the windows of the shop and plugged in my laptop. Maybe I enjoyed coming to the coffee shop, because it was a combination of good coffee, great atmosphere, free internet, and a window to peer out at the real world passing before my eyes.

Sam ordered a hot tea and sat down across from me, setting his bag on the floor and pulling out his books.

For some reason, today was one of those days, and by that I meant one of those days that your vision changes, your mind becomes hazy, and you cannot focus on any goddamned thing. I looked over at Sam and saw something incredible. Sam reading and being productive. I have been around the bastard for too long. I knew when he is actually thinking, because he rubbed his facial hair, and that was exactly what he was doing now. I stared at my computer screen that projected a half-complete paper before my eyes, and I let my eyes wander from examining Sam, to watching the lady across the coffee shop with long, brown hair and gorgeous eyes. She sat there reading some novel, biting her lip intently, and I imagined my dreams that I could not summon. I envisioned a beautiful women like her overtaking them, controlling my mind and leading me through an entirely different dimension of reality, showing me life and love and beauty, leading me through the darkness of my life out into the golden, radiating light. If I couldn't remember my actual dreams, I figured that I might as well day-dream about inventing them. My eyes were then distracted by moving figures outside the window. Various people moving down the street shuffling their feet. I wondered where they were all going or where they were all coming from? Were they going to meet someone? What were they all thinking? Did they notice me peering through the coffee shop's glass at them, wondering what I was thinking or why in the hell I was staring at them?

And then I saw her walking down the street. A girl that showed up in my one class before but was not there earlier the past week. I asked Sam if he had ever seen her before or knew anything about her.

"Nope, never seen her before in my life, but I'm damn glad you got my attention. I sure as hell don't mind looking at her at all," Sam said kind of trailing off, watching the figure move down Forbes, and then I ignored what Sam's eyes were doing, because I was following her too.

"I don't know her name, but she is the one from my class that I was telling you about. She's something right? Smart, beautiful, very easy on the eyes," I said, even though I knew Sam wasn't listening to anything I was saying, and I wasn't really either.

"Yeah, you should talk to her."

"She wasn't there today. I was thinking about it, though."

"You can work your nihilistic, pretty-boy charm, telling her about existentialism and the works of Joyce. She will fall for you immediately. I'm willing to bet any sum of money on it," Sam articulated these words with a mock-aristocratic air, deliberately poking fun at me.

"Yeah, that's how I impress all the ladies. Besides, the closest you've come to an intimate interaction or a meaningful relationship would probably be when you were so drunk you accidentally washed all your underwear with Maria Caldrone's clothes in the laundromat in our building."

Sam broke into a loud laugh, trying to stifle it since we were in the coffee shop, and everyone began to look in our direction.

"I completely forgot about that. I need to provide this world with more humor, even if you are the only poor bastard that appreciates it," said Sam, and then, "I'm just saying that you shouldn't be a pussy about that girl. Actually talk to her."

I partially ignored him and just decided to nod, because I didn't want the conversation to go much farther. I was going to pretend that I was reading, while I thought about this unknown woman, who abruptly entered my life and waltzed around my thoughts for the past couple of weeks. Yes, I decided to just shake my head and smile at Sam, so I didn't make the mistake of encouraging him.

I often referred to Sam as the quintessential iconoclast of our generation. I will admit that this only encouraged him, so later I decided to refrain from such encouragement, because I realized he didn't need my help to be himself.

When I met Sam freshman year of high school, he was already very outspoken, and I knew all the shit he had gotten himself into. He really hadn't changed much since high school, he just continued rapidly to become more intelligent. And in many ways, I envied him. His pattern of character tended to repeat and present itself to me, when I would witness his newest acts of, what he termed, "revolutionary scale." Now he certainly did not partake in violence of any sort. He was a natural-born pacifist. Even if he wanted to be otherwise, it was never in his physical or mental character. No, he did most of his damage with his intellect. No one would believe it at first, since Sam was mostly stoned, but he was a supreme intellectual. He had graduated third in his class and was an honors philosophy and science student at the university. Sam was much smarter than me, but I was thankful for his companionship, because I was able to bounce ideas and new concepts off of him, and I trusted his feedback to be genuine and critical.

~~~

In his public speaking class, Sam presented an essay he had written about America being founded by assholes and continued on to debunk most of American history. He attacked America's most beloved historical figures: Washington, Jefferson, and Lincoln. He revealed that they were merely violent slave-owners, racists, genocidists, and moral egoists. He argued that power has only been allotted to a chosen few since the founding of the country and those in power perpetually use their hegemony to oppress and exploit the poor. He wanted to purport a different view of such idealized figures, because with most things in America, people loved their freedom of ignorance and aimed to believe that everyone or everything about the United States was all great and gold-frosted roses; instead of researching and looking for accuracy, they resorted to turning a blind eye to most things and believing everything to be perfect. But don't get me wrong. Sam never fell into any sort of idealism, or one end of thinking. The Left or the Right. When it came to everything, Sam was entirely himself and was outside of it all. Overall, his teacher was mortified, the students were shocked, but the professor had no choice but to give him an excellent grade because of his superb presentation, argumentation, and research, and he even said that his teacher was mildly impressed. He didn't really care about any of it all that much, but he did it simply because he could. He really was a miraculous son of a bitch.

I think I got along with him so well, because I could associate mostly with his ideas, beliefs, and radicalism. In my literary excursions, I aligned my appreciation and reverence with some of the most rebellious figures in literature's history: Shelley, Byron, Thoreau, Joyce. We got along just fine, and I thought that maybe I might dream about a meeting of such radical minds. What the fuck would the world do then?

•

Friday had blurred almost into nothingness, and nighttime was rapidly approaching. Sam was back at the apartment, rolling all his joints, getting ready for tonight's "big journey," as he called it, so I decided to go out into the city for a stroll and just enjoy the sun dimming as the city lights began to brighten and become more vibrant. I decided to head down Forbes towards the Hillman Library. I turned right onto Schenley Drive, passing the Carnegie Museum and Library, noticing the words "Drunk in PGH Again," slurred with Sharpie across the steel box that controlled the street lights. I continued towards Phipps Conservatory and Botanical Gardens. The leaves had changed to their fall hue. I could smell the quintessential smell of autumn: dead and dying leaves. And as sad as it is, there is something calming about the smell of the dead leaves. They mix perfectly with the coldness of the air.

    I had been trying to make sense of life for a long time, perpetually and constantly asking questions, but I mostly never got any concrete answers. I wanted the answers, and I wanted truth. I was willing to pursue it deep into the darkest areas of human existence, delve further into any of the depths that most people were petrified of even contemplating. Yeats said that "it takes more courage to examine the dark corners of your own soul than it does for a soldier to fight on the battlefield." That's exactly what I intended to do. My beliefs went entirely against everything that I had ever been told and everything I had ever been taught. From the time I was a child, I was sent to two preschools, both at religious institutions, even though my family was probably more secular than most conservative families. The one was in a Presbyterian church. I can safely say that I didn't learn much, or even anything at all really. We would ride around on tricycles and make hotdogs wrapped in Pillsbury dough crescents. The other preschool was in a Catholic church, and I don't really remember much of what we discussed. I am sure that it was dogmatic and similar to a catechism, but why would I remember that when I could remember riding a tricycle and eating crescent-wrapped hotdogs? From the time I was young, religion had been gently nudged in my direction. Public school made us recite the Pledge of Allegiance, which to me now just seemed somewhat oppressive. It's not that I am not patriotic; I simply don't believe in the concept as strongly as most. Nationalism seems misguided to me. A delusional pretentiousness based on geography. It seems too narcissistic for me mainly. I blindly memorized that pledge though, refusing to analyze what it actually meant. I ignored god's name in it. I overlooked the fact that I was even pledging anything to something, something I was being brainwashed into, it seemed like. All of those kids reciting over and over again like in a cult. It was something that I certainly could not form a rational opinion about, seeing how I was only five years old. I was brainwashed and taught to speak those words, to revere them, and to absolutely never question them. But the haziness of what it actually meant burned itself into my brain. However, I refused to dwell on them and I never really listened to them. I heard them but I refused to listen. It was just a mechanical process that I had to perform, like consuming water. I knew it must be done for some reason, but I didn't waste my time to contemplate it for long or at all.

    Then from kindergarten up until the eighth grade, I was forced into attending Sunday school at the Catholic church I "belonged" too. Quite a peculiar phrase. I never really paid attention, instead my friends and I would be the terrors of the class by pranking other people or saying crude statements. In fact, one of the only things I remember is getting a spontaneous erection in my fourth grade Sunday school class, feeling like I was being punished, like everyone knew. It was no wonder that I was seen as some sort of demonic creature in the presence of those holy people. No wonder they endeavored tirelessly to save my soul. I applauded them, even though they obviously had failed. I went through the motions, more concerned about the playtime we would have as an interval break to relieve all the anxious children. I would run to the wooden chest in the back corner of the room and lift the lid only to find an array of various toys. Oh, how divine that moment was in my childish existence. How was I to focus on the creator of this earth when I was only concerned with riding my bicycle, playing with my friends, watching television, and eating junk food?

    I continued through the motions, receiving my communion, my first confession, and eventually confirmation, which I don't know what they believed to be confirming in me. That I bought all the bullshit they had to say? I remembered making up lies in the confession box, because I was only eight years old and couldn't possibly think of any mortal sins I had committed that were going to send me into an eternity of torture and agony after my far-in-the-future death. It wasn't until I was in the 6th grade. That is when they started to actually fuck with my head. They convinced me, in the back room of the church, in the hall where every Friday during Lent old people and believers gathered to eat fish, that if I were to masturbate I must go to confession to be forgiven for my horrible sin. For about a week or maybe a couple months this startling revelation had completely traumatized me. I had just recently begun to explore my body, and I had just started to masturbate. My life was revolutionized by the incredible power of an orgasm, and then it was destroyed and shattered by this statement, echoing prophetic power through that church hall. I was horrified and mortified. I had never really listened to anything that they had to say before. I went to the Sunday school but would race home afterwards, instead of going to mass, hoping to be saved *from* them, not *by* them.

I had just crossed the bridge and admired the luscious, expanding green grass of Schenley Park on the left and stared disillusioned at the statue of Christopher Columbus. I hoped that one day they would take that statue down. I never could agree with the veneration of such a man. I thought of smashing the statue to pieces, making an Ozymandias of him, and then throwing the remains onto a funeral pyre. Then I noticed Phipps Conservatory standing there to my right, and I wished that I was inside admiring all of the botanical wildlife.

In my Sunday school, I heard mouths mumbling about Jesus who had apparently died for me, because I was evil, or the people before me who were evil. We were and are all evil, they said. At my communion, I had to sit in the middle section of pews in the church, in the back row on those horribly uncomfortable wooden benches, standing and kneeling like I couldn't decide on which I preferred. I admired the stained glass windows with various saints and martyrs. They looked beautiful with the light coming through them from the outside. Oh, how I had wished to only be outside then, not cooped up inside that church. I looked to my left and there were some wooden doors in the wall, and I knew inside those doors the priest would sit listening to people confessing all their deepest, darkest secrets, or maybe they all just made up shit like I used to. Then, I looked at the back wall and there was a stations of the cross quilt that hung from the ceiling, showing the progression of the life of Jesus, my saviour, our saviour, your saviour, their saviour, somebody's saviour. Everything about that church smelt and felt weird, uncomfortable. I never understood what the hell anyone was ever saying, why everyone was smearing that water on their heads, mumbling to themselves. The second grade led to my first holy communion, where I marched up to the altar like I was in the food line in my elementary school's cafeteria, except I was holding my hands awkwardly to receive some cracker that dissolved a little then stuck to the roof of my mouth like a tacky substance. I would spend twenty minutes in the pews attempting to peel it off the roof of my mouth, then I would finally break it free and it would dissolve and be gone as if it were never really there.

      I walked to the left past the botanical gardens further into the park, listening to the birds chirping up in the trees and hearing a girl laughing off in the distance. I imagined her sprawled out on a blanket on the grass, her boyfriend holding her hand laughing too. The sun was getting lower on the horizon, which was no longer visible through the buildings or the tree line, so I knew I should be heading back soon, because Sam would be waiting. I decided to walk a little faster, strolling further into the wooded area of Schenley Park, the trees arching overtop of the road and overtop of me, providing an oddly comforting and protecting feeling.

At that young age, I never questioned religion or god or the recitation of things. I was merely told this was that and blindly believed like most people. I don't know if I ever really took it all that seriously or not, though. I believed that there was a god, mostly because I never had any reason or desire to think otherwise, but I didn't know how much I believed the people who were telling me such things. Ever since I was young, I had a problem with authority figures, and I always found no harm in questioning them and their authority; naturally, they did not find these things as enjoyable for them as they were for me. I believed that power was merely an illusion propagated by the few onto the many. To me, it had no bearing; it had no grasp. So, I was persistently in trouble with the authoritative figures, never anything serious. But go figure. Who would've ever imagined me to appreciate the writings and lives of such radical people. But I realized that I wasn't wrong, at least not in my approach to life, they all were. At least that's what I thought and still think. Most of the radical figures in history have changed civilization and society for the better, and they changed it by challenging authority figures. If something seemed wrong or unethical, we had and have to challenge it and question it, bring its flaws to light and attempt to change it or improve it. I didn't know how it would come about, but I knew I needed to push the limits of my life and the lives of others if this world ever had any hope of improving. I believed that that should be the task of everyone. I was a chosen one, who had the courage and mentality to pursue such a radical lifestyle, challenging authority and asserting new ideas and concepts and belief systems, despite the reaction of society and the condemnation that was naturally bound to follow and fall upon me with the weight of the world. I wanted to change things. I wanted to challenge the top of the hierarchy of authority that looked solid and reasonable from a distance, like a child with their head tilted back attempting to look towards the top of a tall building against the sun's blinding rays. But I had learned with most things, once you get a closer look, they are never quite what they seemed to be in the first place.

My cell phone started ringing. I pulled it out of my pocket and looked at the screen: Sam.
"Hello."
"When you coming back?" Sam said, coughing then laughing.
"On my way now. I'll be there in ten," I said, turning around and hanging up my phone and beginning to speed walk back in the direction of our apartment.

I jogged up the street, out from underneath the awning of trees, out of Schenley and past Phipps. I crossed the bridge and counted the parking meters outside the Carnegie Library. I thought, "Carnegie was a real fucker, but I do have to thank him for the libraries. It's just too bad only assholes like me actually go there. The world would be a lot different if people still asked questions, strived to understand things, and weren't too lazy to pick up a book every once in a while." Or as Márquez has written, "The world must be all fucked up when men travel first class and literature goes as freight."

I crossed the street, through the outdoor pavilion, across the other street, in between the Hillman library and Posvar Hall. Students were sitting outside on the benches, talking and laughing about mostly nothing. I wondered what they were studying at the university. I hopped up the steps and crossed the street into our apartment complex, up to my room where Sam waited, ready for everything and anything.

•

I entered our room, and it was filled with smoke. Sam was nowhere to be seen. I called out his name as I looked through the refrigerator for a beer. No answer. I called again, opening my beer and sitting down on the couch. I saw that his bowl was sitting on the coffee table, so I lit it up, figuring he was probably already really baked and was either in his room or in the bathroom. The weed burned good and tasted even better. It burnt my lungs but in a good way. I blew out the smoke, figuring that I might as well contribute to our smoke-filled room. As I was taking another hit, I started coughing uncontrollably like a person with severe bronchitis, and the door opened up and in entered Sam, carrying a large pizza box with a huge grin.

"The pizza shop down the block has five dollar large cheese pizzas. I love humanity, and I love this stupid fucking depressing city."

"It's not that bad, and I hope you are planning on sharing with me," I said, smiling and taking another deep hit off the bowl.

I passed the bowl to Sam, and he opened the pizza box, took a bite then leaned back in his chair. He sat the piece of pizza on his lap and then lit up the bowl and took a real long hit. The smoke came out of his nose and then his mouth. He took another bite of pizza, and I reached across the coffee table to grab a piece for myself, cause I was starved, since I hadn't really eaten too much.

"What time's the show?" I asked, curious since I had never been to one before.

"Midnight, man. Midnight Floyd is obviously at midnight," he said, talking strainingly but delicately, because the inhaled smoked was still in his lungs.

"Well, why are we smoking already?"

Sam didn't answer, he just sat there eating his pizza. I repeated the question.

"I thought you were smart?"

"And what the hell is that supposed to mean?"

"Why wouldn't we be smoking now?"

And that seemed to settle the argument. I supposed he had a good point. I personally enjoyed the initial high of the pot, feeling it progress. When I smoked, I typically wouldn't feel anything at first, not for a while. Then a couple hits later, I would start to rise up into a higher level of consciousness, where my perception of things would change, and that was the state I envisioned myself being in for this laser show. I enjoyed the peaceful and relaxation state that followed, but I wanted to be at the absolute height of my high for this experience.

"I wanted to be in that awesome high state for the laser show. You know, when you completely culminate on your journey, and everything is unreal," I told Sam.

"Oh don't worry, I got some special blend especially for us for tonight. You'll be flying that high for a couple hours. The show's in a few hours. I'm gonna go get ready. You keep smoking, and you'll see," Sam said, standing up and walking down the hall, disappearing into his room.

I smoked another bowl and ate three pieces of pizza before Sam returned. I wasn't feeling that high, but I often felt that way if I smoked in a dark room or outside at night, then once I got into a lighted area, it all became real and hit me hard and made sense.

We sat there and smoked some more. We finished the rest of the large pizza, and the warmth of the pizza felt spectacular inside my stomach. I could feel the warmth spreading all throughout my body, and I knew that Sam did get some good shit and tonight was definitely going to be a good night.

The time passed quickly, in fact, I don't really remember it passing. I looked at my watch and told Sam that it was time to go. We stood up, and I ran to my room to get my hoodie. It was fall, and it was slowly starting to get colder and colder, especially at night. I came back into the living room and Sam was standing in the kitchen making a peanut butter and jelly sandwich. I looked at him quizzically, trying to suppress my laughter, and he told me that it was a snack for the show. He told me it wasn't like the movies, that they weren't dickheads and that they allowed you to smuggle in snacks. In fact, they were fully aware that most of the people showing up were completely stoned, and Sam even thought that most of the employees were too, or at least he would be if that were his job.

We were out the door and onto the street, standing at the corner waiting for the bus to show up.

~~~

We bought our tickets and climbed the stairs in the Science Center. Sam was really stoned by now, but we had time to kill, so he amused himself by yelling crude obscenities into the long echo tube inside the building. The words left his mouth, and then you could silently hear the waves of sound rolling along the inside ridges of the tube, growing in intensity and finally reverberating back to where he had put his mouth, "God is dead; Neitzsche lives." He continued, whispering, "fascist fucks and the cunts of wheelbarrows." Sam also managed to say several more statements, before the employees standing at the doors up the ramp announced that the show was going to begin in ten minutes. I was so stoned, and I knew that the dudes at the doors would know. And I was surprised that somehow Sam and I, or at least Sam, didn't get kicked out for him yelling that shit in the echo tube. I guessed that everyone else really was baked, and no one really cared. They opened the doors, and everyone began to amble up the ramp into that dark dome, sitting down and reclining in those soft-cushioned chairs.

After some time moved out of infinity and died, the doors were closed, and an ominous, baritone voice began to speak like the fucking Wizard of Oz, welcoming everyone to the Midnight Floyd laser show and announcing the arbitrary choices of the technician-conductor who was going to provide the auditory and visual stimuli upon the concave dome above us. Something about his voice was mildly threatening and disarming, but I knew it was probably just the mild paranoia effect. He told us that he would be starting with "Welcome to the Machine" and then picking songs randomly from *Dark Side*, *The Wall*, and, if we were lucky, he'd play "Echoes."

I slumped deeper into my chair, allowing my mind an attempt at processing my sense receptors. The remaining lights in the room were dimmed, and the projector projected constellations upon the dome, and I felt my body lift up into outer space. I was an astronaut floating. Gravity no longer existed to my mind or body, and the song began with those churning gears and perpetual helicopter propellers rotating in slow-motion. The puppet master behind the switchboard was simultaneously in the song and standing in the box behind us, controlling everything, every little fucking moment and every little fucking piece of reality.

David Gilmour's voice entered into the song, and the synthesizer keys were pressed down into chords, and we were all space cadets moving through time and space, floating through eternity, blissfully moving out into the vast openness of the universe, where time moved slower. And time really did move slow because we were so stoned. But we moved more quickly, and I felt my body lift up into the sky and my mind became pulled into the sight before my eyes. I was sitting in the chair, but I wasn't sitting in the chair. Something in my mind had changed, marijuana or not. I was in the dome, projected there myself. I was in space. This was real, it felt so fucking real. The stars moved rapidly through my line of vision, and I knew my body had completely detached itself from reality now. I was no longer alive. I was no longer sitting in a chair in the Science Center. Pittsburgh. United States. World. Universe.

I was in space, outside the realms of the atmosphere, in the universe. I was dead and floating through eternity. I was a part of some grand whole.

The songs changed and the images transmuted with their melodies. "Comfortably Numb" began, and we were immersed into a corridor where bricks covered the walls, and we were all moving through a narrow passageway in search of something. Perhaps, we weren't in search of anything. We pursued the great unknown, the great perhaps, the great nothingness that hovered high above the abyss of life. The panoramic shots changed and flashed before my eyes, deluding my senses and deceiving me altogether. I was in another world, and I was still alive. I could still breathe, but I could touch the world of eternity, where things always were and always would be. The sounds rose and fell in cadences, and eventually, the hands of the unknown gradually lowered me, further and further until I was gently laid back in my body and swaddled with reality. But who was to be the judge of the line of reality anyways?

•

I have been contemplating that laser show experience that Sam had exposed me to, and now I struggled to define what reality was to me. I felt that what constituted reality was only what I perceived in the present state of being. All the past was founded upon faulty memory, sketchy photographs, stories, videos, songs, and whatever else we built up in our minds. Even in my memories, I misconstrued facts, and I described things solely from my perspective, but I often wondered what it would be like if there were someone else who followed me along throughout my entire life and kept a journal. I wondered how different it would be.

    I decided to abandon such philosophical endeavors that I knew all too well would only regress until infinity, and I had more important things to do.

    I sat there, staring out the window in Kiva Han, meditating on the nothingness and meaninglessness that descended upon my life like a black storm cloud. I envisioned how quickly the sad people living in the plains of North America are overtaken by treacherous tornados, and then I pictured this metaphorical storm enveloping my life.

To me, there had always been something beautiful about apathy. And as the time seemed to pass, I became more and more apathetic and detached. At least to a certain extent. However, my level of apathy reached dangerous limits, because I developed the ability to cut off the tentacles that connected me to love and other people and dislodge them and throw them away. I not only had the capabilities, but I found joy in both dissecting and analyzing my life and also in severing it into several pieces, because I learned that those severed pieces were capable of not only continuing to live but also of thriving and growing stronger. From this particular point of view, I realized that not only did I burn bridge after bridge in my life, but I watched them burn and marveled at the separation they made between me and everything else. The flames would return to my mind and a smile would come upon my face, because there was an erratic feeling of freedom that would overtake me.

I found that I had been drinking a little bit more than normal and seemingly falling into a state of dissolution, but I couldn't figure out what was coming over me, until it seemed that it was already consuming me. People passed by outside the cafe, wearing light clothes, because the coldness of the fall had temporarily vanished, and the people were being deluded by nature, not knowing what time of the year it actually was, and how cold it normally was at that time of the year. But a drink sounded good even sitting in the cafe. I closed my eyes and wished that I was in a cafe in Paris, either now or in the era of the lost generation, bullshitting with Hemingway in the cafe, drinking. "Hey Hem, how's the writing coming?" I would ask as I sipped some liquor from my glass. Then we would discuss his ideas about writing and technique, and I would give him my input, helping him with his work, and vice versa as we'd get drunk off wine in the afternoon. If I could only think of some great lines or capture a fucking moment, I would give all of my being into writing a great novel. Hemingway was 26 when he wrote *The Sun Also Rises*, so I felt that I still had some time to fuck up my life before I needed to start to achieve things and get things together.

    Sitting alone, drinking my tea, a strange feeling came over me. For most people, loneliness consumes them when they are left to themselves, because they are overtaken by a feeling of complete unbearableness. For a long time, I fell into the same category, and I couldn't handle the thought of boredom or being alone. And not alone in strictly the sense of being without a loved one, but also in being just by oneself. A feeling of anxiousness and insecurities sets in, when the person is in a public place, like myself, sitting in that cafe, and people feel that all the eyes of the room are drawn like a parallax towards them, and those eyes are all silently judging and mocking that person's lonesomeness. However, that has no longer been the case with me. I have been completely contented with the idea of being both by myself and alone, romantically, sexually, spiritually. I don't know when, why, or how that feeling came over me, but it had an element of terror, because I felt nothing at the thought of never spending my life with another human being or feeling that strong emotion of love or the thought of dying alone. It produced nothing, no sort of pang or sounds in the hollows of my being. Maybe I had become so contented with myself that I was able to face the harshest realities, or maybe I was so fucking delusional that I was unaware of reality. I no longer cared if the spotlight was on me or not, whether people were silently judging me or completely unaware of my existence, because I felt that I was attempting to embrace myself for who I was, regardless of surrounding factors and circumstances, and what I believed to be the reason and purpose for the existence that surrounded me.

    And as I had been drinking, I had the desire to drink more. It consumed me, and the thoughts of being unproductive floated to my mind, like they were swelling up so much in the abyss of my brain, because I wanted to do something so badly, but I continued to push it to the back of my mind, to push it all away, and instead pursue pointless, empty activities, that could not fill the void, but instead they attempted to seal over it and bury everything deep and pure inside of me. Those feelings initially began when I started to piece together when I got really drunk and had some pathetic self-loathing that desired to reach out and find consolation in any other human being.

~~~

    Her eyes were looking at me throughout most of the night, across the dark room of the bar and dance floor, but I continued to pay little to no attention, just enough to notice that someone was watching me. The lights were constantly flashing through the darkness of the room, and the music was loud enough that shouting was only remotely audible.

    A few friends and I had been drinking since 9:30, and the night was approaching a close, or more rather the bar was, as I looked down at my watch and noticed that it was what looked like almost 1:30 a.m. The hands of my wrist watch were mildly blurred as I continued to drink heavily, drowning something, drowning nothing, pouring poison into a hollow well. Between the constant drinks and the music and the dancing, I had completely lost all my conception of time or the existence of time as an abstract concept. The only thing that matter to me was the music, the movement, and the thoughts that flitted through my mind more like electrical sparks than dense matter containing substance.

    At some point during this brief interval of time from when I last looked at my watch and the bar closed, she came over to me and started talking to me, or I went over to her. I don't remember either way, and I have no recollection of what was said; probably the normal drunken talk between two belligerent, lonely fools.

However, there was a haze that seemed to enshroud the evening from that point in time, until we made it to her apartment or her friend's apartment, then the image cuts in and out and becomes black, mostly until the morning, with a few brief flashes of recollection. But I ended up at some apartment. I remember her telling me that her, her roommate, and I took a taxi to get there, but I didn't know where "there" was, and wouldn't until later, and I definitely didn't remember being in a taxi cab.

I remembered that she struggled getting the apartment keys out of her purse and even more trying to unlock their old, rickety wooden door. There was an awkward silence and aching anticipation in the act that we both knew was instinctively stupid but unavoidable at this point. We were both just waiting. I don't remember climbing any stairs, but I remember descending them as I left in the cold morning air later that night after regaining some consciousness.

In the living room of the apartment, she threw her coat and purse on the couch, and her friend disappeared into her bedroom without saying a word and passed out cold for the remainder of the night. The moment that this girl dropped her coat and purse on the couch, she turned, without saying a single word, and locked her lips to mine. She tasted like vodka and mint as she put her tongue into my mouth. The taste made me somewhat nauseous, but we continued kissing for I don't know how long. Then the darkness fell over my eyes, and the rest became hazy and vague.

...her skin was soft...

...

...

...

...the room was dark.

...

...

...

...And all I felt was a growing sense of **emptiness**.

The closer that we came to each other, the further I felt, and I could feel my insides rapidly beginning to feel more and more hollow.

I must have passed out for a short while, but I remembered waking up, regaining consciousness, feeling completely belligerent and confused by waking up in this girl's bedroom, this complete stranger. I was still really drunk, so I didn't try to question any of my previous actions or to wake up this girl that was lying next to me. In fact, she looked beautiful sleeping, and it actually made me feel even worse, even more repulsive. Instead, I just looked at my watch and realized it was almost five in the fucking morning, so I found my clothes and shoes by using the light on my cellphone, and then I staggered the fuck out of her apartment into the cold morning air, shivering and stumbling to find some street signs or buildings that looked familiar, so I could determine whether I should walk home and walk off this drunkenness or try to find a cab to guarantee that I actually made it home. I remembered coming down her awkward, crumbling stone stairs outside her apartment; there was a plastic swan in a pathetic-excuse for a garden, so I pissed near it and walked towards the road, down a horrible, trapeze-act style of cement stairs that appeared as if they floated in the air, defying gravity. I was on the back hills of the South Side, coming down, looking for a street sign: 18th street. I knew it had looked familiar, but I was still really drunk. Soon I'd be back on Carson, and I'd eventually find my way home.

I walked the entire way, cold rain pelting and soaking me. I walked down Carson Street, past all the abandoned bars, feeling an unexplainable, overwhelming form sadness that no human has yet been capable of capturing with language. It is only capable through personal experience, like some type of pathetic enlightenment.

By the time I woke up the next day, it was two in the afternoon, I was hungover as hell, and I was sleeping on top of my nicely made bed sheets with all of my clothes on. When I finally woke up to head to my classes, I envisioned this poor soul awaking to find her bed sheets disheveled and the delicate imprint in her mattress where I had been briefly. I could see it perfectly clear in my mind.

~~~

These particular interactions happened a few more times, and after each one, I began to become consecutively more repulsed. There was a gouging hole that was tearing and the abyss was growing darker and deeper.

It all sadly made me think of Tomas from *The Unbearable Lightness of Being* and how his only pure joy in life was finding these small differences in the women he tore through and then discarded, and I wanted to vomit, thinking about the hollowness and emptiness of it all. He thrived in that and dissected the most beautiful thing in life by reducing it to a mechanical process and scientific inquiry, whereas I felt this tear that I could see deep inside my being that looked like a wormhole that was about to suck all of the tiny bits of emotions and meaning that I was capable of desperately hanging onto into pure and total oblivion.

Nihilo Sanctum Estne? I remember the line in Latin from a movie. "Is nothing sacred?" These thoughts of meaningless sex created such a strong nauseous feeling that spread all over my body to the point that I gave up caring about sex at all. I had realized through my foolish actions that the apathy I applauded inside of me was only a sham. I learned that the initial feeling of euphoria from disconnecting myself from all of human life and human relationships had quickly begun to rot and corrode my insides. The nervous tearing away of some invisible parts of myself and the hollowness that I persistently felt became amplified and almost unbearable. To me, if it were going to be meaningless, then it was totally pointless. At some point, our instincts tell us otherwise and those are the only thoughts that deluge the brain, but anyone is capable through strength to challenge those thoughts; however, there are not many people who are truly strong, because I often see weakness persistently around me, and sadly find it deep inside of myself sometimes too. But I believe the strongest weakness to be the inability to see the sacredness in pure sex. Fucking a stranger may be good, or feel good rather, but making love with someone that fills your entire mind and body with happiness and pleasure, someone that you have overwhelming feelings for that you can't even explain, someone who, to avoid the cliché of the missing puzzle piece, instead is your spiritual missing piece like the Greeks spoke of, that event provides you with an unknowable and indescribable experience that is capable of touching your deepest, darkest depths and shedding light on, what the naïve and inexperienced would call, the soul. To me, there is something that is more in us and transcends the concept of the soul, whatever it may be, that the art of love making between mutually enamored companions brings. I feel that this kind of sex is the most sacred thing in the world that anyone can ever experience, whether you believe in a creator or nature or whatever, this type of love has been and always will be the greatest blessing of all.

●

As admirable as it may seem to die for what you truly believe in, it is a paradox. To willingly die and deprive yourself of life is quintessentially the most utterly stupid of ideas. Attempting to defend a brilliant idea with a stupid action renders it the epitome of futility. One can much better serve a long life of defending their beliefs with an open mind and the persistence to live.

But finding the persistence to live is sometimes hard when life seems the most bleak, empty, and meaningless.

It had been a long, demanding day of classes. So I sat inside Hemingway's on Forbes Ave, finishing up my second pitcher of beer by myself. I hadn't actually gone to any of the classes, but that was the justification that I ran through my mind and told myself as I swallowed down the cold beer that settled my thoughts and enabled me to think clearly for once. Hemingway's drew a decent crowd, and I have to admit that I particularly liked and approved of the name. It was more than fitting.

All the other bars in Oakland were shit. They were typical college bars: drunk fraternity brothers with tribal tattoos, narcissistic complexes, rufilin tablets stashed in their back pockets, and girls that decidedly wore the same dresses and skirts with matching heels that made them look more like degenerate streetwalkers than the future educated majority of our generation. And I wasn't just the cynical, neurotic, nerdy intellect that was segregated from going to such places. Well, actually, I was all of those things, but there was nothing worthwhile in any of that lifestyle to me. In fact, I believed it to be the ultimate antithesis of "lifestyle" or "living." Pretending to be like everyone else, who are all pretending to be like what the media and culture tells them who they should be and how they should act. I am also influenced by the culture and time that produces us; the only difference is that I am aware I am in the waters and I swim however I please, while the others take no notice and float on, allowing the stream to take them wherever, much the same way the driftwood is carried, floating and crashing onto the embankments or cascading into pieces over the waterfalls.

  I knew that with a bar named Hemingway's, chances were high that none of that crowd would stumble into the place, and if they did, it would be similar to them accidentally stumbling into the campus library thinking it were a strip club.

  I knew that Sam should be on his way home from work, and more than likely, he would instinctively know that I would be ruminating over my thoughts and drinking inside Hemingway's and would stop by. I emptied my last glass from the second pitcher and ordered another, wearing a faint smile on my face and a lasting glimmer in my eyes as the waitress looked at me with a heart-rending sadness in her face. I could tell that she wasn't sad at all in her life, but she was accidentally showing a deep compassion that burned within her soul at, what she thought was, my pathetic and disillusioned existence. More than likely she was right; I felt as if I were dissolving, but part of me enjoyed and reveled in the feeling. Like salt or sugar dissolving into a glass of water, but I had a strong desire to stir the contents as quickly as I could to see if it would entirely disappear. I felt like I used to be different, like there were layers that were thicker and denser and the delineations between them were distinctly formed, but all that seemed to be quickly fading and drastically changing. In my aching frontal lobe, I could feel the hollowness inside of my being, and I couldn't help but believe I was running towards the precipice of a cliff inside my mind.

When I was sober, it felt as if I wasn't entirely myself. At least, my honest and genuine self. It felt as if my entire brain were separated like islands, but, whenever I drank, the synapses began to connect everything with fine threads, and all those independent islands quickly became a large mass of land, profound and littered with rapidly growing crops of thought and truth. Not eternal and absolute truths, but little, possibly insignificant, personal truths. The I, the am, the *sum*, the whole. That is who I longed to be whom I am. The gates and battlements were lowered. All the devices and neuroses and natural instincts that flood the brain naturally on a constant basis and cloud the unconscious, they slowly became assuaged and liberated.

The blonde-haired, empathizing bartender brought my third pitcher of beer over to where I sat at the bar and slid it across the counter to me. I leaned forward on my bar stool and slid a five and some ones over the lip of the bar-top to her. I began filling my glass and glanced to the left, towards the windows, in an attempt to get a look at the street and all that was passing by in the world outside those windows, but the curtains hung and sealed off my view. I put the pitcher down and took a long sip from my beer, when I noticed the entrance door opening and in walking Sam, looking haggard from a long day of work and possibly sleep-deprivation. His hair was greasy and stood up in a couple different places, jutting out in various directions, but his face wore a gigantic, beautiful smile as always when we see each other. I smiled too, because it was infectious and because Sam was my best friend and I loved him. I stood and we hugged for a second, before he sat down, and I filled the empty beer mug that I was holding on reserve for him.

Letting out a sigh of exhaustion, not desperation, Sam sat down on the bar stool next to me and asked me how I was doing before taking a drink of his beer.

"I'm doing alright, I suppose. Attempting childishly to hold onto the ropes of my sanity. How about you, buddy? How was work and everything?"

"Work was real busy, as I'm sure you figured out, since I am getting done about a half hour late. But other than that, I am doing pretty good."

"Good. That's good. I'm glad you're done and can share a beer with me. It's been a long day and is definitely needed."

"Yeah, I agree."

Sam then asked me about my classes that day, while I was looking straight ahead at all the different beers they had on tap and sipping from my beer, and I couldn't help naturally producing a mischievous smirk on my face. The caught culprit of the crime. I glanced over at him and told him that I had skipped all my classes again.

"Why, man? What's up?"

"I don't know. I just wasn't really feeling it today. I had a lot on my mind, and I just couldn't bring myself to go. It was just one of those days, where I'd much rather lie in bed and sleep, and then once the sun goes down, roam out towards the bar for some beer like the raccoons with rabies blend in at night with everyone else."

Sam started laughing at what I said, but I could detect something deeper in his laugh: concern. He paused a while, so I would feel and recognize it, then he took a sip from his beer and turned to me:

"So what was on your mind all day?"

That was a very good question. I had been mulling over, what I would term through sheer inadequacy as, millions of things; however, I knew that in comparison to literally a million, the thoughts were not very diverse and instead were quite infinitesimal, but the crucial part of my thoughts were their frequency and persistency and density. They weighed down my brain and my body and filled me with a feeling I would attribute to being similar to paralysis. Hence, the abandonment of all sense of responsibility for the attempt to exude and purge everything from my mind and soul by lying in bed and sleeping for the entire day. Though, there were a myriad of thoughts that recurred and new ones that crept up into my mind, while other ones flickered like brief, dying flames that I would never be able to conjure their shape or texture ever again.

"I don't know. I just didn't have any motivation to get out of bed, no desire for class. It just felt pointless today, you know? Just one of those days, I guess."

"Yeah, I know the feeling. I get like that every once in a while."

Now that Sam was here, sitting next to me in the bar, I felt a little relieved, not that I felt anxious or anything before, but it was comforting to have him around. We are indeed social creatures, regardless how hard we try to unclench that grasp upon us, there is a hidden contentment and serenity in some form of solidarity. Plus, with Sam being present, the pitchers of beer went down much more quickly. The bartender set another pitcher of beer in between Sam and I, and Sam laid some money on the bar for her. I watched her delicate hands, across the other end of the bar, tilting the pitcher and pouring the beer from the tap into it, gauging it as it slowly filled up then sifting the foam from the top and filling it up just a little bit more. With each pitcher, the beer began to taste even better, and the bartender's smile appeared to become more pure and genuine, as well as more frequent and pronounced.

The beer was beautiful and loosened my tongue as well as the judgmental and parental god thumb that pressed upon my subconscious to suppress it.

"I've been feeling like a sifter recently. You know, like those soil sieves that just sift through the dirt. It's with my thoughts though and views on life. I feel like I am just running my hands through water. There's so much going in and out and through, but there's nothing of substance, everything just leads to emptiness or nothing."

I finished the beer that was in my mug and Sam was already holding the pitcher waiting to pour the remainder of its contents into my glass and hail the bartender for another round. I nodded and thanked him and took a sip, while trying to gather my thoughts before continuing, because I knew that Sam's facial expression and silence overtly revealed him switching into the role of the inquisitive listener.

"Everything, man. Everything. It all seems like it's collapsing, but then when I think about it more, I think differently, because I feel like most of these things were never supported with anything, but instead they all just seemed to float in my mind out of pure delusion. Love, life, the world, humanity, god, everything. I am afraid that too much has revealed itself to me too quickly, and the weak incapacities of my brain cannot handle it."

My eyelids began to feel heavier and my tongue began to feel invincible. I wasn't sure anymore how many pitchers we had gone through, but I was feeling really great, and I knew that was all that mattered. I looked around the bar a little bit to try and catch a glimpse of the crowd that had snuck in as the old one left without my noticing. There were perhaps only ten other people in Hemingway's, one other at the bar and a couple of groups scattered about the room at tables, all with differing looks and hidden desires, but all essentially the same.

A girl sat in the corner with another girl, one was drinking a long island ice tea while the other was drinking, what looked like, a cosmopolitan. One sat talking while the other sat listening. Essentially, they were Sam and I transported into different bodies, with different lives, different problems and different existences, but there was a hidden thread, invisible, like spiders throw in the nighttime across the trees and bushes that occasionally you will walk through and you will feel it, and it may send a shivering chill down your spine as you are overwhelmed by it, but then you will quickly forget and move on with your life as if nothing ever happened or as if it were never actually there; but the truly incredible and truly profound moment is when, from a distance or up close, one becomes aware of that beautiful, magical thread and recognizes it from a very unique, rare angle where the moonlight hits it ever so perfectly and elegantly, so that the inquisitive looker may recognize its form, if only for a second, and ponder on it and see that it potentially connects everything and spreads on infinitely. Then that person honestly admires and understands the world, by acknowledging that thread, bowing their head in admiration as they duck underneath it and leave it unharmed.

Those two girls, in all their differences and similarities, awakened something deep inside me. Perhaps, it was really what had been on my mind all day. They were probably talking about their days, what was good and what wasn't; their significant others or the one's they wished or wished they didn't have; their plans for the next day or the weekend; they would probably go home and laugh or weep to themselves or with someone. They were a piece of the gigantic whole of existence that continues on and perseveres, like the infinite spokes on a wheel, some may break and fall off, being utterly left behind, while others continue, unnoticed, not noticing, and completely unaffected by the broken or lost spokes, because there are so many that keep the whole moving unfazed and entirely unchanged.

That was how I felt and that was what had been burdening my mind persistently for the entire day; however, I wasn't quite capable of putting it into words. I felt like a broken, left behind spoke, that became aware of the wheel only to watch it persevere and shrink upon the horizon in the distance, compassionless to my predicament.

"I don't know how to explain it. It's like, everything I ever believed in has revealed itself to me to be completely false. Not to mention, almost all simultaneously. So my head is just swirling, trying to take everything in, but it's on complete overload and cannot process anything."

"It's hard man, and it's even harder trying to sort things out and make sense of it. That's why the beer definitely helps," Sam said, with a chuckle and lifted his glass towards mine.

I lifted up my glass also and touched it lightly against his, and we both finished off our glasses even though they were both more than half-full. Between the beer and Sam's companionship, the distorted, kaleidoscopic lens that I was viewing the world through, shifted enough for the lines to line back up and produce an image worth perceiving, if only for a brief instant.

"But honestly man," Sam continued, "it's really rough sorting through everything by yourself in your own mind. I know what it's like too well, and you know you can always talk with me. Personally, it's really overwhelming at first when something powerful overcomes us, like with anything. Love, death, or anything that is life-changing or thought-altering. It comes as a drastic shock, but we work through it over time and it seems to either even its self out over the fabric of time or reveal the sense behind it once the initial shock is taken away from it. I guess it really all comes down to adapting and having the proper mental capacity. For when you jump into the cold waters of a river, automatically all of your senses are bludgeoned by the overwhelming quality of only one sense that blocks out all the others, you *feel* the cold. But you don't understand it and you aren't aware of anything else around you, because that is so instantly overwhelming compared to everything else. But over time, whether brief or extended, that coldness begins to dissipate, losing its overall strength as you adapt to it, and then your other senses are capable of returning to their normal state and revealing themselves again, and you begin to recognize a myriad of different things. From not just feeling the cold but feeling the texture and weight of the water, tasting it on your lips and tongue, seeing all of the moving, living things underneath and above it, and hearing everything around you. Once you return to that state, everything becomes crystalized again and begins to make sense, once you adapt. However, panic throws itself over every living thing like a blindfold whenever that initial shock sets in."

Sam stopped briefly to re-gather his thoughts. He hiccupped, burped, then took a drink of his beer to moisten his throat from his long speech that slowly helped to alter and shift my view through the lens back into a passable perspective. I looked square at Sam's face, but his eyes were thrown upwards and towards the left. He was clearly thinking, attempting to remember the thread of his logic, inquiring whether he had forgotten anything, and then all of a sudden his eyes locked onto mine, and he smiled with the look of a completely absolved, childish heart and said to me, "Besides, in my personal experience, whether you jump into the water of your own free will or slip down the muddy embankment accidentally, once that initial coldness wears off, you are always much more glad to be swimming about those waters freely than standing on the dry land."

Sam was my intellectual and emotional saviour, because he was a compassionate genius. He may not have sorted out and made sense of my thoughts for me, because that was something that I, and every individual person, must do for themselves; however, he instilled me with the nudge, perhaps a spoonful of hope, that only close companions are capable of, to continue on with everything, knowing that in time it was all going to unfold itself and lay maybe not all the answers but glimpses and bits and pieces of them before me to attempt to make sense of everything.

The feeling that had been dwelling in me for the entire day, that felt like my insides being filled up with helium, such a light gas that it has the desire to move upwards against gravity, like a balloon, but filled up so much it almost feels nauseating and as if the balloon or your insides were attempting to turn themselves inside out or buckle and collapse under the various, differing forces acting against one another. The infinite sadness, that unbearable lightness. As I devoured the weighty words that Sam said to me, the gravity of them seemed to weigh that feeling down again and anchor it deep inside me. Between Sam and the beer, everything was slowly slipping back into how it should be, back into the realm of normalcy or the closest thing that could be considered such.

I finished my beer and looked over at Sam and thanked him for talking to me and helping to put things into perspective, and then I ordered us another pitcher, because, well, why not? I felt that we deserved it, and that perhaps everyone else should be enjoying that crisp, cold taste of fresh beer from the tap, and delving deep into the human mind in an attempt to understand it, to understand the thoughts and emotions that drive and consume us, to understand us and ourselves even if it is only minutely more than we did previously. That's why I lifted my glass and drank, among hundreds of other reasons. The breath in my lungs, Sam, the love that I've had and hope to have more of in my life, the things that I've seen and learned in my life and hope to learn and see. Everything, everything, everything. The waters rise up and they may be cold and swallow you briefly, but you learn to tread and then you learn to swim and they become so beautiful that you never want to leave them and you only want to explore them further.

Sam and I continued talking for a while, slowly finishing our last pitcher, transitioning the conversation from life dilemmas and philosophizing towards casual bullshitting and jibing. Most of the crowd inside

Hemingway's had cleared out. A couple had come in about forty-five minutes before closing, and the time was approaching ten till two, before Hemingway's closed at two. They sat at the other end of the bar from Sam and I and appeared as if they were barely speaking to each other. They looked like a couple that had been together for quite a while, and both of them seemed to be equally morose at the thought of continuing on, so much that it began to have an effect on me, and I was glad that our pitcher was almost gone, and the bar was almost closed, and Sam and I would be leaving soon, because I didn't think that I could bear to see them looking so lachrymose and dejected together. I thought that maybe they were standing on the embankment next to each other, unaware that the waters lay behind them. I finished my beer and stood up, removing my feet from the bar stool and placing them on the ground, feeling for the first time the level of my intoxication as I wobbled a little bit. I looked back at the couple as Sam finished his beer and I pulled my jacket on, hoping and thinking that soon they'd find the boldness to liberate themselves by jumping into the water, whether they decided to do it individually or holding hands.

    I pushed myself through the doorway of Hemingway's, out onto the sidewalk, turning to the right to head down Forbes, stumbling towards the apartment. I swaggered a little bit crossing the street, which was natural for how much beer I had put away. I smiled for an instant because my drunken mind was communicating with itself and saying to me or someone or something that hopefully I had made Hemingway proud, drinking myself close to oblivion and accomplishing next to nothing.

    "What do you think Hemingway would be like...you know, like here, right now, hanging out with us, in our time and age?" I let these words out of my mouth and they were directed at Sam, who was walking next to me, apparently deep in his own thoughts, as we walked down the sidewalk and turned down the side street.

Sam looked over at me and let out a little laugh that was followed by his typical giddy smile: "How drunk are you right now?"

"Drunk enough," I managed to mumble somehow, knowing that only half of myself was being honest, while the other half revolted in disagreement, so I followed it up with, "well...not *quite* enough."

On my emphasis of the word, Sam began to laugh loudly, unable to control himself, not that he wanted to, even though we were outside at two am walking down the city streets. Sam was obviously very drunk also, and with the thought of that, mixed with our conversation and our current situation, I felt a sudden overwhelming gladness and happiness that I couldn't quite define or control. I was just so content for that moment. It was one of those moments that you wish you could capture in a glass bottle or a still frame and keep forever to look back upon, but instead it only sleeps in the core of your memory and you try and try to preserve it for as long as possible, hoping that even in old age, you are capable of recalling those exact moments even if you cannot relive them. That moment with Sam and I was one of those moments, and what was even more miraculous was that I didn't know why it was. It just was. There was an explosion of serotonin thrown into my frontal lobe and the world lit up with bright colors and filled my entire body with an incredible and swelling euphoria.

We turned onto our street and continued slightly laughing to and amongst ourselves, then stopping as we turned onto the pathway that led to our apartment. I looked over at Sam and asked him if we still had that case of beer in the refrigerator and he said that we did, so we climbed the stairs and drank more and laughed more and talked more, about both important and nonsensical shit, until finally I said all that I could muster to say and crept down the hallway, through the door and into my bedroom, where my beautiful bed awaited me with patient, open arms, and I slipped soporifically off into one of the most beautiful sleeps that I had ever experienced.

•

I never really had the privilege to travel much, but it was always one of the dreams that slumbered in the back of my mind that I desperately hoped to enliven and make it become a part of the fabric of reality. I wanted to see the world, and I mean really see it. I wanted to be its most eager pupil, who sits at the front of the class, soaking up every last lesson it has to offer.

    I desperately needed to just get away from the city and clear my head, so I decided to leave late Thursday night; besides, Sam was home visiting family over the weekend. So I spontaneously decided to get out of Pittsburgh and take a trip to a bigger city. I bought my train ticket for New York City and possessed a childlike eagerness as I had my ticket checked, and I boarded the train. I was looking forward to a peaceful excursion out of Pittsburgh, glancing out the window and reading a book.

    I set my bag down on the empty seat next to me and got comfortable, reading through my book and, every once in a while, looking up to take in my surroundings: the atmosphere of the train, the people who were sporadically spread out around me on the train, and the buildings then trees that flickered by on the other side of the window as the train continued to maintain a steady speed, bouncing down the tracks towards the destination.

We changed trains in Philadelphia and then were back on the tracks, heading towards New York City, and the anticipation and eagerness grew as the miles for the destination decreased.

Stepping off the train in Grand Central Station was equivalent to entering a whole new world. The subway was filthy and smelt like the homeless people who were obviously sleeping on the benches, but there was a strange element to it all that possessed a quality remotely similar to beauty.

The sun slowly lurked over the tops of the big buildings, illuminating everything, especially since the train ride had taken place in almost complete darkness. The light was a revitalizing stimulant. I had barely slept at all on the train; I only dosed off for about twenty minutes or so, and I felt a strong sense of emotional purging from a powerful dream, but I had no recollection of it. For some reason, I felt more rested than if I would've slept throughout the entire train ride.

As soon as I first stepped out into the city in the chilly, autumn air and saw the sun up in the sky, lighting up the world, reflecting light off of all the massive buildings, I knew that I had instantly fallen in love with the place. I really had no overall goal or purpose for being in the city, but I just wanted to roam and experience it to the greatest extent that I could. It was still too early to check into my room, but it was interesting watching the inner-workings of the city: all the business people shuffling with their coffees to their office buildings or stopping to buy breakfast at all the street vendors, and the early morning sound of taxi cab horns honking and the site of the seemingly chaotic methods of driving. I recognized patterns in chaos.

I honestly wasn't that familiar with New York City, so my goal was to simply just drift around and stumble upon things. I knew I wanted to kill some time until I could check into the hostel, because I didn't want to have to carry around my heavy bags all day. Without sleep, carrying almost sixty pounds on my back, I walked twenty-some blocks up 5th Avenue to the beginning of Central Park, across from the subway station and Trump Plaza. I entered Central Park, passing a street-food vendor, the smell of roasted nuts rising potently into the cold morning air, and a homeless man that look exactly like Charles Manson, making eye contact with me and beginning to speak, what sounded like cling-on or some dead language, in the highest falsetto voice I've ever heard. I just smiled, nodded and continued walking into the park.

I had never been in Central Park before, but I felt like I had chosen a perfect time of the season for experiencing it for the first time. Winter was late, and some of the leaves still hung onto the boughs of the trees. There were plenty of leaves that had already fallen to the ground and swished and crunched as I walked down the path through the park, but the morning breeze that perpetually blew through the park that morning was delicately dislodging the remaining leaves from the trees, and I was present for it, watching the season change before my eyes. Death was stagnant in the cold air that morning, but somehow nature made it appear to be so overwhelmingly beautiful. Birds were singing, car horns were blaring, children were joyously screaming, and as I watched the wind, which I knew belonged to the winter, gently tear the dead leaves from the living trees, I could sense an unexplainable, poetic, and potent emotion within me. Something felt like it was beginning to make sense. Like I had a higher realization and understanding of things. Like everything was somehow going to be okay. That all the living continued to live in some way or another, regardless of the death that patiently waited for everything.

As I explored Central Park, I was reminded of the perks and overall euphoria that only being alone can bring.

I was surrounded by millions of people, but I didn't know any of them; so to me, I was completely by myself in the city. I walked on, completely contented and couldn't think of the last time that I was that happy.

I was only able to explore about half of Central Park, and then I exited onto 5th avenue and across to Madison. I began making my descent southwards, back in the direction to where my hostel was located on 45th Street. I admired all the shops but was also disgusted by the absurd aroma of consumerism and wealth that the shops and street in general gave off. I continued down the street more impressed by the architecture of the buildings than what latest fashion trend lay inside, waiting and aching for some poor-minded but affluent person to stroll in and splurge. The buildings spoke to me more beautifully than the futile goods that they harbored.

By the time I made it to 45th Street, I realized that I was still about an hour too early to check-in for my room. I had underestimated how quickly I actually walk. But I was desperately eager to lay down and rest, because my legs and back were beginning to ache and throb. I knew that the Public Library was nearby, and I wanted to see it, so I continued down Madison Avenue and turned down E 40th Street, then made the left turn, crossing the street, with the massive, architecturally-incredible library staring at me across the street. I climbed the stairs in the front but decided not to enter the building itself, instead I chose to sit outside on the platform that overlooked the road and nestled close to the building. The air was still relatively cold, but it was beginning to warm up as it approached noontime, and I had been sweating from all the walking I had been doing, so it was relaxing to rest my legs and take off my sweatshirt to feel the cold air on my damp skin.

Sitting in the metal chair outside the library, I closed my eyes and just took in all of the myriad sounds that surrounded me. People chatting on cell phones. Cars and buses accelerating up and down the streets. The sound of the crosswalk signs signaling the pedestrian's diminishing time period of safety. Beep. Beep. Beep. Pigeons' wings flapping, all gathered around the library to binge eat on all the food scraps thrown onto the dirty cement. Old cheesesteaks and fried rice containers. It felt incredible to just rest my tired legs and eyes. The weight of everything had been bearing down on me all morning, walking the city streets, and it felt incredible to have it finally lifted from me. Even the heaviness had reached my eyelids, so I just kept them closed.

     I'm not sure whether I fell asleep or not, but if I did, it were only for a brief period of time. I looked at my watch and it was almost one. I couldn't wait any longer. I had the insatiable desire to check into my room and get it over with. I stood up and pushed my chair in and then began walking towards the front of the library to head down the stairs onto the street. I was slowly walking down the stairs and coming out onto the street when I noticed this woman. Most importantly, I noticed her eyes, and I was mesmerized by them. I couldn't stop staring, and I knew that she noticed me looking, but part of me couldn't stop myself and the other part didn't care to try. She glanced back at me and our eyes locked completely, and I saw a faint glimmer in them that looked so vaguely familiar that my heart began to speed up, and I watched her facial expression change slightly into an unforced smile. The relativity of time is a miraculous thing when you experience it first-hand. Time doesn't stand still or slow down drastically; however, at particular moments in time, time itself tends to either speed up or slow down even if only slightly perceptible. I felt it slow down at this moment, when her eyes met mine. There was an overwhelming connection. Not sexual. Not emotional. But in some way, spiritual and unexplainable. It was like we were instantly stripped bare and were able to view each other purely: a quick glimpse, peering into the soul. But like Shelley's analogy for the creative genius being a waning candle, we were only present for the viewing of the flames extinction, but we felt something profound that we carried with us: the knowledge that the flame had existed, no matter how briefly. And a gladness brimmed from the depths of our hearts.

    The moment had passed. The beautiful woman was gone. But there was a deep, unexplainable, contented sadness that lingered within me afterwards. I continued walking down the street, not looking back but knowing that we had some pure connection. I knew that we would never see each other ever again. Statistically, it was near to impossible. I tried to piece together what happened as I continued walking towards my hostel. There wasn't a romantic connection in any way. It felt like merely a recognition of some sorts. We were both human. We were both similar on so many unexplainable levels. We were all unable to separate ourselves from the human condition.

    I crossed the street and turned left down onto 45th. I kept thinking about the woman I had passed in front of the library, and the depths that I perceived in her eyes. How it felt like looking deep within myself. Then I began to think about everything. And I felt like everything aligned itself in some hidden reality that I knew I would never be able to understand.

    After checking in at the hostel, I entered the small room to find it empty. There were two sets of bunk beds and bags that were thrown on the floor by the beds. The room was probably only ten by ten and was a little crammed, but it was okay by my standards. I picked out the one remaining bed that was left untouched and set down my own bags and made the bed with the fresh linens that the woman at the desk gave me. Once I finished making the bed, I sat down on the edge, leaning my head forward to avoid hitting it off the bar from the bunk above mine, and I grabbed my laptop out of my bag. I tried to get on the internet to check my email, but the wifi wasn't working, and I was too tired to try writing anything, so I ended up just turning my computer off and lying down on the bed.

I had fallen asleep and slept for only about a half an hour before two of the other three people sharing the room with me returned. I pretended to keep sleeping, since I wasn't able to actually fall back asleep. As I lay there, part of me was hoping that they had just come back to grab something and were planning on leaving again, so I could try to sleep a little bit more, but another part of me wanted them to stay. They were speaking in a language that I didn't understand. It sounded harsh like German, but I wasn't entirely able to tell for sure. Eventually, I slowly began to get a little stir crazy being awake and unable to understand what they were saying, so I started to restlessly move on my bunk. Finally I rolled over and opened my eyes slowly, pretending like I was just waking up, yawning, squinting, and stretching a little bit. The whole theatrical make up. I don't know why I did it, but I enjoyed pretending.

I opened my eyes up more and there was a man and a woman sitting on the top bunk across from mine. The man looked at me and I waved, letting out a semi-exhausted, "Hello."

"Well, hello there. I'm sorry if we waked you."

His accent was strong, and his English was imperfect but good. The woman just smiled and waved.

"No, not at all. I was just taking a quick nap," I said as I swung my legs around to hang over the edge of the bed and sat up.

"Did you just get in? In New York City?"

"Yeah. This morning. I took the train."

"Ahhh," he said at first. He seemed like he was thinking, and then he asked me where I was coming from.

"Pittsburgh."

"Ah, yes. Pittsburgh. I haven't never been there, but I've heard of it. Where is Pittsburgh at?"

"It's in Pennsylvania, about seven to nine hours from here, by car or train."

"I've heard of Pennsylvania," he said, and then it was quiet for a brief moment of time. A silence filled the room, and so I yawned and stretched again, then reached for my bottle of water I had in my bag. I opened the bottle and took a really long drink, then capped it and tossed it onto my bag.

Then I asked, "So where are you guys from?"

"We are both from Vienna. Do you know Vienna?"

"Oh yes, I know Vienna. I've never been there, but I know where it's at. That's awesome."

Then I asked them if it were their first time in America or New York City, and they told me that they had been to New York City once before and that they have been to Chicago and Sacramento. They didn't like Chicago that much, enjoyed Sacramento but preferred New York City. They told me that they were in New York City for a week and were leaving the next day to fly back to Vienna. They explained to me all the different highlights that they went and saw for their week in the city. They had gone and seen the broadway version of the Lion King and recommended that I went and saw it too. They were sad that they had to go back to Vienna the next day but asked me if I wanted to come to Vienna some time and go to the bars and clubs with them. I agreed that I would if I were ever in Vienna. I told them that it was my first time in New York City and so far I was in love with it. And I told them that I hoped to come back when I had more time, but I was actually only staying overnight and then leaving early in the morning to take the train out on the Long Island peninsula up to Montauk.

"Where are you going tomorrow?"

"Montauk."

He asked me to repeat how to say Montauk a couple of times, so I said it slowly and tried to stress the vowels and consonants. He attempted it several times, slowly and deliberately, then nodded his head.

"And where is that? This 'Montuck'"

"Well where I am going is Montauk point. It is all the way out Long Island. Until you can't go any further. Long Island juts out into the Atlantic Ocean. Montauk is as far as you can go."

"Ahh, okay. And why do you wish to go to Montauk?"

He seemed more confident in his pronunciation, and I believed that that helped him actually pronounce the word correctly, instead of constantly thinking of whether he were going to say it correctly or not.

"I don't know really. I was just looking for something random and spontaneous to do. I mainly just needed to get away from Pittsburgh. I needed to just go somewhere by myself. I wanted to go as far as I could on land out into the Atlantic Ocean. Montauk was the closest to Pittsburgh that went out the furthest. Plus it is supposed to be absolutely gorgeous up there. And I wanted to see New York City, because I never had before, so it just seemed like the best decision."

"What do you think of the New York City?"

"I absolutely love it. I was always skeptical of it at first. But now I understand what the hype is all about. There is just something unspeakable and powerful about the city. It's totally different than anything else."

"Yes. I completely agree. It is wonderful. We already can't wait till we can come back again in the summer. We have been here for almost all the seasons. The fall now. The spring before. Next, we come in summer, then maybe the winter."

I laughed a little bit, and they looked at each other and smiled, then laughed a little bit too. I could tell that they were really in love with each other just by the way they looked at one another at that moment. The smallest, nonverbal signs often reveal the most.

I realized that we had been talking for nearly twenty minutes and I didn't have any idea what their names were.

"My name is Owen, by the way," I said and stuck out my hand to shake theirs.

"I am Étienne, and this is Stéphanie," he said, gesturing towards the woman sitting on the bed.

I shook both their hands and asked him to repeat the names, so it would help me remember and to make sure I was pronouncing them correctly, or, more rather, as correctly as I possibly could.

"It is very nice to meet you," Stéphanie said.

I could sense that she was a bit shy, because she didn't speak English as well as Étienne.

"Your English is really good. The both of you," I said, hoping that she wouldn't feel as self-conscious speaking around me. I had no intentions of judging her English skills. I wanted to hear them speak more than anything, and I wanted to learn a little bit about them.

They both laughed, and she had a big smile on her face. Then they began speaking in a foreign language that I didn't understand. Then more laughing.

"What language are you speaking? If you don't mind me asking. It sounds like German"

"It is German, but it is a little different between German they speak in Germany and German they speak in Austria."

"Okay, that's what I was thinking. It sounded like German, but it also had elements that seemed unique to me."

"Yes, absolutely. We are from Austria, but we speak German and have French names. Funny, don't you think?"

Étienne began laughing and so did I. Stéphanie wasn't laughing and began speaking to Étienne in German. I figured that she wasn't sure what Étienne had said in English, so she was asking him to tell her in German. I tried to reassure her by smiling. Then I said:

"Well at least your English speaking skills are much better than my German speaking skills, because I can't even understand anything you are saying."

We all started laughing, and she said something to Étienne in German, then looked at me and said, "Thank you very much," and I knew that she meant it.

I had sat back down on my bottom bunk, and the three of us sat in the room talking for what turned into almost three hours. We shared a lot about one another and learned a lot.

Étienne and Stéphanie went to school in Vienna but then dropped out, because college degrees weren't viewed as being crucial for most jobs. Stéphanie worked for the government and said that it was a pretty boring desk job, but the pay was relatively decent. Étienne also worked for the government, but a different part of it. They asked me about my schooling and American colleges in general. I told them that in my opinion they are generally overrated. That they are turning more into businesses as opposed to centers of education. That most of the university presidents and professors are only concerned about their massive pay and couldn't care less about actually educating. And also that the students are born thinking everything should be given to them and that they already know everything so there is no point in going to class or actually picking up a book and reading it. On both ends of the equations, the products that were put into the formula didn't add up to anything worthwhile. However, there were rare glimpses of an indefinable hope that brought on the unexplainable joy of solving such a mind-rattling math problem. Those were the teachers that had pure hearts and truly wanted to educate. Those were the students who were humble and eager to learn.

They were European and loved America, but they were also a little cynical about 'Americans.' I could tell that they were glad that I was unabashed in discussing and criticizing the ignorance and arrogance that is ubiquitous across the United States.

"I mean, don't get me wrong, I love America. But being born as an American, it seems to be instilled in our brains, subliminally, that we should be pretentious and ignorant strictly on the basis that we are Americans. Now, I know that every country and every different group of people all believe that they are at least a little better than everyone else, but I think America tends to go a little further than most. My problem is with it all. Because it is nothing more than futile labels and childish nonsense. All this superior thinking. We are all the same in more aspects than we are different, so why is it so important to say one is better than another. Yes, one may be better in a certain aspect, but I guarantee that it is weaker in another aspect."

I felt like I was getting a little preachy and that my sleep deprivation was loosening my tongue. Étienne was translating a summation of my rant into German for Stéphanie. He was smiling as he was speaking in German, and Stéphanie began to laugh about half way through.

We changed the topic to traveling in general, and I told them how I had only been to Europe once, and briefly, and how I hoped to be able to live there someday, and potentially teach literature or creative writing. Then we discussed plans for their last night and my first and last night in New York City. They planned on taking a nap to rest up for this club they were going to. I asked them what time their flight was the next day, and they told me that they had to leave at eight a.m. I laughed, saying I didn't know how they were going to get up if they were going out. That's why they were napping now, they said. We talked a little bit longer, then I told them I was going to go out and explore and find something good to eat for dinner, and I would let them sleep. I said that I hoped to see them later and they agreed.

I left the room and walked down the hallway, then down the three flights of stairs out into the lobby of the hostel, then out into the street. It was now dark outside and the lights of the city looked incredible. I roamed aimlessly, not knowing where on earth I was going but not really caring either way. Eventually I stumbled upon Time's Square, realizing that it was just a couple blocks from the hostel I was staying at, but I accidentally found it when I made a massive loop through central New York City. The vibrant lights in the city at night were bright and beautiful, and I allowed myself to become entirely lost.

When I came back later that night, Stéphanie and Étienne were already dressed and just about ready to leave for the club. I had stopped at a Mediterranean restaurant near the hostel and got some falafel, hummus and pita bread. I only came up to the room to check my computer again to see if I had any mail, but the internet still wasn't working, so I just gave up and talked to Étienne and Stéphanie for a little bit. Then I told them I hoped they had a great last night in New York City and had a safe trip home, because I probably wouldn't see them again. They wished the same for me, and we exchanged some information, so I could contact them if I were ever in Vienna.

After they left, I went downstairs and ate on the back patio at the hostel. It was one long, bare picnic table and metal chairs on the wooden deck. There was a pay phone attached to the brick wall outside. I sat down and opened up my container and began eating. The food was delicious, and the night air was surprisingly warm. The city and buildings had spent all day heating up from the sun, and at night, all the heat was radiating and keeping the city alive and warm. One other person sat outside on the patio with me. A man, by himself, sitting in the corner on his laptop, attempting to upload the photographs that he had apparently taken from earlier in the day. I sat there for a while after I finished my food, just looking straight up at the open sky, framed like a portrait by the straight lines formed from the tops of the buildings. The city was so full of life and Time's Square was so close that the sky was lit up and it looked like it was daytime, but it was actually almost eleven p.m. I sat there, watching the clouds slowly floating by through the sky, and eventually, my eyes began to get really heavy and I started to feel very tired, so I went upstairs to lay in bed, even though I couldn't fall asleep.

I eventually dozed off sometime after three-thirty in the morning, then I was woken up at about four-thirty when Stéphanie and Étienne stumbled into the room from the club completely drunk. They turned on the light and rattled around through the room for a little while, before they turned off the light and lay in bed. I think that they forgot I was there, so I just lay there pretending to sleep still. They passed out rather quickly and began slowly snoring, and I continued to lay their unable to sleep. Then at about five, the French girl who was the fourth person in our room came in and got into bed. She tossed and turned a little bit, seeming to also be restless and suffer from insomnia. But eventually I heard the soft, labored breath of slumbers, and I lay there wishing that I could just fall asleep.

~~~

I was only sleeping lightly, so I noticed the morning light slowly starting to creep through the window a little before six in the morning. I had only gotten a couple hours of sleep, but I was used to operating on little or none at all, so I forced myself out of bed. Étienne, Stéphanie and the French girl were all still passed out, sleeping deeply. I had slept in my clothes, so I was pretty much all ready to go in the morning. I just had to pack up my bag then strip the sheets off of my bed and turn them in at the desk with my key. I checked out of the hostel and hopped down the steps onto the sidewalk. The sun was still coming up and the air had a crisp chill to it. It bit but only slightly. It certainly helped me wake up more quickly than I normally would have. I started walking, and walking quickly towards the train station, because I needed to catch the early train out to Long Island if I had any hopes of making it all the way out to Montauk.

As I walked to the train station, I was able to watch the gears of the city slowly begin to start churning again, after never really coming to a rest the night before.

Businessmen and businesswomen were walking in small masses that were becoming larger down the sidewalks, and people were hailing taxicabs on both sides of the street and for as far as anyone could see up and down 7th Avenue. The machine was perceptible to me, but I was completely on the outside of it, watching all of its most minute inner-motions.

    I only had a couple blocks to walk, so I made it to the subway station in time. I got to the station and bought my ticket for Long Beach. I was actually early, so I just sat down and waited for the train. After about twenty-five minutes, the train showed up and everyone boarded, lots of people were running to catch the train. I watched three people that were too late. I saw the frustration and disappointment in their faces as the train began to pull out and they realized they were too late, and I sat there not able to do anything to help, just watching the change in their exhausted faces.

    On the train, I got a decent seat, where it wasn't too crowded, and the ride seemed a lot shorter than it was in actuality. In Long Beach, I got off the subway and started to make my way to catch the railway train that goes all the way up to Montauk. I made it to the station and bought my ticket, then I was waiting again patiently for the train to depart. This time it was a little longer, but I was in no hurry. At the station, I stopped and bought a fresh black coffee, and it tasted beautiful in the cold, fresh morning air, as I stood up on the port waiting for the train to show up. I stood on the platform waiting, because I had no desire to sit down. I knew I would be sitting on the train for hours. I was just glad that I had my bag and everything, a good cup of fresh coffee and a good book to read on the train ride.

    I ended up reading for a little while for the beginning of the train ride, then I passed out for not quite an hour. When I woke up we were more than halfway there. We had already left the big cities on Long Island, and most of what I could see out the windows was just tons of dead bushes and trees and pine trees. The view looked so bleak, but there was something beautiful and poetic about all of it that I couldn't quite put my finger on. Maybe it just all seemed honest.

~~~

After exiting the train, I didn't realize how far of a hike I had. It was the complete end of the line. Montauk. The last stopping point for all people traveling up Long Island.

I was walking more quickly than I normally would, because I was excited. I had been so eager to be there for quite some time, and now that I was finally there, there was a moment of it being surreal to a certain extent. I stopped at the small building at the end of the tracks to buy my return ticket to New York City, so I would already have it when I came back to catch the last train out of Montauk that evening. The building was more like a shack than anything else. The woman at the counter, who sold me my return ticket, smiled at me. She knew that I was only a temporary visitor there. I stashed my ticket in my pocket, so I wouldn't lose it, then I left the train station and began hiking up the road towards the town.

I walked for about a mile down the road before I reached the small town of Montauk. As old women tend to say when they describe such things, it was rather "quaint." In my opinion, the town looked very peaceful and lax. To me, it embodied everything that I admired and thought of as being associated with Montauk. It was why I wanted to travel there in the first place. It was calming. It had a strong enough aura in its simplicity. I longed to clear my head and hopefully refill it with answers. That was why I came to Montauk at all.

Once I reached the small town, I turned left and headed up the main road towards the point. There was only one main road that led straight through Montauk, up through the state park that was near the tip of the peninsula, then to the complete end of the land, Montauk Point.

I made it down the road, walking at a steady, quick pace, a few miles before my legs and back really started to bother me, and even at that, they only were beginning to ache a little bit. I had remembered to bring a big bottle of water and a couple of power bars to snack on for energy and to prevent muscle cramping. I continued on, persevering up the road, only resting at the two overlook spots that I came across on my way to the point.

At the first overlook, I rested on a wooden blockade that was set up to mark the end of the parking lot, where all the cars would pull in. I leaned up against the wood, breathing heavily and looking around at my surroundings, attempting to take everything in. There was a wind that started to pick up and was very strong. I could tell I was getting closer to the ocean, closer to the point, because the wind was getting stronger. I watched the overlook sign blowing and almost turning horizontal from the wind. There was one lone seagull that was walking around the parking lot, afraid to take flight in such a strong wind. I watched him hovering low on the asphalt ground of the parking lot with his wings tucked-in closely to his body.

Eventually the wind calmed down a little bit, and the seagull flew up to the post of the sign. Then the wind picked back up, and he ducked his head down and fought against the wind by reducing his resistance against it as much as possible. He knew it was futile to fight against such a strong force, a force that you could never have any hopes of winning against. I thought that the bird and I had a lot in common. We were both alone in such a remote part of the world. I thought that I still had a lot to learn. I looked up and realized for the first time how vibrant and beautiful blue the sky was. I had never seen it such a color. I knew that only this part of the world, with this kind of ocean and this kind of sky, could produce such a unique shade of blue. I took a drink from my water bottle, then I watched the seagull fly off over the field of dead grass and dead bushes, into the distance, towards the bright blue ocean that started to open up into the distance, then I threw my bag onto my back and continued my journey.

The second overlook was not much like the first. It provided a better view of the Montauk Lake that was off to the left from the road, but other than that, there wasn't much to look at or explore. I analyzed the bright green pine needles that grew off of the mini-pine trees that contrasted heavily against all the other dead and dying plant life. I thought that it may have meant something, but I turned my attention to the gorgeous view of Montauk Lake over the hillside that ran down off the left side of the road, then decided it was best to continue walking if I had any intentions of completing my journey.

The stretch between the last overlook and Montauk Point was filled with an endless road of trees on both sides, almost like a tunnel but without the overarching of the trees across the road. They stretched on as the road entered into the state park at the tip of Montauk. After about two hours of walking down the main road and taking a brief rest at the two overlook places, I had finally reached the lighthouse at Montauk Point.

When I finally got to Montauk Point, I was surprised how deserted it actually was. The State Park and everything on that end of the peninsula was closed for the season. Closed for the upcoming winter. There was one car in the parking lot, and it belonged to an older couple, in their late forties, who were coming up over the dunes, towards the parking lot to leave. The lighthouse itself was actually barricaded off, since everything was closed, so there was no way of getting closer than a couple hundred feet away, which was fine by me, because I didn't come to Montauk to see the lighthouse up close. I don't know what I really had come for. It was more of the atmosphere and the environment and, I guess, what I hoped that they would reveal inside of me.

I was surprised I wasn't more tired than I actually was from all the walking I had done. I guess all the excitement of finally reaching where I wanted to be had slowly overwhelmed my exhaustion from walking. My mental euphoria far surpassed my draining physical excursion. I thought that perhaps that is how triathlon competitors or mountain climbers felt at the exuberance of finally reaching the end or the top. Not that my personal feat was on any level along those lines, but it had a similar psychological component.

I looked around for a while looking for a way to get to the beach since the lighthouse was closed off for the season, and eventually I found a narrow, human-made trail that wove down a hillside. I had to walk down the road away from the lighthouse and parking lot a couple hundred feet, climb over the guardrail on the side of the road, then descend a dirt- and gravel-covered hillside that led downwards through a pull-back fence opening. I climbed down the hill and through the fence, and then I was walking down a narrow pathway that dug its way through the trees in the woods, and I noticed that it was becoming more difficult to walk. The hard dirt and gravel ground was slowly turning more and more into a soft, finely grained sand, and my balance was disrupted by its surface. I began to walk slower and with more effort. Finally the pathway came out into a clearing, and the sand changed back into a hard-surfaced ground with grass growing wildly upon it.

Out from underneath the shade of overhead trees and across the field of verdant green, I could see the ocean, stretching out and out farther. To me it looked to stretch on for infinity, but I knew that eventually it would meet with the shores of Europe. I walked across the grassy field, and, at the end of the field, I came to the part where I finally saw the shoreline for the first time. There were rocks that I had to traverse to get down to the actual sand of the beach before I could get to the water. I stepped on them strategically, hoping to not lose my balance and fall.

Then after some careful maneuvering, I had managed to reached the sand again and feel it underneath my feet. I walked down a small sand dune and was met by the calmly crashing waves of the Atlantic.

The beach was mostly rocky, covered in large pieces of driftwood, but the sand that was there underneath was the softest sand I had ever felt. It had clearly been churned and ground into such a fine particle under the strains of the water and the rocks. I had become so overwhelmed with the sights of everything, and all the thoughts that were flitting through my mind so rapidly, that I had not noticed how close I had actually gotten to the water walking, until one of the gentle waves rushed onto the sand and over my feet and lower legs. The sensation pulled me back into reality. The water was warmer than I would've guessed. Altogether it was an incredibly beautiful day for that time of year. The sun was shining bright against the bright blue sky, and the ocean was reflecting the bright rays of light off and illuminating everything. It was a warm day for autumn, and the water reminded me that I was definitely, most certainly alive.

My sudden realization was quickly altered when I looked down and saw that all along the beach, there were dead baby jellyfish that lined the sand. I looked down the beach farther, and it appeared that there were more. There had to be at least thirty or forty of them, just lying in the sand. I bent down and picked them up, knowing that they were long dead, but I tried futilely to save them by throwing them all back into the ocean. There was a feeling deep down inside of me that was somewhere between lament and nausea. After throwing about fifteen into the water, I sat down on the sand and watched the water crashing over a massive rock that was about five feet out into the water and rushing up and onto the shore.

I had been trying all of my life to understand the indifference of the natural world. A world where there is no justice, no right and no wrong. Only conceptions of such ideas that humans have created through abstract thinking and they have labeled as virtues or morals or ethics. I knew that all of these ideas and feelings had to have some sort of origin. Altruism tends to work the most fluidly if it is reciprocal, and, for a species to survive, they must learn to coexist and cooperate with one another. Not just human beings, but all species, from elephants in the animal kingdom to the lowest forms of organisms. The bee that takes honey from the flower and in the process gathers the pollen on its body to carry, share, and inadvertently propagate the genes of the flower. The Anglo-Saxon who found the sweetness of the apple in the fields of Kazakhstan and decided to spread it across Europe and into the Americas for his benefit, but in the process, he helped to spread and propagate the apple seed, making it superior. Everything is intertwined and interacts in some way or form with every other thing. The invisible thread that connects everything in the world. Oftentimes, invisible. On rare occasions, perceptible to the trained eye and the intellectual mind. Sometimes what appears to be the most simplistic, when analyzed more closely, presents itself to be the most elaborately, convoluted, complex entity. And in this grand scheme that has allowed us to evolve and spread so rapidly ourselves, we have developed such powerful abilities in thought and emotion. We are now not only capable of sympathizing with our immediate family, but we are capable of sympathizing with a picture of a starving child half-way across the world or an injured robin that we've found in the backyard of our suburban homes. We have such potent empathy that we tear up when watching an animated cartoon about giraffes or anything else. From this empathy, we have devised societal rules that govern what actions are considered praiseworthy and others which are not. From this empathy, I felt a strong loss that cut deep into me, and I didn't know why, when I looked down at the beach and saw those dead jelly fish stretched across the sand. There was nothing I could do, and I knew that. Was I lachrymose because I was impotent to such an unknown phenomenon, such as death? Or had I recognized that thread glistening in the sun at Montauk Point that connected me in some way to those jellyfish and everything in the world that surrounded me on that beach?

There are moments that you reach in your life every once in a while when you just think too much about everything, all the little things that hide deep in the far corners of your mind, and you just get so depressed that you can't understand anything. In the back of everyone's mind is the thought of their imminent death. It is only natural. But naturally, we all hide it far in the back of our minds, so that it may only creep up slowly and stealthy on a dark evening when we least expect it, but it is quickly checked and put back into its place before it starts to weigh too heavily on our cognition. A book we've always been ambitious to explore, yet we only dust it off from time to time. We crack its back and turn the pages and quickly reshelf it, the longing in our hearts. However, it's those moments that are the most real, the most intense, and the most honest. We really begin to explore ourselves and attempt to understand ourselves and the world and the meaning behind everything when those moments take us by surprise. What is the meaning of life? *Is* there any meaning to life, or is everything just random, arbitrary or meaningless? Why do things have to die? These were the questions that tended to surface quickly in those moments. It always recurred for me when I would see anything dead. Those jellyfish stretched across the sand reverberated the feeling deep inside to make it much more poignant. And then something crystallized and came forth in my mind: I had become a byproduct of the indifference and apathy I saw so vividly before me in the world.

But I realized that I had gone too far. I had lost sight of everything that was worth holding onto in life, because I was too busy keeping my eyes shut. I realized that I thought I had ingeniously developed a system of disconnecting myself from the indifferent world I was placed into, but instead I was separating myself from those tiny fragments of reality that most people refer to, generally, as happiness, or the wells that it springs from. In *War and Peace,* the character, Prince Andrey Bolkonsky, enters into the war on the Russian side against France and Napoleon in hopes to gain grandeur and immortality, but instead he is wounded on the battlefield and has a life-shattering change on his mentality of life. He realizes that all the pursuits he had were in vain and entirely meaningless. He looks up at the sky, and it is the most beautiful thing to him, because it remains eternal and unchanged, and even more important, it is calm and un-phased by the horrible war and ruthless killing that is going on right underneath it. He watches peaceful clouds moving through a beautiful blue sky, and he can't fathom an explanation of such a harsh contrast between that sky and the war that surrounds his wounded body. That realization enables him to see not only the meaninglessness of his own foolish pursuits, but also the meaninglessness of the entire war which was perpetrated under the similar meaningless pursuits of Napoleon himself. I had finally realized that I had that similar feeling overtake and leave me feeling bitter and cynical, except I had applied the meaninglessness of life to everything. With most people, the doors of disillusionment are slowly, creakingly opened, but for me since I have always been a curious and eager person, I pushed on the doors and they flung themselves open wide for me to take in everything in one large, bitter dose.

    I had receded entirely into both a cognitive and emotional reclusiveness that I now realized was necessary temporarily but not permanently. I learned to become entirely content with myself as a human being, which may be the most difficult task there is for us in our lives, with the exception of the egomaniacs, of course. For most of us, loving ourselves is more difficult than loving fictional, cartoon characters on a television show. Why is this the case? I don't know. But to solve the problem and to embrace yourself for just who you are, that is the most rewarding answer there ever will be. If anyone ever hopes to love another human being completely and unconditionally, or to help other people in the world, or live a fulfilling and meaningful life, or even strive towards progressing humanity towards a more peaceful world, we must start within ourselves. We must find who we are and what it means to be human, before we have any hopes of acting humane.

    As I gazed farther down the beach towards a massive cliff face, there was a large group of seagulls that had all flocked close together and were lying on the beach. The entire shoreline for as far as I could see in each direction was completely deserted, aside from me and the flock of seagulls. Noontime had already past and time was slowly beginning to creep into the early afternoon, and the sun hung bright in the deep blue sky, refracting light in all directions as it hit the ebbing and flowing ocean water.

    I walked down the beach in the direction of the seagulls, trying to not come too close as to disturb them, and I sat down on a big rock and looked out across the vast ocean before me, not able to truly fathom its end or its magnitude. I closed my eyes and listened to the water slowly whooshing and crooing onto the sand gently. Kerouac under Bixby Canon Bridge. Big Sur. I immediately felt relaxed and peaceful and could feel any problems or thoughts I had being instantly washed over by those same waves, washing and cleansing my mind. With each wave that made it ashore, my body and mind became more calm. All the thoughts I had of the world, all the thoughts I had of loneliness, all the thoughts I had of love, all the thoughts I had of injustice and violence, all the thoughts of death or any sort of life after death, all the thoughts of a god or an arbitrary and meaningless existence. They were all becoming purged from me in one giant, natural and pure catharsis.

Then to my right, down the beach, I heard faint squawking and flapping wings that seemed much farther away than it actually was. I held onto my meditation, but I could feel it delicately slipping away from me, and I could feel my eyes instinctively trying to open to explore the sounds and the world before me. With my eyes closed, was it all really there? Was it all real? Did any of it actually exist? That Joycean, Protean ineluctable modality of the visible.

I opened my eyes and had to squint at first, because the sun was so bright that day, more bright than I had ever seen it, and then I noticed all the seagulls flapping their wings and taking flight from the beach, all soaring up into the salty air. More and more and more of them, all flying up into the sky, creating a multi-colored patchwork against such a blue sky, almost looking dark against the contrast of colors. When I noticed them all lying on the beach, it looked like there were only twenty or thirty of them, but when they took flight out over the ocean against the backdrop of the blue sky, forming a flying formation that looked like cresting waves, I realized that there were closer to a hundred of those seagulls. They circled around in the afternoon sky and landed on the water of the moving ocean.

•

On the train ride home, I had passed the time by reading *Big Sur*, sitting in the snack car, drinking coffee and eating a cheese Danish. I peered out the window and tried to drown the sadness I felt inevitably rising up within me with my coffee. I thought of the last time I had been loved, or under the impression that I was loved. But I realized that she never loved me, even though she tried.

    Before the end finally came, I knew that things were over. There was nothing between us, and if there ever was it was long gone and irretrievable. I hadn't been blind, but I had been deluding myself in denial, unwilling to accept the inevitable reality.

    One of the last times we were together, I remembered the sad, soft words she spoke to me in a quavering whisper, as my blood ran cold and it felt as if I were dying. She said she had never seen eyes so blue, sunk into such a sad, cynical face. And there was a sadness that gripped my whole being, and trickled like rain water from my mind down into my heart as I remembered this event almost perfectly. And as I was leaving a place that I had fallen in love with on that bitter, lonesome train, I couldn't help feeling those emotions again in some way, like I was leaving her all over again. And I felt that deep, hollow pang of depression, yes, that sad, bleak chorus that sings in your chest to remind you of your voids like a sadistic echogram, as I watched all the beautiful things of the world moving quickly before my eyes, my blue, blue, deeply oceanic blue eyes that she loved, or that she said she loved, and all those beautiful things, fleeting, passing, and paying not the slightest attention to my general existence. They were utterly un-phased by me. They had seen my kind before. I thought she was the only one who could perceive my beautiful squalor and the agonizing love that swelled in the core of my heart, my whole heart that I was so eager to dissect to cut out all the bad parts and offer up the small remaining fragments of pure golden purity to her.

But it was all too late, or it had never even began. Her love had grown tired of me, and now I finally was able to understand her, and in a way, forgive her. There wasn't anything that happened between Liz and I that caused everything to dissolve. It just naturally did by itself, quickly dissipating over time. Falling apart like a poorly-knit sweater, one fine thread followed by the next. And for a while, I had lost all of my faith in love completely, believing that the human heart was the ficklest of all our organs.

It was almost as if it were never there. There was a shroud of forgetting that seemed to obscure the lens of the past, and there were vague memories that flickered dully from the unsalvageable wreckage. A hollow melody, a flatline. Blurred into a pinpoint: a singularity of nothingness.

But what seemed to be the most frightening was that even though I wasn't bitter at all, I had become so goddamned cynical about love, because it seemed that as the human race progressed, we progressively got worse and more terribly selfish and pathetic at something so simple as love. I understood that it was hardly ever simple, and never would be. But as the time and ages passed, people tended to become much more idiotic when it came to loving another human being. It was so hard just to love oneself, but everyone seemed to become so hung up on and delusional with the idea that love was so pure and beautiful and easy and exactly as it is portrayed in the movies and music. Love at first sight, et cetera, et cetera. Maybe it really was, but the world that I perceived told me something entirely different. I saw the members of my generation failing miserably at loving one another, and I couldn't possibly attempt to argue that I was much different, but I just couldn't figure how that had become the issue, or more rather, the norm. Why were most men so fucking egotistical and in pursuit of as many easy fucks as they could possibly attain? And why were most women so naïve and foolish to allow men to perpetually use them in such a manner? There's that old evolutionary argument about males needing diversity in propagating their genes, but it seems like a cop out to me. I believe that people were led into the selfish delusion of mass culture that portrayed a male and female image. Distinctive stock roles. To me, they defy our better judgment and overall happiness. They destroy purity in human connection.

    I wanted to believe in love, but it became so difficult to believe the boats we put ourselves in would continue to float when we could see all the holes when we first stepped inside the vessel. I understand that the feelings of love are going to make a person feel, and most often go, insane, in the sense that they feel their love is so unique, yet they embody all of the clichés, they believe that everything works through for itself and that loving is easy. I felt like I was still so cynical about love. I believed that love, as Rilke has said, was the most difficult task of our entire lives, and perhaps the purpose, the true meaning, for our lives, and that we needed to fight and constantly work towards attaining, and maintaining, such a delicate thing. No human beings could possibly love one another or spend their lives together without having disagreements or disputes, and anyone that believes that

that is the case is thrown into the heap of delusional assholes who believe love is the creation of the Hollywood machine. What human being can spend their entire lives without having disagreements or disputes with themselves, let alone someone who may be an incredibly good match for the other but obviously will feel differently about something at some point in time? It is unique peculiarities in our loved ones that make us love them, that make them perfect. Not some fallacious ideal.

That was the love that I wanted to believe in anyways. Not that movie bullshit that's so unreal, even though there are some components of love that I believe they do capture, but they tend to amplify and magnify the small fragments of actual love that are usually the peaks, the best moments. You have to fight for your love, you have to constantly work at it and attempt to be as objective and selfless as possible, which is extremely difficult. You have to love yourself and be comforted with who you are and be just exactly yourself and take that risk of the other person loving you for exactly who you are. Doesn't that make sense?

Modern society has everyone programmed to be able to possess everything instantly. And at the slightest displeasure, we are taught to flee and dispose of things apathetically. These mentalities can never be positively applied to love. Love is exemplified in patience. Love is the product of slow, precise craftspersonship. Love is learning. Love is allowing two objects to come as close as possible without becoming one, without losing the purity of their selfhood, their uniqueness, all the things that make them loveable in the first place; everything that defines them.

We've constantly fought and continue to fight for our survival, so why should love be any different? I hardly think that as our Neanderthal ancestors forged through the tundra climate after the last ice age, ruthlessly fighting for food and survival, found it to be an easy task. And if men or women continue to make the animal excuse, then explain to me about members of the other animal kingdoms. There are very few species that are monogamous; however, there is still the element of love that is present. It may not be the same as ours, or maybe it is all too similar. Most birds are polygamous, but the males will persistently attempt to woo the female in order to exhibit their superiority to pass on their genes. But, most of the men in the world who believe themselves to be that superior male when they aren't, yet they falsely seduce the female and win their goal, then leave her alone forever. Then there are the few and far between men, who are much like the bower bird who diligently works to build an incredible nest and patiently over time impress and win the heart of the female in order to mate, to make love with her. That is the type of love I would aim to pursue and fulfill. One that requires my entire being and captivates the entire being of another.

     Nothing on the earth or in our lives will ever truly be easy. Now I believe that people who clearly are not compatible should never be together, yet it seems like they are the couples who fight the hardest, maybe they are foolish, maybe they are stoic, maybe they are the only ones truly in love. But I believe that love will be more rewarding and fulfilling and meaningful if it weren't all golden sunshine, because I believe it makes everything more honest and pure. But I knew it was all worth fighting for in the darkest hours, fighting for those moments when it wasn't pure golden radiance. But part of me felt that I would never even bother with that realm of life, and that I would just let it all slip past me, before my eyes, and that I would just leave it up to the fools of the world, that I didn't want to even be bothered with it. I felt that I had more important things to do, whatever they could've possibly been. I thought that I would remove myself from that area of life to slowly wither into old age with only my thoughts and my own life. Maybe someday that would change, I thought. But for the time being, I was content and didn't have plans to alter my life. I continued to believe in my own skewed vision of love, even though I remained highly cynical about it, as I watched the dead souls of my generation float through life, hurting one another over and over again because they thought they could attain some ideal that did not, and never would, exist.

There was such a potent depression that seized my life that I thought I'd never be able to recover from.
However, time can be surprising and work in slyer ways than even humans are capable of, because the dark skies that consumed me and the fog that hazed over my mind slowly began to lift. I had allowed my perspectives to be altered, as I let the pain go with the love that I thought I had.
Every once in a while, those remembrances of such a transformative time period in my life would slowly awaken from their slumbers deep inside of me. And it was no longer painful or sorrowful, but it felt merely like a part of my past that I had come to accept.
But in fact over time, I slowly began to realize that the love I thought her and I had was all wrong. I felt like there was constantly the weight of some heavy yoke bearing down on me, and so much was required of her from me, while she always seemed remotely cold or detached whether she showed it or not. And once that feeling was lifted, a feeling of consolation filled my heart and soul, knowing and believing that there would come a love someday that would be so pure and so honest that it would set me free.
And I thought that finally I'll shed this foul skin, then I'll be pure again. For, is the serpent truly supposed to recognize that old husk of its past life as a part of its true self?
I remembered Sam and I had a conversation a couple months after Liz and I had separated, and I remembered saying to him over a late night cup of coffee at a diner, "I know that it sounds and seems rather lame,

but now that everything is done and some time has passed, I have to agree with the cliché that declares that 'it is better to have loved and lost than to have never loved at all.' For me, past love has brought such a potent form of depression. However, to me, there is something so sadly beautiful in it all, and I am glad for it. It feels almost as if I were reborn. That I know what it is to be alive. Because in all love, there is such a strong human connection and bond formed that creates such a strong physical and emotional pain when it has been severed. So in my personal opinion, to have experienced the heights of love and pure human connection and the lows that only its extinction brings, far exceeds any sort of life lived without experiencing a connection remotely similar to that. Besides, I feel that I have been able to learn a substantial amount that will lead my future into a life of love, by seeing the flaws and shortcomings of the past."

And Sam said, "Yes, I'd have to agreed. I had been numb for a portion of my life, that to feel, even if it's pain, is a beautiful thing in its own right. To be reminded of life, that you are actually alive. Besides, I think that there is a profound genius and love that can only be acquired through pain."

I knew Sam was right, even back then. But sitting on the train, it was sad being and feeling alone, and I was thinking more about how I had thought so much about just giving up and letting myself die at first, but then my attitude changed, and I began to believe that Liz and I were never meant for each other and that someday I would find that person who just fit snugly and perfectly with me, and then I started to remember the trip that Sam and I took to the woods in Autumn.

•

I sat in the car as the music melodically sang through the speakers and vibrated through the subs in the back of the car. Minus the Bear's *Highly Refined Pirates* album, rocking, and hard. The city far behind us in the car, and I was already immediately beginning to see more green as it grew over the horizon and on both sides of the car. Trees passing by quickly and quicker as I turned my head more and more sideways. I have always been impressed at how the guardrail and trees, in this case, but honestly anything that would appear on the sides of the moving vehicle, seem slowed down when looking at them through the windshield and then they rapidly begin to speed up as you turn your head to the right, if you're in the passenger's seat, towards the side window. I guess that's relativity for you, the way Einstein explained it to be. At least, I think. In some form. The objects appear to move more quickly or slowly through space-time from a different perspective, relative to another perspective on a coordinate plane. I am the embankment, and she is my train. I watch her go, dropping a pebble from the train, and I admire the parabola it makes; however, she perceives the pebble to fall straight to the ground, while I watch it's true, beautiful trajectory.

We pulled into a gravel lot off a side country road and parked at the end of the parking lot even though it was empty, with the exception of one other car. Sam asked if I wanted to smoke before we went into the woods, so naturally I answered in the affirmative. So he packed up the bowl and began lighting it up, and we passed it back and forth, with the windows up, the flame curling into the opening of the pipe, and the car filling up with smoke.

After a couple of minutes, we grabbed our gear and I pulled my coat on as we got out of the car and began to walk through the parking lot to a wooden staircase that led down a twisting set of stairs to a massive outgrowth of rock. I could hear the running stream moving quickly, before we had even reached the stairs, but once we started to descend the stairs and I first saw the waters, it all hit me at once how much I loved the beauty of nature and how nothing could compare to it and how I couldn't even honestly attempt to capture it with words and how fucking stoned I actually was and how being stoned somehow made everything in nature so much more right and peaceful and serene.

Once I got off the stairs and onto the rock, I began to feel so much better. I couldn't explain it, but everything began to feel perfect. I felt as if I were returning to my natural state and I were entering into a heightened sense of being in-tuned with nature. I walked across the rock to the narrow channel where the water was rushing violently through the crags in the rock that were maybe only 3 or 4 feet wide. I stared in amazement at how something so violent, like the quickly moving and raging waters of this stream could be so neutralizing and beautiful while being so powerful and violent at the same time. I thought about if I were to fall into the water, whether that would change or not. Would I remain peaceful as those same waters more than likely would obliterate my living corpse? Or would something change drastically, and the peace and serenity that then filled my soul would be replaced with utter and sheer terror as my body was ripped to shreds against the rocks as that beautiful water continued to push me through the complete process of my total undoing? I envisioned those waters rushing with the frothy white foam, filling with the red of my blood, and I was unsure, but for some reason, I felt like I believed more in the former. I believed that it would somehow be a peaceful death to die out there among the beautiful green pines and the raging waters.

Death has always been something that, as I'm sure is the case with mostly everyone, consumed my thoughts for quite some time, and I always wondered how I would die or what it would be like to die or what the hell would happen after I did finally die? I would like to say those thoughts are far from my mind, and although they are indeed much farther, they are still near and resurface every once and a while, so I focus on them greatly and deeply and try to work them out or work through them.

It is certainly hard to tell what death actually brings, because to date there is no record from the dead actually telling us, not considering near-death experiences and séances and Ouija boards. The white light seen by people who have experienced a near-death situation can be explained by the chemicals released in our brains at that particular moment of trauma or experience. It has been simulated in humans that are not anywhere near such a deathlike experience or situation, but instead when the human brain is under such stressful situations, it basically goes into a protective state, much like a tortoise returns its head and limbs to the core of its shell when it feels threatened. It is instinctive and appears ubiquitously throughout the species. The white light is indeed an inherent instinct in human beings, and if anyone of us were to incur such an experience that triggers that instinct, we would all see relatively the same thing. Besides, we all should know that our eyes are only gauged as being mildly reliable, because they love to play tricks on us quite frequently, so therefore, the white light scenario of death or anything similar to it is hardly worth seriously considering as some form of definitive proof of an afterlife for us or our souls once we die. However, I will admit that stories along those lines often send chills up the spine regardless, and we endlessly pursue meaning and understanding on the grand scale in the most mundane and easily explainable scenarios.

      I walked along the stream and watched it come out of the crags and enter into a wider area, and the water became much more calm as it spread out and slowed down. Sam and I decided to follow the water downstream and see where it would take us, so we climbed down some of the rocks and passed through a narrow passageway, as the rocks jutted out over our heads and we squeezed through. I noticed that on the inside walls of this cavern-type passage that people had managed to graffiti the walls, not in the sense of spray-paint, but just with marker, and I thought that we have been graffitiing the inside of walls from as early as we developed forms of writing with pictographs and hieroglyphics. I smiled and continued on moving, surprised at how my body was so agile while being so damn stoned. I descended and traversed a lot of steep and sketchy rocks, only to approach a narrow passing, where I had to hang onto the rock in front of me with only one foot on the ledge below me, as the water, that was probably just above freezing temperature and seven feet deep, rushed behind me right at the heels of my tennis shoes. Somehow I crossed that section of rock perfectly and continued on to, thankfully, the much more open expanse of rock that was cut into various lengths and heights but hugged close in between the water and the trees. Looking farther down, the water began to widen and stretch itself out through the wild forest that surrounded us.

The water certainly opened up, but farther down, the trail narrowed and then became non-existent and impassable, so eventually, after we strolled around and explored everything we could there, we turned around and headed back from the way we came, hiking and climbing back over the rocks, somehow avoiding the hazards of falling into the freezing water, then up those wooden stairs and back to the car to smoke another bowl before we went exploring a different area of the woods.

After we finished smoking, we exited the car. This time I really felt like an astronaut moving through antigravity in space. The gravel in the lot beneath my feet didn't help as it shifted and constantly moved underneath. We climbed over the guardrail and crossed the road, down a path on the other side that widened then narrowed then widened again and passed through a yard. We walked down a gravel driveway and through the grass of this yard, then down through the shrubs to what turned into an actual path. It was a miniature path about two feet wide, and there was actually sand, fine-grained beach sand on this narrow trail. We walked down the path towards the rocks in front of us, and it was weird walking across this sand in shoes, weird because it was difficult high and weird because I couldn't figure out what the fuck the beach sand was doing there. We came to some rocks and had to climb up them onto where they flattened and spread out. To the left was a little pond, obviously where some of the water from the river seeped in through the narrow cracks of the rocks and filled up this little area, and to the right was the massive river that had widened staggeringly and was about fifty yards wide. I realized that it was difficult terrain to tread, but we continued on, staying focused and realizing it was for the best.

Personally, I just hope that death is a process with as little suffering as possible. Now I know that is not the case with most people, but I hope that maybe at some point in the progress of humanity and technology that we will be able to insure more people with a painless death with no suffering.

I am certainly afraid to die, as I think every person should be, because I am afraid of the fact that I will slip into a complete ceasing of all that I have ever been and worked so hard to become, but then I convince myself that it is inevitable, it is a part of living itself, and that when that moment actually comes to face me, death, then I won't care about any of those problems or concerns, because death will have already consumed me and I will not exist; ergo, I will not worry about not existing. However, as much as a consolation that may be, it only tends to go so far.

Death is quite a mysterious thing and, as most people are afraid to admit or notice, it does indeed have an element of beauty. As Keats has said, "I have been half in love with easeful Death." The reason why I think it has an element of beauty is because it makes living all the more precious and everything in life fleeting and beautiful. Love, new experiences, your favorite foods, your job, everything would seem to lose its savor, or they would at least not smack the tongue as Thoreau's friend has said, with that "bow-arrow tang," if our existences were stretched out over the span of eternity. It feels like we live for quite a long time, however, we still view it to be a short time. Certainly some people live to one-hundred years, and most of us wish to live a long healthy life that will let us see one-hundred. It's hard to tell with anything though, because some people that reach one-hundred years old just want to die, while others want to keep living and experience new things. However, comparing one-hundred years to the greater span of the existence of our species and the planet, even if it only spanned back to 3,000 B.C.E. or even 10,000 B.C.E., it is such an infinitesimal span of time, the lives that we all live. Could you fathom living to 200? Doubling one of the highest lifespans? How about living to 1,000? What would you do? Certainly the school loans would cease to constantly burden my mind, because paying them off over a thirty year time period would seem like nothing, whereas now it seems like half of my life, or my whole life if I die young. It is a crazy concept to contemplate in your thoughts, and it is certainly interesting to ask yourself what you would do if you could live that long?

But that takes things too far down the road of life and the living, when what I really want is to get into the heart and core of death for what it's worth, at least for as much as I can as a living human being.

My vision of death is a rather bleak and haunting one at first glance; however, I feel that it is the most accurate, honest and, once you've really thought it over logically and truthfully, settling. I do not believe in any type of afterlife. Now, that doesn't mean that I hope that there isn't one. And indeed, there may be an afterlife; however, I just don't believe in the concept of heaven or hell as it has been created and evolved over the time of human existence through religious institutions and literature. If there is an "after life" that we go to after death, or our souls go to after death, I believe it will be much different from our current conceptions of heaven or hell as they are described and defined now. Now, I certainly have no idea if there is an afterlife or not or what it would be like anyways. There could be a heaven and hell described as perfectly as Dante or Milton explain them. Anything is possible. If it were different, I don't know if it would be any better or worse than the conceptions we have of heaven or hell now, or if we could even consider it to be better or worse. In fact, I feel that if such a place, if it would be considered a place, did exist, we probably couldn't even begin to fathom what it would be like.

Instead of an afterlife, I believe more along the lines of what Bertrand Russell had to say on the matter, "when I die, I will rot." As horrible and dysphemistic as that sounds at first, once looked at coldly and seriously, it begins to make the most sense and to seem less frightening and terrible, and philosophically, that is honestly what will happen, and all the farther we know, whether something comes after or not. The first human reaction when we experience something frightening or terrible, we immediately reassure ourselves that it is absolutely and entirely false, and then we refuse to analyze or examine the matter farther. However, if instead we fought through the terror and analyzed the matter at hand, we would all probably learn a great deal more. I believe that if we can learn to face such a bleak view of death, it doesn't matter whether there truly is an afterlife or not, because we learn to *live* much more beautifully. Once we begin to analyze the impending death that looms over all creatures destined to live, we can start to learn a lot about death. For, if death is a natural process to all things that are alive, then death must affect and result in the same for all things that experience death. Some would argue then that perhaps it would be better to never experience life, because that is the only way to avoid death. But I would say the opposite, because the impending death is what makes our lives and living all the more memorable and meaningful. We all only have a limited time to spend our lives, how will we spend it? That's what makes life unique and undeniably beautiful.

Whatever breathes life into the heap of matter that we are, we have a choice on how to learn to live.

Returning to the commonality that all living things share in common, with relation to death, I would like to say that as the seasons change, the tree may lose its leaves, as they brown and wither and eventually fall to the earth where they are consumed by the earth, much like our corpses are, those of us who choose to be buried. Now, what is different between those leaves and that person who is buried in the dirt underneath the shade of that same tree? I will tell you that in death, there is nothing different between them, while the religious or spiritual person will tell you differently. The way they lived and perhaps died were different; however, in death they are the same to me. Their life has ceased and they are no more. The peculiarity in humans that raises a lot of questions in death is our ability of sentience and thought and consciousness, which indeed it should pose questions, but the cold, hard fact is that without a beating heart to pump blood throughout the body and to the brain and without oxygen to flow into the lungs and be sent to the brain and oxidized into the blood, there is no sentience, no thought, no consciousness. All cease at that moment. Therefore, in my opinion, at death, all forms of sentience and thought and consciousness, everything that you consider to be you, your entire being, your soul, all cease and are no more. Everything stops, never to start again, but yet the world continues on unfazed, ebbing and flowing eternally, just like waves created far out in the ocean, unsuspecting of their ultimate doom of crashing against the shoreline and the sand; but they are beautifully sucked back underneath the other waves, back into the water and pulled out to be recycled and feed the future waves. I believe that to be the same case with all living things. Just as the tree leaves rot, die and fall from their branches to the earth and soak up into the soil, they feed that tree that continues standing and produces new generations of beautiful foliage every spring that returns on earth; all humans once placed in the grave, in the dirt, their bodies slowly decay and rot and feed the soil and all the creatures that feed upon their corpses, only to promote life to flourish in other realms, only to keep the giant rotating wheel of life moving.

    But concerning our sentience, there are small memes of our consciousness and our lives that continue to eternally live in the hearts of all those people that we've loved. The great metamorphosis from the concrete to the abstract.

Everything in our universe is made up of atoms including us, and everything on our planet is made out of chemical compounds including us, therefore we are a part of a giant cycle that is so much larger than us, so unfathomable and misunderstood, and so crucial to the continuance of eternity. So looking at things that way, potentially there is proof for the eternal soul or eternal being, or even eternal recurrence, because we provide the continuance of new life through our deaths, but we don't know what it all means and we will probably never know what any of it means. We must be humble enough to admit that as far as science advances, they are only continuing to answer the question 'how?' We must face the fact that we may never know the 'why.'

But as frightening as it is to confront death, it is also essential for us to confront it as a living species. We have been blessed with highly evolved brains, at least as far as we are capable of understanding, so we try diligently, and for good reasons, to understand as much as we are capable of understanding. Broadly, nihilism claims that everything is nothing and we will never truly know anything, and as silly as it honestly sounds when trying to apply it pragmatically, there is a certain small component of it that is truthful, or presents itself as a truth. To a certain extent, we can only pretend that we know anything. Even everything that we hold dearest, all of the things we claim to be truths, could potentially change at any moment. Now, chances are that most of them won't; however, allowing your mind to widen and expand by contemplating that it is *possible* that they could change and change at any minute, now that thought is mind-altering and enlightening. The uncertainty of everything.

As we continued on farther down the rocks, we came through a clearing that looked more like a wilderness trail we could hike on. The path led into the woods, and trees enclosed us from all angles and they arced over the pathway, but the sun's rays still found their way through the foliage of the tall trees and the waves of light shined in and reflected and refracted and illumined certain, tiny portions of the woods. The light had found us there somehow, in that remote part of the world. I could see distinct, particular rays of light, cutting through the trees and shining down in set areas. It amazed me, and I was taken aback by its overpowering quality that it had over me, something so simplistic, yet so stunningly overwhelming. Those delicate rays of light, shining down from a massive, burning star, a staggering distance away, cut down and reduced in these woods to such a tiny, little beam of light that I could see the lines where it didn't effectively reach. A place where the darkness meets the light.

The walk through the woods was mostly a blur for me. I remembered seeing severed trees, ones that had clearly fallen down across the path and were chain-sawed by the trail maintenance people, and then I saw ones that were out of the hikers' way, that just laid across the hillsides of the woods. Massive trees that weighed tons, just came crashing down at some point in time and no one was there to notice, only to show up later and find them in that position as if they had always been that way.

The trail was narrow and continued up and up farther and farther, and I watched the water slowly appearing farther down from where we were at, up in the woods at the bottom of the mountain, and the sound that it made became lower but still audible. I watched it through the trees over the hillside as we continued along our path, hiking and climbing through the woods, ducking underneath trees and traversing rocks and other obstacles. Finally we came to an area where we began to descend from the mountain and the path began to widen; we were coming back down towards the water, and the closer we came to the water the trail became wider. Eventually we were standing alongside a stream, and the trail opened up into a big area with sand all around, and a new path began to the left that led to a waterfall that was just barely in view from where we stood, at the interim, transition period between the path we were on and the path we would soon be on. The sound of the waterfall was very distinct, and I could see icicles formed on the branches of trees and roots that were sticking out of the water, as the cold water continued to rush in curves and streams and vortices, cascading and rushing farther on down their stream from the waterfall into the calm body of water that was the large river that we had been following from the beginning of our journey.

~~~

    I removed my water bottle from my bag to rehydrate, then placed it back in my bag and started to walk over towards the new path, ducking underneath a branch that jutted out overhead and squeezing in between two bushes that were acting as a pseudo-gate to the new part of the trail. The waterfall was now only a couple hundred yards ahead of the trailhead, and I continued walking tirelessly up the path toward the loud, cascading falls. The path was relatively straight but winded gently, and I attempted now to follow it as expertly as possible. With Sam behind me, I walked and walked, until finally I had reached a hill that went upwards to the left, towards a cliff edge and cave wall that wrapped around the waterfall, and to the right, there was a section of the stream that narrowed to about three feet wide, then farther down widen and gained speed as it rushed toward the big river we followed.

    I traversed the gap where the stream was narrow, then I began to carefully and strategically place my feet onto rocks that stood out of the water and allowed me access to continue traveling towards the base of the waterfall. I climbed over several rocks and made some sketchy leaps, until I was finally within twenty feet of where the water was falling over the cliff face and crashing onto the pond that had formed, spreading out into two streams that went into different directions.

There was a smooth, massive rock that stood about five feet out of the water, so I climbed up onto it and sat down, resting my legs that were beginning to become fatigued as the adrenaline from hiking and climbing was slowly dwindling away.

Admiring the water rolling over the cliff face and watching it plummet into beautiful splashes, I let out a deep sigh and closed my eyes, so I could only hear the sound of the water and the birds fluttering and chirping in the trees above my head.

As I sat there with my eyes closed, listening to the sounds surrounding me, a deep sense of serenity took hold of my entire body and mind, and it was remarkably similar to the feeling of slowly drifting off into a deep sleep. And as in the similar moment of sleep, those thoughts that seem both random and arbitrary began to deluge the mind, and they came in such an overwhelming way lacking all sort of cohesion. Hypnagogic. Proustian.

Then finally one fine thread settled. It was some koan or story that I vaguely remembered, one that I had heard a long time ago. I couldn't remember where I heard it from, but for some unknown reason, it was slowly but potently rising from my subconscious to the surface.

It has been rumored that a story was once told to a man, or maybe a group of people, by a wise man who lived in a cabin, on a hill in the deep, dark forest. This wise man had no known family, friends or trade. In fact, there was very little known at all about the wise man. Though once a year, he would travel to the village, before the leaves began to change colors upon the immensely large, beautiful oak trees, and he would startle the entire populace with a profound story.

Around this time, the wise man had a distinctive full-white beard that occupied the majority of his face. He walked with a cane, but most assumed he did not need it.

The villagers often wondered how he lived his life in the woods, all alone, or why he only decided to visit them in the beginning of autumn. But nonetheless, he did.

As the wise man stumbled into the village, all the men, women, and children began to gather around. Now, in the center of town, the congregation began to assemble and multiple. The crowd began to approach, often whispering quietly amongst one another or merely shuffling in awe and perplexity.

Once the crowd had gathered around the wise man and settled down, he softly stroked his beard and opened his mouth slowly. He said, "Upon the autumn day that surrounds us, ages ago there stood a great wise man and his student who had always sought out for the meaning of life, of eternity, and of wisdom. The teacher one day, while walking through the same woods that surround our beautiful village, was with his young student. Now the teacher had been silent for several hours and the student started to become anxious. The wise teacher sensed the student's uneasiness and therefore stopped walking and looked him in the eye. The wise teacher said, 'If you are so restless with my teaching, then I will give you a question to occupy your thoughts.' So the wise teacher reached down before him and picked up two identical rocks from the ground. The student stood confused, admiring his teacher when the teacher threw both rocks into the air simultaneously. In a matter of mere seconds the one rock hit the ground. However, the second rock never hit the ground. The student stood looking around in awe and the teacher said to his student, 'Tell me, son, where the other rock has gone.'" The wise man looked around the crowd of villagers and said, "I ask of you the same question that the wise teacher once asked his student. I will return when the snow has come and ceased, and I will leave you to contemplate your answers."

After the wise man had spoken, he turned and walked straight out of the village into the vast, deep forest that changed and shed its most polychromatic attire and seemed to blush as it returned its possessions to the soil underneath its feet.

The sun blazoned around the earth, radiating a golden magnificence upon the blue and white sky, as nature's ephemeral tears froze and gracefully bathed and purified all that was blessed and touched by Her celestial presence. The ground froze then thawed, and She wept for her lost children no more.

The wise man sat in the woods, observing the wild birds flying about and singing in their exuberant manner, the leaves softly swaying and whispering to one another, the creatures and animals running up and around and about the freshly green and revitalized trees, and all the wild flowers and wild fruits sprouting through the vast and bountiful land. The sun rose high above the village as the wise man entered and rested at an old, sturdy, wooden table in the center of the village. A crowd much larger than the first circled around the wise man, and he looked up at them and either appeared to smile a bit or squint his eyes and face in a bunched up manner as the sun shined overhead. He was truly a beautiful old man, but it was apparent his age weighed upon him heavily.

Just then, a young man stepped forward, panache and centralized in heart and mind, and spoke to the wise man. He said, "I have determined the correct and only logically possible answer to your question." The wise man sat staring at the vivid and sundry flowers that grew throughout the garden and said, "Continue with your presumed answer." The young man's chest swelled, and he said, "In the case of the rocks thrown into the air by the wise teacher, the first rock was brought back to the earth by the natural laws of gravity; the second rock was interrupted mid-flight by some secondary force, assuming the scenery of the woods, it could be hypothesized, as one of many hypotheses, that the second rock was caught in the branches of a tree over the wise teacher's head." The wise man did not alter his vision from the blowing flowers and said, "Your assumptions are natural to the manner of your mind and the disbelief that stirs within your naïve heart. Your answer is incorrect, but not entirely. Search deeper within yourself, and you will be surprised when you find the truth. All answers of truth slumber also in the heart, not only the mind."

The young man slipped back into the crowd with his head hung low and a second man, in the middle of his life, approached. He said, "Dear wise man, I believe that I have the true answer to your twisted riddle." The wise man took in a deep breath of air; the aroma of the flowers pleased him. After a few moments of silence the wise man spoke, "Provide me with your answer, if you believe that my question was merely a riddle." The middle-aged man said, "The wise teacher you speak of was nothing more than a magician who successfully deceived his young and naïve student with a sleight of the hand. The first rock was thrown into the air, but while the student focused on the rock thrown into the air, the teacher put the second rock into his pocket."

The wise man watched as the breeze moved from the trees, to the flowers in the garden, to the cheeks on his face and continued on into eternity and back again. The wise man said, "The wind is truly a peculiar and divine thing. As for your answer, there lies not one meter of truth but quite the contrary. It is filled with miles upon miles of fear and untruth. To properly clear up this misconception: the wise teacher had no pockets."

The wise man picked up his cane and rested it upon his lap and looked around the crowd. He said, "Are there any amongst you who has truly thought about this question and is willing to provide me with the answer?"

An old woman from the crowd slowly began to shuffle through, emerge and approach the wise man. She nodded before the wise man and said, "Please grant me the privilege to speak to your worthiness and holiness." The wise man said, "You may speak. Please make it worth meaning and truth." The old woman said, "I believe deep within the core of my heart and being that the wise teacher had displayed the meaning of life to his student. The first rock symbolized the naïve and fearful person who curses god and, in result, when they are thrown into the air they are dashed to pieces against the ground and sink away into nothingness. The second rock symbolizes the righteous person, whose heart is filled with love and truth, who in turn is not thrown into the air at all but is slowly lifted up like an ethereal being into the gleaming light of heaven by a divine one."

The wise man stood up and looked among the crowd, then he smiled and walked over to the old woman. He said, "You have answered wisely, truthfully, and from the depths of your heart." Then the wise man kissed the old woman on the cheek and handed her his cane. The wise man turned and walked into the woods, as the bright sun continued to burn above the beautiful landscape, and tears flowed down the cheeks of the old woman and across the indelible smile upon her face, because she knew they would never see the wise man again.

I think that's how the story ended. It all seemed vague. But, perhaps, there's no such thing as endings. Either way, I couldn't remember where I had heard that story or why it was rising from the depths of my mind at that particular moment. The sound of the crashing water, the wind rustling the trees and the animals filled my ears, but it was distant. The story stayed, running through my mind, and I couldn't help wondering why. Why was it there and what was the point of any of it?

I tried to ignore the story as I climbed down off the rock, carefully traversing my way back onto the pathway, the waterfall cascading behind me and the point of the story stirring in my mind like the water in the pond at the base of the falls.

My eyes followed the stream rushing beside me as I walked down the pathway, and I realized that I was now following the stream. I passed through the two bushes, ducking my head to avoid the branches and exiting the trail. Climbing down several rocks, each one progressively larger than the previous one, I could finally get a clear view of an opening that led out onto a plateau by the river's edge.

As I came through the woods and the clearing, there was a huge slab of rock that started at the edge of the forest and spread about twenty feet out into the river. I walked slowly out onto the rock, towards the water's surface, looking up and down the river, unable to see either a beginning or an end. I sat down on a part of the rock that had a deep curvature in it that closely resembled a chair.

Time was slowly creeping by and passing, and I could feel it. I stared at the water for a long time, just watching it flowing downstream, moving rapidly, twisting and turning, crashing and cascading over rocks in the river and carrying debris with it as it moved without ceasing. I was in some deep trance, where I just stared at the water, and it felt as if my mind went completely blank, but I knew deep down that it hadn't, even though I couldn't remember what the thoughts were that were flitting about, and then a splash in the water brought me back to reality and diverted my empty, unimaginable thoughts.

The trout in the stream were jumping. I could not see them leap from the water, but I could hear the splash and could see the ripples of the water that followed and accompanied the sound. I hadn't noticed it before, but once I heard the first one, I began to hear it every couple seconds. Then I noticed the ripples of the water as the jumping fish created gentle waves that spread out from their splash. I sat there, watching the ripples on the lake and realized they were everywhere, tiny but everywhere. The wind was blowing, and it was stirring up the water. I began thinking about how all those ripples in the water weren't just created randomly and arbitrarily by the wind and the fish, but that instead they were all cohesive and one like they all were attached to the same string. They waved up and down and from side to side all across the water. They looked like the genius brushstrokes of some artist. The creation of beauty; the beauty of creation. I had to stare long at it before it finally formed in my mind and before my eyes, but then it was there. It was all one and continuous. Then the story came back to me.

    For a large portion of my life, I had thought about committing suicide. Looking back on it, I honestly couldn't pin down one particular reason, but instead there seemed to be myriad reasons. A severe depression had crept into my life and smothered my existence entirely. I had no idea where it came from or how to overcome it. The only plausible, logical thought I could conjure in that mindset was to defeat it. And I thought that if I were to kill myself, then I would effectively kill the depression. As I would lay awake at night, and I could feel a sharp pin jabbing inside of me, in some unknown, indefinable region that I never even knew I had, I would talk to myself in my head, saying, "I would rather pursue the nothingness that suicide will successfully bring me, opposed to being burdened with overwhelming sadness and melancholy. At least in death, the pain shall cease." Not completely faulty logic, but certainly unsound to a sound mind that has never experienced those bleak, sleepless nights, where the rain is falling outside and tapping out the tempo of pure melancholy on your windowsill and echoing the sound in the hollow core of your soul.

    Over the period of several years, I was able to train my mind into finally overcoming the veil of depression that had slipped itself over my entire being. However, its dirty claws would occasionally find its way out of its cage and wander down the halls of my mind and back into my life. Mostly, these relapses would occur on dark, lonely and insomnia-induced nights. Then the thoughts would return, until my mind was able to fight them off. And eventually the thoughts became less frequent and less poignant, until eventually they stopped.

But there is something that is forever changed in the depths of a human being who for years has the constantly recurring thoughts and images of their own death brought about by themselves. I was always in a reserved state of anxiety and fear, because I knew that creature still slept deep in my mind, and I knew that it could potentially be awakened at any moment.

These thoughts began to surface as I thought deeply about the story of the wise man.

What is the meaning of life or why is it completely devoid of meaning? And if so, in either case, why would the thoughts of suicide exist in a living creature? The first series of questions, I believe, is a futile exercise in philosophy that is incapable of yielding any true results. It's too broad; however, the second question poses quite an interesting problem that I had never been able to honestly put my finger on. Evolution declares the doctrine of the survival of the fittest: the necessity to survive. So how could such a thought, like suicide, present itself cognitively and psychologically at some point in some living things as a logical option? Perhaps there are an indeterminate amount of potential answers. Perhaps there are none. For me, it seemed that the bleakness, the emptiness, the meaninglessness, and the excruciating pain of existence had become so disgustingly potent that the only logical leap was to cease to exist in order to bring a cessation to such overwhelming thoughts. For some reason or another, those thoughts had welled up and flooded every last hidden corner of my mind and bullied it into wanting to give up.

In the story, the wise man presents the village with a riddle, which is essentially the meaning of life question, which is more of an unsolvable enigma, as opposed to a riddle or a question. The story explicates the idea that both the young man and the middle-aged man are wrong. The young man for his naïvety and utter belief, to the point of blindness, in all science. The middle-aged man for his atheistic and overly-cynical outlook on life. But the old woman, who apparently answers with the belief of faith in some god and in some perception of a meaningful universe and existence, is revealed as answering correctly. The old woman seems to prescribe to some sort of belief in a supreme being and even in some afterlife, because she says the two rocks symbolize the faithful versus the unfaithful. Whereas, the one falls to the ground, the other is lifted by the hand of god; however, in the riddle, as in reality, the second rock vanishes, much as we do when we die. Nothing remains, except the faith of some people that at that moment, the moment of death, some sort of intervention occurs, whatever that may be, as different belief systems believe in different theories. Regardless, it is improvable and not worthwhile in attempting to prove. What is more important is not whether life itself has any meaning, but how to make our individual lives have meaning for ourselves. In death, there's a haziness that we simply do not have the answers for, or the capabilities of fully understanding. However, the essential point that arises is that we must find some sort of faith in something. We must find meaning *for* our lives, if we simply do not believe it to be inherently present.

    I had always found it hard to believe in a god or a purpose driven world, where everything had a reason, and fate and destiny reigned. Not that it was a hard concept to wrap my mind around, it was quite easy and straightforward, but I was skeptical. The ideas and belief systems did not align with the world that I viewed through my eyes or saw unfolding in my own reality.

    As I began to defect from the beliefs of society, I felt a great divide swelling between myself and the rest of the world, and as that gap began to grow, I felt more alone and guilty, as if I had done something wrong. I became more introverted and felt rejected from everything and everyone, and shortly afterwards, the meaninglessness of life and the emptiness from within began to bloom like a terrible, rotten seedling inside of me. It was the first time that the meaninglessness, exhaustion, and pain of existence weighed upon me. That was when the thoughts of suicide began to rise up in the depths of my mind.

I eventually realized that there was nothing wrong with me. In fact, I became quite proud of myself for thinking the way that I did. At first, it was painful, but then there was an acceptance that began to settle in eventually, shortly after I began to start working through the depression that seized my mind. I was proud, because I was thinking, and thinking independently, refusing to be persuaded or influenced by the powerful forces around me. The story of the wise man had for some reason risen from my subconscious and brought back that particular moment of my life. I had not understood my own meaning to attach to my life. I had learned that life was utterly meaningless, and it suppressed me so much that I then thought it must therefore not matter, or have any repercussions, or it must be meaningless also, if I were to commit suicide. However, it took a while before the thoughts sifted through the depression and surfaced, revealing to me that all life is meaningless until you find what is meaningful to you and your existence and attach whatever it is to your life and pursue it completely.

Overhead, I heard squawking noises, and I was distracted from my thoughts and looked up over my head. There, flying through the sky, were two geese. I watched them flying a hundred feet up in the air, then they flew out over the river, circled around and began to descend, landing on the water, skidding and splashing up water on the sides of them both, as they swam over into an almost-hidden cove near the side of the river. I continued to watch them as they floated around for a while, swimming over to one another occasionally, tapping one another with their beaks and squawking at one another. Then finally they swam over to a little patch of island that was about twenty yards away from where I sat. They climbed up onto the land and began plucking and eating the grass. I watched them eating, and every once in a while, they would get close to each other, brush up close together and cuddle with one another, and then eventually they finished eating, and I watched them take off, flying out over the vastly wide river, slowly getting smaller in the distance, as they flew towards the tree line and the mountains off onto the horizon. I didn't realize it until they were almost out of sight, but I was smiling uncontrollably, and I wasn't all that sure why.

I returned to my thoughts, and at that moment, when I began to think again about my past and the story and everything else, I felt different. The anxiety and fear that lay hidden in my mind, fearing that the thoughts of suicide may rise up again, were no longer there. I was still smiling uncontrollably, and I began thinking about the absurdity of it all, and I felt like the meaning finally aligned itself in my mind. I still disagreed partially with all the answers given in the story, but I had become content with the answer I now possessed. I felt like that was all that really mattered to me, because now that weight had been removed and everything seemed to become illuminated.

After wanting to die for almost my entire life, I finally felt the strong urge and desire to live. I stood up on the big rock and glanced out across the water of the river, then turned and headed back toward the forest. I no longer wanted to die, even though it had constantly weighed on my thoughts before, even subconsciously. But it was all gone. I leapt off the rock and down onto the dirt and sand, walking and feeling the earth and snapping twigs underneath my feet. I could hear the river still rushing behind me in my ears, and I thought about all the ripples on the stream being cohesive and continuous and all inner-connected, and then I thought about those two geese, nuzzling one another and then flying off over the river and into the distance, side by side, and I began to smile, honestly, for perhaps the first time in my life, then I turned and continued to walk away from the water into the forest, down the narrowing then widening sand- and dirt-covered pathway, out and beyond into a whole new realm of life.

●

We stood upon the precipice of autumn, waiting for the winter and the cold it brought to rapidly wrap us up and shake the joy and life out of all the living. The winds would rage more frequently, blowing the frost in our direction, and I knew that soon the city would be covered in snow, smothering all the people and all the buildings and all the street lamps that would burn long into the night.

    I planned on going across to the South Side to hit some of the used book shops looking for something good to read. I found pure euphoria in bookstores that was often hard to match in other realms of life, other than pure, unconditional love of course. But I was in the pursuit of some books, and anyone who is a bibliophile can easily recognize the imperative that this instills somewhere deep and unfathomable inside the mind. Yes, I convinced myself to ride my bicycle across the hot metal bridge and cruise down East Carson Street, looking for a new book that would captivate my entire being for at least a couple of days, perhaps a week, until it would itself slip deep into my past and memory like an obscured, antique photograph.

    The wind was cold on my face, but it felt beautiful and invigorating blowing against my sweat. Regardless of what people say about catching colds, I say fuck them. This is what it often felt like to be alive, and sometimes we simply have to remind ourselves what it's like to be alive into order to truly live.

    I cut down the back streets onto Boulevard of the Allies, across onto Bates, then down under the underpass and across the hot metal bridge. Everything began to feel surreal, and my blood was beginning to move more quickly through my veins, and I was sweating more. I crossed the river, looking over the side into the water, allowing my eyes to roam, gradually following the current's movement. There was a euphoric feeling about that evening that left me feeling invincible.

    The Southside Works radiated their lights in the darkening sky, and I made the decision to cut down the side street behind the main building and ride alongside the river. It was beautiful watching the sun collapsing onto the horizon after a long day's work, reflecting its rays off the water's surface. The city on the other side of the river, rising towers. I road down for a couple miles and then turned off the trail and up a side street, out onto East Carson. I turned off 18th street and headed towards Station Square. I stopped outside the front of the bookstore's building, chained up my bike, and walked inside, the City Books neon light illuminating the glass in the window.

    There has always been something about bookstores that captivated a hidden part of my being entirely. Once I'd walk in, there was no telling if I would ever leave. I could spend hours, merely browsing through the books, through genres that didn't even interest me. I often spent more time and outlasted the employees who were paid to be there. I always knew there was a part of me that lusted after knowledge, and I believed books to be the opiate that would provide me with just a small sliver of that nirvana. And also, there was a feeling of calmness that pervaded my body once I entered a bookstore, absolving all my problems temporarily.

I closed the door to the shop behind me and felt a heavenly light radiating upon me as I looked to the left and then to the right, gazing at the bookshelves that stretched from the floor to the ceiling and from one wall to another. All of the shelves were filled with used books. The books on the shelves were like old, broken lovers. Someone had selfishly used them and then discarded them as if they meant nothing. I slowly walked through the store respecting these books, because I had been a broken lover before. The chamber. The library of lost souls. I knew that they only longed to have a hand reach out and touch them to remind them. Essentially they were massive pieces of someone's life and someone's mind. These books were filled with brilliant ideas and passionate emotions and philosophical questionings and truths. In a way, I found the meaning of life to be buried somewhere deep within these pages, and most people overlooked that plain fact. Whether they were bored or too anxious or too conceited or too ignorant to notice, I may never know. Either way, books were my narcotic, and like a drug addict who can't pass up a hit when offered, I couldn't pass up buying at least one book when I entered a bookstore.

My eyes adjusted gradually inside the store as nighttime came and the lights inside the store played a more important role. I perused through the novels, scanning alphabetically over the names of familiar authors, looking to see if there were any books I had read or had heard about or planned to read, and then I continued down the aisle, browsing through the books on philosophy and then psychology and then ornithology and then biology and then evolution and then I returned to the fiction section.

I was standing in front of the letter L when I first noticed her. She had the most beautiful dark hair, waving down her neck onto her shoulders. A color I had never known existed. It looked like a work of art, like the poetry that can only be found in a bird's nest. Perfect, pure. She had a pair of white sunglasses resting on her head and wore a sexy pair of black jeans, ballet flats, and a grey cardigan. I watched her out of my peripheries as I pretended to be intrigued by the books spread through that area: Joyce, Kafka, Kerouac, Kundera, Laurie, Márquez, Meno. I picked up *Hairstyles of the Damned* and remembered a particular fondness for that book in high school. Oh, how fucked up high school was. I stood there, casually flipping through the pages but obviously, secretively, glancing in her direction. I felt like an undercover detective, spying on the suspect, taking mental notes of her body language, her every movement, her every detail. Black-painted fingernails attached to her delicate fingers reached up onto the shelf and removed a familiar-looking book. What book was that? I knew that I'd seen it before. I felt like I had read that. I just couldn't put my finger on it....That's it! *The Perks of Being a Wallflower*. That's the book. I knew I remembered that bright green cover. I could recognize it anywhere. It was one of the best books I had ever read. And it was so distinctive.

    The book was placed back on the shelf, and she shifted her hips and turned her legs to stroll off in the other direction. I watched her hips move, and there was something magical about it. I was thankful for evolution to lead to the female body. Her curves were enthralling, and it sent the blood pulsating throughout my veins, reassuring me that I was definitely alive. Standing there still holding the book, I checked her out, not creepily but sincerely. I simply could not help being overwhelmingly attracted to her. She was one of the most beautiful women I had ever seen, and I was convinced that there would be none to rival her. I instantly adored everything about her from afar: the delicate tone of white skin that snuggled against her bones, the very structure of her bones, her flowing hair, eyes that I felt could possess me, lips so genteel I couldn't prevent the thought of tasting them, white teeth that made me want to exhibit my own.

I wanted to approach her, I mean for Christ's sake I was an adult, but I couldn't even fathom what to say. I thought of all the lamest pickup lines and all of the most captivating lines of poetry I had ever read, but I felt that nothing could be adequate. I believed that she was on a level entirely above anything else this world had to offer.

And then I figured, fuck it. There was nothing that I could possibly lose from trying. That bastard Sam was right. I needed to put myself out there. I decided I would just casually approach her and say hello, so I started to walk towards her, not knowing at first that I was still carrying that book I was pretending to look at. I took in a deep breath and slowly exhaled like some sort of Buddha meditation exercise or technique in yoga and felt surprisingly relieved, which was good, because I stood next to her, and my mind was churning the words to say and my mouth and vocal chords were slowly beginning to respond.

"Hey, how are you?" I said, exhaling the words almost tantric-like still in the Buddhist mindset.

She looked up at me, her eyes seeming to blink in slow-motion, me watching the fine hairs of her eyelashes moving perfectly, and a smile taking over her face as she said, "Hey. I'm wonderful. I see you around a lot."

The last part of her greeting took me somewhat by surprise. She had clearly taken notice of me before and on several occasions, at least enough to keep track of it and make a mental note of it.

"Yeah, I see you around campus sometimes. And I think you're in my psychology class on Tuesdays," I said, still feeling a little anxious, my stomach producing the butterfly effect, the endorphins began dancing throughout my body, then I started to calm down.

"Oh...I'm not actually in that class. I just like to sneak into random classes that I think sound interesting."

"Really?" I said, almost laughing but utterly inquisitive, squinting my eyes and tilting my head.

"Yeah, it's just kinda something I do. If I hear a lecture that sounds interesting, I'll slip in and sit in the back," she said, still smiling big.

"That's really random but pretty awesome. I don't think I would have the guts to do that. What other classes have you snuck into before?"

"Well...let me see. Uhh, oh yeah, there was a world religions class, a Latin American history class, an astrology class, Russian Literature. A bunch."

"So what made you choose my psychology class?" I asked, prodding her with questions, so I could get to know her more, and because I was falling in love with her voice.

"I heard your professor talking about cognitive psychology, and its explanation of thought, emotions, and relationships, and I was sold at that," she said softly.

"Well I hope you got something interesting out of sneaking into the lecture."

"Multiple things, that's why I stayed, and why I'll return," she said, laughing to herself.

I had immediately fallen in love with everything about her. I wanted to learn more and know more and hear her speak more and hear her laugh and smile and watch her eyes look into mine. Her face was so beautifully structured, perfect. High cheekbones and a jawline with a perfect mouth and nose and eyes that beguiled me.

"I look forward to seeing you in class then. My name is Owen by the way."

"Lilly. It's nice to meet you."

"Very nice to meet you, Lilly."

There was a brief pause, so I said, "So, I couldn't help noticing that you were looking at *The Perks of Being a Wallflower*."

"I knew I could see you spying on me from over there. Pretending like you were reading that book, but you're not fooling anyone," she said, laughing and gently nudged my arm.

I couldn't help it or prevent it, but I immediately blushed a little bit like a child, feeling completely idiotic for having been caught in a harmless crime.

"It's not a big deal. I was watching you too, obviously. I was just more sly about it," she said, winking.

These words made me want to blush more, but instead they made my heart feel like it was lifting up, almost as if someone were filling it with helium while it was still beating inside my chest. I couldn't help but smile as I stared hard into her breathtaking eyes. I wasn't really sure what else I could say at this point, since I was so overwhelmed by her.

"I can lend you that book, if you are interested in it. It is one of my favorite books, and I would love to be able to let you borrow it," I said.

"Really? That would be great. You can bring it to psychology class on Tuesday, and I'll be sure to give it back to you as soon as I'm done, cause I hate when I lend people books, and they never return them."

"Me too. I have generally made it a rule of mine to not lend out any more books, but I think it's okay to make an exception for you."

At the sound of my lamely pseudo-chivalrous-esque statement, she broke out into a laugh that she attempted to suppress by covering her mouth with her hand. It made me smile too, and before I knew it, I was laughing also. I watched her shoulders shaking with laughter and her body slightly leaning forward. I could make her smile. I could make her laugh. I would've given anything to have kissed her. Time. Patience.

All of a sudden she stopped laughing and looked at her watch, saying, "Oh shit, I gotta get going. It was a pleasure meeting you. I'm sure I'll be seeing you around, and I look forward to psychology on Tuesday. Bye, Owen."

I loved that she swore so casually.

"I look forward to it too. I'll bring the book. It was great to talk with you," I said.

And as soon as she entered my life, she left the bookstore, out onto the city street and into the night.

For the first time in my life, I left that bookstore without buying anything. I felt like I had gained more than I could have ever purchased inside that store. I walked over to the bike rack on the sidewalk and unchained my bicycle. I swung my leg over the seat and adjusted my weight as I pushed down on the pedals to start moving. My messenger bag oscillated on my back as my initial pedaling rocked the bike back and forth. I gained speed and continued to pedal harder. Then I turned sharply, hopping off the curb and into the street, beginning to pedal faster, churning my legs mechanically. They slowly began to burn as my body was shooting acid inside my calf and thigh muscles. The night was dark and the air was cold. The bars and coffee shops and stores lit up the street more than the lamps that hung overhead the sidewalks and streets. As I pedaled faster and harder, the bike rapidly accelerated, and the colors of all the lights slowly began to fade and blur into one. One holy light that burned through the darkness, as I rode farther down the street, past the drunks and beyond the multitudinous voices that all bled into one, and into the night.

•

The ride home that night had an eternal feeling. The cool air was blowing against my face and through my hair. I could feel the coldness; it was breathing life into me through my lungs. I felt truly alive for the first time in such a long time. I almost had forgotten what the sensation was like, to feel my heart beating, racing and pumping blood through my body. She filled my thoughts and when I returned home she filled my dreams. And when I dreamed about her, my heart began to beat so quickly that I would wake up. Yet, all I wanted to do was stay asleep so she was always there with me...and in all those dreams, I would lock my lips with hers and hold her delicate frame, her beautiful body in my arms. So close. There was just simply something about her that absolutely overpowered my entire being, my cognitive faculties, my emotions, and my bodily functions that I never paid attention too: the palpitating beat of my heart. My heart was raging chaotically as thoughts of her raced through my mind. I could feel my heart within my chest. I could feel my heart beat in my temples, in my wrists, in my legs. I felt my blood moving through my veins, slowly then rapidly, quickening then slowing, and I knew that my thoughts were the cause. She was the cause of all of this. I never wanted the feeling to end.

I closed the door to my bedroom and collapsed fully upon my bed face down. I lay there for some time before I moved. It could have been eternity. It could have been only an infinitesimal fragment of a second. In strange times, time passes so strangely. Either way, I regained my composure slightly, rolling over onto my side to look at the clock: 10:43 p.m. I wondered where she was and what she was doing now, if she were thinking about me the way I was thinking of her, if she were actually looking forward to seeing me on Tuesday or if she were only being polite. These thoughts kept replaying through my mind, over and over again, until I eventually felt dizzy. I actually could feel vertigo. It was absolutely insane. I was rising too quickly from the depths of the ocean floor, the light illuminating the surface of the rippling water as I travelled faster and faster towards it, and the bends were shaking my body down. But no, I lay in my bed imagining one various imaginary scenario after another, only hoping and wishing that there would be an invisible force that pulled us together and became unbreakable.

Someone's bony knuckles knocked against my door, and I knew instantly who would be standing there, even though I fantasized it was someone else. I heard Sam mumbling words against the door, but they didn't make it any farther. The words were either absorbed into the wood of the door and became one with the door, or they collided with it so forcefully that they slumped to the floor dead.

"Open the door, asshole. I can't hear you," I yelled at the door from inside the room, sitting on my bed. That unfortunate door, being verbally abused from both sides. And then that same door, creaked and cracked from the turning of the door knob, and then it slowly opened, and there was Sam standing in the doorway completely sober.

"Heigho! What are you doing tonight, buddy?"

"I dunno, I was planning on maybe just reading for a little bit then going to sleep. Why, what brilliant act of rebellion or mental and physical annihilation are you concocting?" I said, smirking and staring at his surprisingly sober looking face. I had forgotten his true appearance when he didn't have slurred speech or bloodshot eyes. But then again, I had pretty much been the same.

"I was thinking of either smoking and watching a movie or planning something epic, but for the latter I need a co-conspirer," he said these words with sober sincerity.

"Are you actually sober now?"

"Yeah, why?"

"I don't know. I thought you were. I just couldn't remember the last time I saw you truly sober like now."

"I know I'm sexy, but this isn't going to get you into my bed tonight," he said winking and laughing.

"Damn, I figured it was worth a try," I said with a laugh, then I paused, thinking of her standing in the dimly lit bookstore, her bright white teeth smiling as she spoke to me, but then I finally remembered what I was saying mid-sentence and continued, "what movie were you thinking about watching or what plot were you going to conjure up?"

"I was either going to watch The Darjeeling Limited or try to create something big, you know, like something prominent. Revolutionary. You know, the norm for me."

"Hmm...good fucking movie. It's tempting, but now I'm intrigued by this idea of yours," I said, squinting my eyes and scrunching my lips together to overtly declare interest through my body language.

"I don't know. Something radical. Yeah, definitely something really fucking radical. That's the only shit that changes society. The dumbass conservatives are afraid of change and radical new ideas, and the liberals are often too fucking stupid by focusing on their pseudo-intelligence to come up with anything remotely intelligent to pursue."

"You're not nearly as fucking stupid when your sober."

"Fuck you, you know what I'm talking about. You're just like me. We don't belong to society or societal norms. We are standing on the precipice of all this shit. We are the ones that have to take the leap from the edge to prove to the ignorant fools that there is solid ground over the edge, and that from that solid ground things are better. Well, maybe not entirely better, but at least potential progress for improvement."

Sam's voice was getting a little louder as he was clearly getting heated up and excited. This was the passion that burned deep within Sam's core. He was a brilliant person, one of the smartest people I had ever met, and he truly and honestly wanted to change the world.

"You know I agree with you on all this shit, but where are you going with it? What the fuck are you or I or anyone else going to do, or more rather, what can we do? We can't just go into the mountains and arm ourselves and start a revolutionary movement. We can't just start shaking things up, but I'm sure that's exactly what you intend? Minus the weapons of course, because your mind is the most frightening of all weapons that exist," I said, knowing that I didn't mind stirring things up, but I wanted to provoke Sam, so he really got going with what he wanted to do.

"Indeed. For, truly, the man in the street with an arm full of books should be feared more than the man with a gun. And seriously, why the fuck not!? Why shouldn't we? The most intelligent and wildly influential people have all challenged the majority, the norm, all the fucked up systems of oppression in place, to bring forth change, to progress humanity into the future. You know this all too well, even more well than I do. You are obsessed and idealize all the radicals of the past. You've lent me your favorite authors' works, and I've read them, stoned or not, so you can't tell me otherwise. We need to write a manifesto. Most of the greatest radicals were misunderstood and despised during their lifetimes but were all adored and credited with advancing humanity in some way after their deaths. That can be us. Ghandi read Thoreau, and it incited the power within him to cause the revolution in India. We are those outcast, iconoclastic bastards of our age that will be hated our entire lives but possibly revered next century. And even if we aren't, who gives a fuck. We have the power to change things. We have the mentality to wage that war. The war of ideas."

Sam said these words with dire conviction and a genuine air of intelligence. He sure was a remarkable creature when he was stoned and even more so when he was sober. I knew a great deal about cultural memes and how ideas traveled and evolved through generations in society. It went all the way back to Plato.

He continued, "The important thing is that we are trying to better things, to improve the flaws that are still so prominent. We, as a species, were destined for progress, for evolution, for growth, for intellect. So why must we all recede into our ignorance like petrified recluses instead of facing the world. Even if we aren't progressing in a way that is upwards or forwards, we can at least widen the humanity of the world."

I laughed to myself for a while, just looking at Sam standing in the doorway of my room. He stood there waiting for my response, anxiously, so I knew I shouldn't make him wait forever.

"I am really tired and have got a lot on my mind right now, but well...let's fuck up this world. What do we possibly have to lose? We can always become expatriates if we have to, but we do have the freedom of speech amendment on our side, so we might as well put some real weight on that bitch to see how much it actually bends. Those capitalist-fascists that purport that lie and illusion of a democratic republic shall soon learn to fear and lose sleep when they became aware of the intellectual youth that are reading in the libraries and coffee shops of the world," I said, sitting up and shifting my body, so my legs dangled over the bed and eventually touched the floor.

I stood up, looking over at my computer desk where my laptop lay, and then I put on my shoes, looked around to see if I had forgotten to grab anything and said, "Let's go for a walk and discuss these big plans. Nothing invigorates the mind and wriggles loose brilliant ideas like a cold, biting autumnal night's air."

L

●

I swear that some moments of life make the revolutions of the hands on the clock spin uncontrollably, rapidly, and other experiences demand those hands to move so slow that only long-exposure photography taken over the length of eternity could prove their movement. Tuesday was the latter.

    Sitting in my literature course, I tried to watch the hands on the clock, but they didn't move. I longed for the time to come, where I would stroll into my psychology class, and she would be sitting there, gorgeous as she was, or maybe she would come after I got there, and I would turn and her eyes would meet mine, and it would be as if the heavens and earth or the sun and the moon aligned. I knew that some phenomenally beautiful event would occur then. It would go completely unnoticed by all of existence, but we would know. That was all that mattered anyways. That was all that was actually real anyways.

    "Lord Byron was infamously known for his reputation of debauchery, like most of the British authors we have been studying. He was not nearly as notorious as the Earl of Rochester, but nonetheless, it was rumored that he had slept with over three-hundred women, which, on many levels, led partially to his self-loathing and descent from society. Byron is one of the most distinctive authors and personas in all of literary history. He possessed such an overwhelming sense of, what only the Germans have been able to term, *Weltschmerz*. Regardless, Byron is still recognized and revered in Greece for his valiance and support of their country during the Greek Revolution."

My professor's voice filled the room, proclaiming the results of profound writing talent and good looks. Good thing I had neither. I didn't care though, because all I wanted was Lilly.

"The other Romantic poets were equally unique and abhorrent in the eyes of society. Shelley was hated by society for most of his life, and it wasn't until about the 1960s that he really became recognized."

My professor's voice echoed through the silence of the room. I looked around, and most people were either yawning or nodding off. I was the only one that was normally interested, and even today I was having trouble concentrating. The little arm on the clock clicked inside its trapped little chamber. Oppressed behind that glass, only to tick forever.

I raised my hand and decided to speak.

"Why is it that Shelley, and mostly all of the other Romantics, were hated by society during their lifetime?"

"Well, as with most movements in history, the message that these poets were attempting to spread completely contradicted British society. Blake was borderline insane, and indeed probably had some form of schizophrenia, but nonetheless he was a brilliant painter and poet, who challenged the conventionality of the Church. Coleridge was mentally overtaken and dejected by his opium and laudanum consumption, and he was also convicted of plagiarism. But the message that Wordsworth and Coleridge wrote in their *Preface* was legendary and changed the scope of poetry. As for the later generation Romantics, Keats evolved into a master craftsman of verse and directed all of his passion to poetry and Fanny Brawne. And well, we have already discussed Byron and Shelley."

My teacher's speech was very straightforward, but there was a hint of sorrow in her message. She continued talking, mostly ignoring the rest of the room and having a direct conversation with me.

"The lives of the Romantic poets were lives filled with complete sorrow and tragedy, especially for the later generation. In society's eyes, these poets were degenerates, but today they are revered for their beautiful words. They all died so young, and the world was robbed of who knows how many more incredible poems. Keats died at the age of only 24 from tuberculosis. Shelley's life, on the outside looking in, was a miserable wreck. His first wife killed herself after he left her, and he and Mary Shelley had several children die either during or shortly after birth. Then Shelley drowned, after the boat he was on sank, and his corpse washed up on shore several days later. And we already heard of Byron's fate, dying in Greece during their revolution."

The clock ticked one more time, and I sat there staring into my teacher's eyes, and I could feel the sorrow, the defeat. The world works in cruel ways.

She looked at her wristwatch and said, "Well, that is all for today. Next class, we will be starting with a brief overview of the Victorian period. We will read a couple more poems, and then, good news for those who hate poetry, we will be moving on to some short stories and plays. Have a great week, see you Thursday."

Shuffling of books and zipping bags commenced, and soon everyone in the classroom was piling out through the door. Some people were still half asleep. Zombies moving through life. I could never understand it. I packed up my books slowly, sliding my chair back in underneath the desk, zipping up my backpack and throwing it onto my back.

"See you on Thursday, professor. Thanks for the lecture today," I said, walking for the door.

"No problem, Owen. It's just nice to see someone intrigued by the lives of such incredible poets and their writing."

She stood there smiling, and I smiled back, then I turned and was out the door. I walked down the hallway of the building, contemplating the lecture and the post-lecture exchange. Then I realized my psychology class was finally approaching. I started to walk faster subconsciously. In no time flat, I was out the building, down the steps and into the street, slowly walking faster and faster. I was crossing the street and walking to my next building. I still had about twenty minutes before class even started, but I couldn't sit or stand around waiting. I would have a mental breakdown thinking about everything. No, I had to get to class, even if I was early and had to watch the clock more, waiting for her to walk through that door.

I entered the building where my class was, and I started to slow my pace a little, so I wouldn't look like a complete maniac, literally running through the halls to get to my psychology course. People always thought I was weird, and I always thought I was too. I just loved to learn new things, and I couldn't help it. I guess it's better to pursue knowledge than power, regardless of how many assholes say money and power, power and money is everything. I thought that the man in the street with an arm full of books should be feared more than the man with a gun.

But all of that was meaningless now, because I was walking into that room, knowing that inside my bag laid that little green book, and I was hoping that shortly after I got there she was going to walk right through that same door too.

~~~

My world instantly became the towns closest to Vesuvius when she blew. Everything was ruins, being consumed with fire and smoke and ash, and there was absolutely nothing I could do. I tried to calm myself down and make excuses for why she hadn't showed up. Maybe she had a test or a paper or an emergency. I hoped she was okay. It didn't make any sense. I had to calm myself down and quickly, because I was acting ridiculous.

    I took deep breaths. Lots and lots of deep breaths. Ash filling the sky, casting a grey haze that seemed like a portrait of the end of the world. Ash flooding my lungs, asphyxiating. Calm yourself. It's not a big deal. I just hoped she was fine. I knew that I just needed to get through this class, and everything would be okay. I would be able to go back to my apartment and hang out and talk with Sam. I knew that he would calm my nerves and help me rationalize things. Sam always had a miraculous way of rationalizing the irrational. But I wouldn't actually talk to Sam about it. He would just help to distract my thought process from getting stuck in a self-destructive eternal loop. That's the work of a true friend. Stop the swinging hypnotist's pocket watch. I am shattering all the clocks and hexes of the world.

    My professor seemed different today. He looked like he hadn't shaved since our last class. The pupils of his eyes were reddened, not the kind from crying or smoking, but it looked like it was from pure exhaustion. I wondered what he could possibly be going through, and if he were going to be okay. I hoped that he was going to be okay. I hoped that Sam and I were going to be okay. And I hoped that Lilly was going to be okay too. Maybe a volcano had erupted in the confines of his life too, but he persevered regardless.

    "The human brain is an absolutely phenomenal thing. Evolution has been more than good to our species. We are capable of cognitive reasoning, complex thought, appreciation for art and music, and we even have some moral sense and ethical decision making components programmed into our brains somewhere. We can love and find humor in simple things. We can live selflessly, regardless of our genetics. Our brains control every part of our body and have the capability of human language and perception."

I wished that Lilly was here, listening to his impassioned presentation about the incredible feat in evolution that lead to the brain of *homo sapiens*. I desperately wanted her here or anywhere really. I just wanted to be with her.

"The emotions that humans express are universal. They are controlled by specific areas of the brain and can often tell us so much about individuals and our species as a whole. At the heart of the emotional control board of the brain sits the amygdala. This little almond-shaped organ receives and processes all kinds of signals and data. It is really incredible. Nature is a beautiful thing, and it is a damned shame that so many people disbelieve or fear evolution. Darwin's ideas were not meant to shatter peoples' faith in life but to reinforce it, showing the world for how beautiful it is and even more so, how much more beautiful it can become."

I thought about his words and never really understood it. Why did people fear evolution? I never really thought twice about it. It seemed to make perfect sense. Maybe it was just my generation, but I don't think I could speak for an entire generation. When I was in high school, there were huge debates about the teaching of evolution, and they still continue. I never understood it. The world's a crazy place, so why was it so insane for people to completely disagree with the idea that we evolved from apes, and that the line of evolution regressed farther back. Darwin's idea went public in the middle of the nineteenth century, and the twenty-first century still feared it. People cringed when they heard about it even suggested or hinted at, but I never did. It never seemed that improbable or implausible to me. I had read some of the *Origin of Species* and *The Descent of Man*, and they were beautifully written and even more beautifully argued. Darwin was drastically misunderstood. He felt that his new ideas would help free humans from various sorts of mental bondage and allow them to rejoice in the beautiful ebb and flow of life. Science has made so much progress over one-hundred and fifty years, and it only supports Darwin's claims further. The churches and the religious people, especially the fundamentalists, fear science and Darwin and will continue to do so. Enduring the religious school stuff in my younger years obviously hadn't totally hindered my critical thinking abilities. On one side of the fence stood a group of people holding piles and piles of evidence, and on the other side, there were only scared people with empty words, desperately and frantically holding onto the dead past and one blindly optimistic idea.

Love

The word hung and echoed through the room from my professor's mouth and grabbed every student's attention immediately, especially mine since I had been temporarily zoned out, thinking and analyzing what he had been saying before.

"Love captivates every last one of us, throughout our entire lives, whether in good ways or bad. But it consumes us, nonetheless. And it consumes society and culture and science and art and literature and Valentine's day cards."

The class laughed in unison like programmed drones. I sat silent, staring at my professor's face, hoping that he was going to reveal some truth, something to help me continue on. Maybe he would let down his own armor and expose himself. We all must learn to perform such a miraculous feat.

"Love transcends all forms of life: scientific, artistic, whatever else. It brings light and mystery into this world simultaneously. According to evolution, it makes perfect sense to be attracted to another human being and have strong feelings towards them, because in a completely biological sense, we are all destined by nature to carry on our genes. Now in our current society that is not necessarily how things actually turn out, but that is how nature intended them. We have homosexuals and sterile couples and couples that simply don't want children and condoms and contraceptives and all kinds of other things. These all go against what we were genetically programmed for, some refer to them as Darwinian suicide, but we have evolved into higher realms than biology alone. We have evolved into the societal and intellectual levels of life as well. There is nothing morally wrong with any particular lifestyle. But the truly miraculous thing about it all is that something remains. Love. Love is still there and felt by millions of people, and most of it is unexplainable. Love connects every last human being on earth, in some form, on some level of intensity. It makes perfect sense to love and care about your family. It also makes sense to feel love for a partner who could potentially carry on your genes. But it is both bizarre and beautiful to love and care for a complete stranger in a distant part of the world that we may never actually see ourselves with our own eyes, but millions of people do that every day too. The world is a beautiful place, and we have the capabilities of making it even better. Through love, anything is possible. Love remains above all other things. The love you have for your family is explainable, just as the love for strangers on the other side of the world is morally explainable, but the overwhelming love that is evoked from someone you meet on the street or in a coffee shop or at a friend's party or in the bookstore is what makes life worth living."

      I couldn't believe he said book store. Where on earth was Lilly when she could have been hearing this lecture? My mind was controlled by my professor's speech, until he combined love and bookstore, and everything became unreal and unfolded itself. I instantly switched my thoughts back onto Lilly, and I could see her standing there in the bookstore again, smiling and bating her eyelashes in front of me. She had to have been flirting with me, because it was so obvious I was flirting with her. I wanted her so badly. I wanted her love. All that talk about love was driving me mad. I needed to find her and just be with her. Love was everything. *Omnia vincit amor*. Love conquers all. It truly does. It must. It has to, because what else is there that remains without love, in a world where there exists not love?

●

That night the city lights filled my eyes up with reflecting kaleidoscopic visions, and music poured into my ears through my headphones as I walked those cold, damp, dark streets through the evening. I passed the bookstores and coffee shops, imagining all of the people inside them, talking to each other and laughing with one another. I thought about being a part of their lives, a long lost friend who stumbles in and lights up a smile upon their face. Winter would be releasing the beautiful, delicate snowflakes from the clouds above soon, and I knew they would soon cover all the streets.

My heart had been beating faster and faster every day, and I just needed to make sense of everything, of life, of love, of living. I needed to finding meaning, and I needed it to all make at least a little bit of sense to me.

I could smell the aroma of roasted coffee lifting out onto the street and into the air as a man with dark hair, wearing a grey peacoat, came out of the coffee shop.

I had been slowly losing my faith in everything that I held sacred, and it felt like my world was unraveling one stitch at a time. The sweater would soon be in shambles, and I was afraid that the world would willingly embrace me in its cold grasp and smother me to death. I had to make sense of my surroundings and find some faith. They say the older you become the more cynical and realistic you become, but I wanted the past back. I childishly wanted my childhood back when everything was a simple organism that worked perfectly, smoothly, elegantly. Now every-fucking-thing was a complex heap of disaster. I needed something to believe in. She gave me some hope, some faith. She shined her light deep into the darkest depths of my darkest being.

School was approaching the end of the semester, and it felt like it meant absolutely nothing to me anymore. It used to mean so much, but now it just felt like an empty void, meaningless. Everything was some fucked up conspiring contradiction trying to destroy my mind. I felt like a schizophrenic attempting to prove my sanity but only sounding more insane the more I spoke or the more I thought. The foundation my life had been built upon had come crashing down immediately, and it didn't make any fucking sense. I didn't feel any different, and I was scared to death it was all going to take me by surprise and destroy me in some cunning way. I burned the church I was born in to the ground, but I was too distraught to tell if I was on the inside or the outside.

I went to sleep believing and praying that god was there looking over my shoulder, protecting me and the ones I loved, but then I awoke and there was nothing. I didn't believe, and I knew that I controlled my actions, and that I needed to do good, because it was right, not because it was god's plan or not because I was going to go to heaven. That wishful thinking no longer applied. It no longer made any sense. If there were a god, why would he give a fuck about me or what I did? That god didn't seem to care about all the atrocities in the world, and I woke up realizing that none of those atrocities were ever going to cease if people were so naïve to believe that it was part of god's plan and god was going to intervene if god deemed it necessary. We need to deem it necessary to treat other human beings decently. We need to deem it necessary to have faith in something genuine and something real, not something that is going to deceive and betray and treat people like worthless pieces of clay that will eventually turn to dust and then nothing. We need to have faith in the common blood that surges through every human being's body and the emotions that we all have in common. That is what is real and that is all that will every really matter in the end. All of this will mean everything or it will mean nothing, but there is no sense in throwing it all away on a slim chance, a false hope, all out of ignorance. Even if there is a god or gods, why must we lie down lazily and leave everything to them. We have the strength and intellect and humanity inside all of us, whether it's instinctive or from a creator, and it has the ability to shroud the world in a persistence to love, to help one another, to live like gods ourselves. Because if there is a god, then I believe in the qualities and intellect that god instilled inside of us: the ability to strive towards beautiful lives and to love, genuinely and selflessly.

   I was afraid of the future, and I wasn't afraid to admit that. I could go to sleep and never wake up. I could walk out into the street to cross and be hit down by a drunk driver or a taxi cab driver or a neurotic cubical worker. Anything could happen. My heart could stop at any second. A blood clot could dislodge and occlude my pulmonary vein or aorta. Anything is possible, never forget that. But I wanted to live more than anything. I wanted to fucking live and breathe and fucking live and breathe for as long as I possibly could. I wanted to live life and never meet death at my door with regret brimmed up in my tear-filled eyes. I wanted at least a small fraction of the world to know of my existence. I wanted to at least touch the lives of some people. I wanted to love someone with all of my being and know that that person loved me back. I wanted to have a child that I could watch slowly growing from infancy to adolescence to awkward angsty teens, slowly sprouting into adulthood. I wanted to see little features and characteristics of my lover's and my traits in them. I wanted to see a smile on their face, and I wanted to see them live life.

    Everything is unknowable and everything will always remain that way. The only thing that is certain is that we should strive to live beautiful lives before the breath leaves our lungs cold and dead, and we travel into the unknown.

    I crossed the street and no cars killed me. I felt the cold night air filling my lungs, and the pressure was clenching my chest. It was always more difficult to breath in the cold. The city was on the brink of the seasons changing over; autumn was collapsing under the weight of the world and dissolving and fading into a slow winter. I knew it would be beautiful. Soon the leaves would only cover the ground like a beautiful quilt, and all the trees would look bare, their boughs exposed, shaking in the wintery breeze. The snow would soon follow, hitting everyone's frost-bitten, roseate cheeks, melting almost instantly into tiny streams of water running down the sides of their faces. The world was gorgeous. Life was incredible.

    The streets were surprisingly empty. Only a few college students lurked about, perhaps some being angel-headed hipsters searching for an angry fix, perhaps others were merely wandering like me, searching for themselves and something. I felt like the answers to the world's most confounding questions lay in our minds, and we need only unlock them through certain experiences, such as contemplating while walking the cold city streets at night, admiring the changing of seasons and the glowing street and building lights. I believed that everyone could find a grand and beautiful epiphany or ultimate realization in the most mundane or everyday aspects of common life.

    I decided to walk into the park, because it seemed like the perfect place for Zen concentration. I strolled across the bridge and up over the grassy knoll, trees passing me on both sides. Then the trees were becoming dense and surrounding me more, closing me in. Soon the city lights were fading and dying down as I walked into the park, into the woods, farther and farther, the trees being the only thing that was present with me. Finally, I decided to sit down on the earth's cold ground, resting my back up against a thick elm tree.

    The world came to me in waves, and I let my mind roam free. Music continued to pour in through my ears and into my mind, enjoying the melody but concentrating solely on all of my thoughts. I thought and thought and thought, and my head began to reel and hurt.

                  flowers

                                  Bloom

        solus ipse

                                        soliloquy

                        À la recherche

is there a god how could we ever wish or hope to know i wanted to make sense of everything but how are we to make sense of anything i want there to be meaning and i want to find it im scaredscared what if there is a hell and what if i am punished but what if there is a heaven and they dont let me in how would all of the people from all of time worthy of heaven occupy it without it being crowded what if i just die and rot in the ground what if nothing becomes of me i think i think i am okay with that i am okay with that for now but what happens when i get older do i get more scared or do i become more accepting i just wish there was some inherent meaning instilled inside of us that was evoked from within to tell us all of our own deepest darkest secrets and reveal the world to us through our own eyes i wish it were all true and all real i wonder what will become of me when i get older will i even live long enough to get old when my flesh starts to pull down gravity and sag on my face and arms and legs and my bones slowly become more and more brittle will i have someone to love me and hold me and reassure me that everything will be okay will she be the one that i have always dreamed of will she never leave me i am okay with the answers i can take them will someone just lay them all on me and quit leaving me in such suspense if there is a god why won't you just show yourself and tell us and quit quit confoundingbewildering allowing us to continue on living belligerentlyidiotically and with no greater purpose i need more than words in a book i need more than fablesallegoriesparablesunrealistic unbelievablerepetitiveapocryphal stories that have been told overover but namesve been changed humans are only capable of so many stories we tell them overover again differentnames slightlydifferentscenarios different circumstances but the samefuckingstories overoverover overover yet we continue to starve for them because we starve for meaningconnectedness because that is ultimately what keeps us alivebreathing what keeps us going persevering against all the odds that stack themselves up against us we continue to strive and continue on fuckitallfuckthefuckmessfucknonsense there isnt goddamn thing in my way thatll every stop me if soso can get through that situation i can damnfuckingwell get through anything too we tell stories of lovebetrayaldeathlifebirthliving mundanefantastical all the stories overover againagain but we cannever get enough we cantever get it out of our minds and it just goes onononononononononononon...

     Birds' wings flapping in the tree overhead. Soft delicate melodies come from their throats, their wings fluttering against the remaining leaves that still grasped onto the tree boughs. Those birds refused to leave just because the winter came; I am not going anywhere either.

storiesstoriesstories realfalsetruefictionnonfiction stories storiesstories shakespeare wrote everything everytype of story theres to tell the lunatic he added mostly tragic inventions to them the lover his stories were meant for stage entertainment as much as they were in the pursuit of the truth the poet and truestorytelling otherwriters attempted to capture the world as they saw it through fictionnonfictionnon whatever those titleslabels are even supposed to mean

wheres god now iam here sams at the apartment lillys at her apartment wheres god why cant god reveal itself whys that the rule doesgodneed rules i just wanttosee i wanttoknow the jokester atheist says if theres a god whywouldhemake meanatheist its all insanefuckingallfuckinginsane imnot afraid to die but i donteverwantto fucking die death is the ultimate test and proof of life lifes a building towards death people have

alwayssearched foreternity it makes perfect sense to create
the consolation ofeternity peoplesearched for the
fountainofyouth gilgamesh searched foreternity
weallpursue eternityinvain of religiongodheavenhellnone
of it matters if the universe is e x p   a   n   d   i   n   g
only to collapse again on itself like a claypotpieced
togetherandcookedinakiln then pushed clumsily by its
creator off a table toshatterintime your precious time this
world will come to an end and ceaseentirely and
wewillbegone long before then time is merely a delicate
concept wovenintoeveryone s delicate littlelives without
time theresnoteternity how could you kill time without
injuring eternity the old adage goes exactly i want to see a
timeless world it would be unchanged for the most part at
least and why did christians come up with the concept of
the devil the jews didnt believe in a satan figure dont
weallfeelbadenough without there being hellsatan pure
corruption in the world the worlds unjust and following
philosophical suit any lifeworldafterlife is likely to be just
as unjust it is nothing we can fix we were not creators in
the beginning weweremerely dirtdustmagic but
wecancreate wearecreators just as much so or more so
whatever caused all this i praise that ifuckingpraise
thebeginning thecreator theeverand alwaysconstant or
themeremiraculousevent i am gladthankful to be here and
thatsallthatreallymatters to me i dont care if the world was
created or if it simply has just always been here idontcare
if i go anywhere when i die because i dont think any other
place could compare to this life this oneandonly life
theonlyone that wewilleverhave things couldhavebeen
drastically different than they actually
      turned out
              for all
                    and

                              most

                                    of us

Through the opening of the trees: the moon, bright and resplendent, shifted into the view of my eyes overhead. I looked up at it and smiled, feeling something deep inside my chest. It felt like my heart was lifting or sinking. It felt uncontained, floating freely by its own will, delicately moving through a gravitationless world. My heart beat fasterfaster and felt lighterlighter as the moonlight shone through the trees down onto me, and I lay there against the tree thinkingdreaminghopingcontemplatingprayingliving.

where could she be now and what could she possibly be doing was she lyinginbed readingabook combingherhair talkingwithfriends watchingtelevisionmovie listeningtomusic writing workingonherschoolwork hangingoutwithfriends laughingout singinghumming tunesoutloudortoherself i held my eyes closed and sawherstanding in my thoughts herhairflowing each delicatefragilestrand of individual hair so captivating i studied each curveandcurlandwaveandsway i breathed in and i could smell her aroma i licked my lips and i could taste hers i envisioned her portrayed in the depths of my mind and there alone i reconstructed her as perfectly beautifully as when i last saw her i knew she must have littleflaws imperfections and i longed to find them soicouldlovethem i stared at her amazing skin and igentlytouched it with my hand tracing her visage those softreddishpinklips like purelittlecloudlikeflowerpetals gently beckoningswaying as she spoke and the melody of her voice rising out of her lungs and mouth and into my earsmindbodyheartsoulexistence then i stared deepinto her darkgorgeous gorgeouslydark eyes i saw the life in her the defined eyelashes flickeringassheblinked like butterflies flittering about from her soul i wanted her purelynaturally i wanted tofeel her body close and holdherkissherfeelher warmthagainstme i wanted to feel my hands exploring her body i wanted to kiss herlipscheeksforeheadneckarms chestlegsbelly i wanted to rub my fingers delicately from her chin across her neck and down her chest over her sternum down to her belly while i kissed the inside of her pelvic bones i wanted her to feel lovepulsating through my fingertips and engageconnectivitywithher in the way that words so often fail i could hear herlaughingsoftly because i tickledher but sheloved every bit of it and shefelt alive exhilaratedloved...

I   standing   foreign room,   she   lying there
       her beautiful   teeth   she laughed
                                    speaking   I couldn't
     make out   words   It must   her room.
       never   there,   imagining
          Posters   the walls,   desk   laptop
              speakers.   see
Piles of books   room   she started
                 couldn't understand   words
regardless   her mouth moving
              drawn to her   read her lips
      futile   matter   just admire
stopped   continued laughing   I was
         too   I   was
         doing.   too focused   was all
            mattered to

The room seemed to recede into nothing.

The   and   and   and   were   gone
    .   walls   bare   vision
looked   beautiful   before me   on
her bed, looking   at me laughing.   smiled   felt
       moving towards   floating   gliding
         all so   she
              smile   out   here   there.
              the floor   didn't make a sound.

155

```
knees touch           her bed           real.
feel    heart                   up again, racing
racing    racing    pulsating    beating    raging
           she      up              my shirt
       pulled me towards her    I lay    top
she kissed        I         back
    her hip    my right hand holding          I kissed
         bodies pressed close           wrapped
      around    waist                  her hands
    my face              she kissed              me
and kissed         her breath       was sweet
         pure      lips moved
         neck              slightly     began
more         we became            . Her
like a cloud       floated      sky
personal world      own universe       contained us.
  felt    lips                against           , no
longer      but whispering                 and
saying     saying     sayin     say     a.....
```

    I caught my head from plunging my body forward onto the dirt as I awoke. I sat there, very alert, sitting underneath and leaning against that tree in the park. Sluggish and soporific, I figured I should probably get back to the apartment and try to get some rest in my own bed. I had no idea what time it could possibly be, and knowing Sam, he probably thought someone in the city had murdered me, because I never came home late alone. Time didn't really matter, but I wanted to be buried comatose underneath the thick comforter covers of my bed, returning to such a pure dream.

•

On Wednesday, I got back to the apartment after long hours of writing papers at the library, but Sam was gone. I figured he was out at class, but I couldn't remember what day it was or when he even had class. It didn't really matter anyways. I walked through the apartment living room for a while, finally sitting down in the armchair. I stared at the television for about ten minutes before I realized it wasn't on. I was a prisoner of my own mind, and my thoughts controlled and bludgeoned my senses.

    I shook my head to try to grasp the world around me, then I stood and walked towards the fridge to pull out a beer or two or three and headed down the hall into my room, closing the door behind me. I placed the beers on the bookshelf beside my bed and lay down. I squeezed my eyes shut hard. I felt a migraine coming again. Leaning over slightly, I grabbed the bottle opener, placed it roughly against the metal lid that contained the beverage, and pushed hard in the upward direction until the metal bent enough and gave way, the cap flying to the ground and the cold escaping from inside the glass bottle. I took a deep sip of the stout, and it tasted beautiful.

Placing the bottle back on my bookshelf, I sat up and reached over to my writing desk and pulled my laptop off and lay back down on the bed, my back and head leaned up against the wall, my legs partially crossed on top of the bed sheets. I flipped open the laptop and pulled up my music player and began playing music and thinking about making a cliché mix-tape for her. I thought that I could slip the disc in the book when I finally saw her beautiful face and I finally touched her delicate hands in the exchange of the book.

I pulled up several albums and scrolled through my mediocre playlist. I played song after song and browsed through the songs that I thought would be absolutely perfect. In the book, Charlie makes a mix-tape, and so I thought that it would be a perfect idea to make her a CD with some of my favorite songs. Music has always meant so much to me, and I guess I wanted to find out if she enjoyed the same songs I did and had a similar musical taste. It seemed cliché and lamer than anything I've done before, but I always thought that clichés were just that for a reason, they meant something, something ubiquitous that we all felt or were capable of understanding. Perhaps, they were really just the best we were capable of describing things and expressing our sad, pathetic selves.

I heard the front door open and close. Footsteps down the hallway. Sam's door opening....still open. Soft rummaging. More rummaging and cursing. Sam's door closed. Footsteps up the hallway, away from our rooms and into the living room. The refrigerator opening, slamming shut. The front door opening and closing seconds afterwards. Sam is gone to who knows where. Out into the late afternoon Pittsburgh city street environment.

The songs changed and changed and played and continued to play out from the speakers and into my empty room and into my ears and empty my thoughts. I stared at the guitar leaning against the wall and tried to think about the last time it had been used: months, perhaps almost a year ago. Too long. I had been staring straight against the wall, listening to Sam's every movement throughout our apartment, thinking and hoping that he either would or wouldn't knock or enter my room or ask me questions or want to talk, and then he came and left without disturbing me or saying a word to me, and by the time I realized I was completely zoned out, several songs had lapsed, and I shifted my gaze back onto the computer screen to continue my thoughts about the mix-tape.

    Lying on my bed, I drank at least four beers with my laptop sitting on my lap, contemplating the right songs and thinking about when I could possibly see her next. I decided that I needed to burn this disc and go out into the streets while it was still light outside to walk and clear my thoughts, and if I were lucky, I might even run into her or see her crossing the street or lying on a blanket in the park reading. Yes, I needed to burn this disk, throw it in my bag, and leave at once.

    I compiled a list of songs and burned a disc. Then I scribbled the track listing on a piece of paper torn out of my journal:

> Lilly:
>
> 1. Yawny at the Apocalypse - Andrew Bird
> 2. Blood Bank - Bon Iver
> 3. Twilight - Elliott Smith
> 4. Delicate - Damien Rice
> 5. It's Not True - William Fitzsimmons
> 6. Oh, You are the roots... - Bright Eyes
> 7. The Sad Waltzes of Pietro Crespi - Owen
> 8. 24-25 - Kings of Convenience
> 9. Sixteen, Maybe Less - Iron + Wine
> 10. Chicago [A.C.E.L.] version - Sufjan Stevens
> 11. I Say I Swim - Seabear; "Love More" - Sharon Van Etten
> 13. St. Naive - Jönsi; 14. Heysátan - Sigur Rós

    The songs I picked mostly from random: a collection of favorite songs and favorite artists, thinking that they had some effect on me, and I was mostly hoping that they would have some effect on her.

    The disc popped out the side of my laptop, and I pulled it out and put it inside the book, then put the book in my bag and pushed my arm through the bag's straps and swung the bag around onto my back. I shut my bedroom door behind me, exited from the living room, out into the hall and outside into the city streets.

~~~

I really had no idea where on earth I wanted to walk to, but I decided that I just needed to get out of that apartment and get out of it as fast as possible. I was hoping that I would see her outside, while I was walking, but I knew that was highly improbable. Regardless of how improbable it actually was, I walked the streets with my eyes alert looking for her shape, her face, her smile, her eyes, her hair.

I knew that I would recognize her immediately, and I would casually walk over to her and make small talk, then pretend I had an epiphany, saying, "Oh yeah, I almost forgot," then reaching into my bag, pulling out the book, and handing it to her I would continue, "since you weren't in psychology, I got this for you." She would smile and hug me, holding on longer than friends do, and she would thank me. But I couldn't figure if the fictitious reels I played through my mind were consoling or more mentally damaging, and also, since I could only think of her, every brief glimpse of every person, or even some inanimate objects, immediately evoked the longing of her actual presence; but then my eyes actually focused, and I quickly realized that I had merely caught a glimpse of some leaves that hung down over an archway a block and a half from where I was standing, waiting to cross the street. My foolishness was overwhelming.

I let my eyes roam, and my mind did the same, imagining all types of scenarios and how I would react, and I continued to play them out through my head.

Walking all the way down Forbes Avenue, I held my backpack straps and watched college students prowling the streets just like me. But they were all different. But they were all the same. They were in groups, but they were still all alone. I could see it in their distant expressions and fake laughter. They passed me, passed the gas station, and continued down the street towards all the Carnegie buildings. I continued down the street, crossing all the side streets, looking around to see if I recognized anyone or if anyone seemed to recognize me. Nothing. No one. She was nowhere to be found.

By the time I reached the hospital, I knew it was time to turn up Craft Ave, then right down 5th Ave, back in the direction I came from, but this time down the other main passageway through this part of the city. The aorta, intertwined with the pulmonaries, connecting Oakland and Shadyside like the atriums and ventricles, flowing to and from and in and out, the vena cavas, superior, inferior. These two streets were the lifeline to Oakland, and I knew I was bound to see or find someone I knew or someone who knew me. But I didn't care if I saw anyone or vice versa. I needed and desperately wanted to see her. Another university on my left. Another hospital on my left, expanding and spreading all along the street and up the side street, like a sly predator slowly creeping up the hillside, methodically crawling towards the top of the hill to control the entire city. Up there, everyone could see them, everyone could recognize them, and everyone could fear and bow before them.

Passing alongside the shops and fast food joints, I saw a couple of people who looked like they were in my philosophy and religions class. As I got closer, my assumptions were confirmed, and the one kid smiled and started to walk over in my direction. He was wearing a knit beanie on his head and carrying a messenger bag that swung from his side, and he had on dark blue denim jeans, black slip-ons, and a button-down flannel shirt.

"Owen, how goes it, sir?"
"Oh, it's going, Lewis"
"Did you read that Russell essay for class yet?"
"Uh, yeah. I actually read it last night."
"What'd you think of it?"
"Well, I think Bertrand was brilliant, man. He argued his points both logically and fluently, not to mention in my opinion, quite humorously also."
"Yeah, he is dead on with that dogmatic bullshit."

"That's an understatement, man."

"I love his question, 'Do you think that, if you were granted omnipotence and omniscience and millions of years in which to perfect your world, you could produce nothing better than the Ku Klux Klan or the Fascists?'"

"Brilliant. Fucking brilliant."

"True. Hey, do you know what you're going to write your essay on for next week?"

"I haven't really thought about it too much. I will probably elaborate on his "The Existence of God" section and write about the application of western philosophical reason to the question of God's existence. Basically, how in logical reasoning, the whole idea of a creator turns out to be entirely illogical based on the way modern religions have explained it."

"You're quite the brilliant madman yourself. Almost like the Russell of Pittsburgh, ha. I was thinking that I might analyze the Abrahamic religious literature just like any other piece of literature that has gone through a rigorous editing and cutting and splicing and changing process. I wanted to note that certain gospels didn't 'make the cut,' I suppose you could say. Judas's gospel that declared Christ's orders for Judas to betray him, in order for the 'plan' to work out as the story goes. But I'm convinced that you will be the next Russell, you curmudgeon. You cantankerous bastard."

"Nah, that won't be me, man. I'd never be nearly that intelligent, nor would I want to waste my life with so much religion or philosophy. It's only a sojourn for me."

Lewis began laughing uproariously, and then began to cough while continuing to chuckle. I smiled to myself, laughing in tiny bursts, but my mind was mostly focused on Lilly. I wondered where she was right at that moment. I could care less about philosophy. It meant nothing to me, when I knew she was in the world, and she was near me. In this shitty, fucked up city, she was somewhere. Within the chaos of all these thousands and thousands of assholes, her perfect and pure body wrestled through the worst of the storm. I knew she was within a mile of where I stood now, but I had no way of finding out and even a slimmer chance of running into her or seeing her smiling teeth radiating as the falling sun reflected against the city's skyscraper sides.

"Well, I don't want to keep you, Owen, but oh, hey, tonight we are having a party at Alexa's house, up on the hill. You know. Off of Forbes."

"Yeah, yeah. I remember exactly where it is at."

"Okay, awesome. People should be showing up around nine-ish. If you see that strung-out fucker Sam, make sure you drag his ass over too."

"Alright, buddy. That sounds like some good shit. I'm sure Sam will definitely be down for partying tonight. I'll see you later then."

"Alright. Peace, Owen."

Lewis turned and walked back over to his group of friends along the side street, and I continued on down 5th, walking past Atwood, Oakland, Bouquet, and then I decided to walk across the lawn of the Cathedral and sit on one of the benches. I leaned my back across the metal vertical bars of the bench, looking out towards the street, watching the college students and business people rushing down and up and across the streets. Then I tilted my head back, and I could perceive the Cathedral, rising up and up into the sky, straight behind me. Lifting my bag off the ground and onto the bench, I unzipped my bag and pulled out that green book, flipped some of the pages and stared at the disc, reflecting the light of the world off of its shiny, silver exterior. I stared at the black marker ink that was smeared into symbols and then words, and I thought about their meaning. I thought what they might mean to Lilly. I hoped that they meant a lot. I hoped I would see her soon. I didn't think I could wait until my next class. I was so eager, anxious, slightly scared.

Fuck it. I closed the book and tossed it back into my bag and decided to continue my walk. Standing up, I put my bag back on my shoulders and crossed the grass lawn in front of the Cathedral, back onto the sidewalk and down the street towards the Hillman library. I was heading home now, back to the apartment, and I knew it.

      Finding my way back across Forbes, I hopped up on the curb, passed the bus stop and the front steps leading up into the library. Turning right, I passed through the familiar passageway that led between the two buildings towards my apartment. I knew I would be there soon, and I hoped that Sam would be back. It was starting to get dark outside, and I wanted to tell him about the party at Alexa's house. I found myself wondering what on earth I was doing, wondering if Sam was sitting on the couch getting baked, wondering where Lilly was and what she was doing and if there were the slightest possibilities that thoughts of me would flit through her mind at all.

•

Walking back into the apartment, I was surprised when I found it to be empty again. Where in the fuck could Sam be? The party at Alexa's was supposed to be in less than an hour, and Sam still was missing. I went into my bedroom to put my backpack on my bed and took off my shoes.

I left my room, leaving the door open, and I saw that Sam's bedroom door wasn't entirely closed, so I decided to knock and see if he might be in there. Knock, knock. No answer. "Sam." Nothing. I pushed the door open, and the room was empty. I looked around a little bit to see if his coat and bag were gone. They weren't. His coat lay sprawled out across his bed next to his bag. Where in the hell could that asshole be? I noticed a small baggie sitting on his desk, so I went over to examine it: some of his stash. I figured he wouldn't mind. I pulled out the top drawer of his desk and laughed instantly when I saw an old-looking wooden smoking pipe. It must have been his grandfather's pipe or something. It looked like an antique, but fuck it. I took it out of the drawer, opened the baggie, took a couple of pinches and packed the wooden pipe. I reached into my pocket and brought out my silver zippo and lit it, slowly pushing its flame into the pipe's opening, taking in deep breaths and watching the fire spread as it began to burn slowly then quickly then stay lit.

    Closing Sam's baggie and shutting his drawer, I exited his bedroom, pulling the door almost closed behind me, and then I walked down the hallway out into the living room, the smoking pipe in my mouth every step of the way. I ended at the couch and sat down, reclining and spreading my legs out across it lengthways. I picked up the remote and switched on the television and began monotonously switching through the channels until I found something worthwhile to listen to as I smoked the pipe and closed my eyes. The music channel was broadcasting a live Coldplay concert, and The Scientist was playing. It sounded beautiful as the smoke filled my lungs and made its way from my pulmonary vein into my heart and eventually into my mind, and the song began to change in time and space and melody. The world continued rotating on its axis, and as I sat there with my eyes closed reclined on that couch, I felt it. I could feel the world moving. I watched it being projected against the backs of my eyelids. The song filled the room and my ears and the world, and it painted particular emotions upon everything its sound touched. I thought about when I first saw the music video for that song. Everything was in reverse. It was when I was about sixteen. It was probably around 3 am on MTV, when they played music videos all through the night. I couldn't sleep; I never slept those days. The sound of the song started being projected from my television speakers, and the video before my eyes portrayed a story in reverse chronological order, while Chris Martin sang those words normally. He travelled through time and the woods, walking backwards, only to end up at that car crash.

    I could also hear that song playing at the end of one of my favorite movies: Wicker Park. The end scene where the lovers were finally reunited and together, as they should be. The song began playing loudly and clearly, and the message was just as loud and clear. Love conquers all, but I had yet to see it with my own eyes. The quintessential airport scene, lovers in love, piano keys touched in the distance across the world and played over the loud speakers. He took her face in his hands and they kissed they kissed they kissed, and it was real, it was so fucking real. I had learned that song on my piano in hopes I would play it for my lover in the airport as I kissed her lips hard and she tasted sweet and perfect and pure.

I had to find you, tell you I need you, tell you I've set you apart. I would stare deep into her eyes and rush up to her in the night amongst the chaos. She would smile and stare back at me, surprised to see me and in disbelief. *Oh, let's go back to the start.* We would stop within inches of each other, attempting to ascertain whether reality laid before us or if it were just some cruel delusion of the mind. Tears would instantly begin to stream down her face, cascading from her delicate, high cheekbones and dropping from her chin onto the cold tiled floor. *Nobody said it was easy.* I would wipe the tears from her face, and she would let out a tiny laugh and stifle her sobs. *No one ever said it would be this hard.* I would move the back of my hand and fingers across her face, tracing the outline of her face. Her hairline, across her temples, down her checks and jaw, along her chin and up to her lips. I would trace her lips with my index and middle finger, and she would smile and wriggle her lips, because my light touch would tickle her. *Questions of science, science and progress, do not speak as loud as my heart.* I would slide my hand across her face, down on her neck and behind her neck and gently take her body in my arms, delicately and softly squeezing her neck in my hand, my other hand alongside the small of her back, pushing her body close up against mine. *Oh tell me you love me, come back and haunt me, oh and I rush to the start.* My mouth would meet hers. Our lips would lock together in a passionate kiss that would be followed by one after another after another after another. Her tongue would slip into my mouth, and it would taste warm, sweet and delicate. I would begin to kiss her playfully all over her face, tasting the wet, saltiness of her tears upon my lips. *Nobody said it was easy, oh, it's such a shame for us to part.* I would continue to kiss her, holding her body close to mine, kissing her hair and letting her rest her head against my chest. She would feel the raging of my heart, and the whole world around us would collapse into nothingness. It would fade into a dissipating blur. It would all fall from the edges, and the only thing that would remain would be the two of us standing on a deserted island in the middle of the world in the middle of nowhere in the middle of the ocean in the middle of all existence and eternity. We would be there, just the two of us. *I'm going back to the start, oh ooh ooh ooh ooh, ah ooh ooh ooh ooh.* The whole world would exist only in her eyes, and I would stare deeply into them, promising to stare forever, for eternity. We would confess our love, and the world would be ours. Our love would be as real as my fingers against those black and white piano keys playing out the notes and composing the tune that filled our ears and hearts and minds and souls.

~~~

  Something disturbed my deep meditation. I heard keys shaking and rattling outside the door, and soon the door cracked and budged and in walked Sam. He eyed me up and down, examining me lying on the couch with his pipe in my mouth for a while, looking a little beyond bewildered, then his gaze changed course, and he looked over at the television and said, "Good concert."

  He was carrying a white plastic bag that he turned and sat on the top of the kitchen counter. I watched him as he emptied the bag, putting a six-pack of beer in the fridge and then turning and asking me if I would want one of the sandwiches he bought. I said sure, and I watched him stroll over and hand me the sandwich then sit down next to me in the armchair. I eyed him up, feeling a little bewildered myself. We knew each other well enough. We didn't have to speak. I passed him the freshly packed pipe, and he lit it up, smoking it and not saying a word. I unwrapped my sandwich and took a couple of big bites. I was starved, go figure. Then the pipe was passed back and forth as we sat watching the concert on television, smoking and eating and sitting in silence.

Finally I remembered about the party, so I told Sam, and he said it sounded like a great idea. He would have to get changed, because it had a been a long day. Even at that last comment, I felt a desire to ask him where he had been and if he was alright, but I didn't. I knew Sam too well. He didn't want any help and didn't enjoy talking about things even if he needed to. Silence was his consolation and confidence. Yes, the calumet we transformed that antique smoking pipe into was passed in pure, unadulterated silence. Well, the silence of speech. The concert music was good and probably even necessary. It soothed the soul of almost any human being. Music was a miraculous phenomenon, and we sat there admiring it with our peace pipe and temporary aphasia.

I thought of my hands against her body like fingers on piano keys, delicately pressing them in a specific and precise sequence to make her sing out the most beautiful tune.

~~~

We were precisely thirty minutes late, but the smoke continued to fill the room as we sat in silence listening to the music coming from the television. Sam and I were always late for everything. Oftentimes, we didn't even show up to parties or events. But mostly, we were just persistently late. Not because we attempted to abide by the philosophy of arriving later and later to the party because of societal status. We simply had poor conceptions of time.

By the time I finally glanced at my watch, I glanced over at Sam and told him we were late for Alexa's party. "What party?" he said. Did I forget to tell him? No, I told his dumb ass. I told him again. He sat up and nodded but didn't say a word. Standing, he handed me the pipe and walked down the hallway towards his room and disappeared. Moments later, he was back out and dressed, apparently ready to leave whenever I was ready. I took another hit from the pipe and knew it was kicked anyways, then I turned off the television as I was standing up and told him I was ready.

The walk over to Alexa's house seemed unreal. We walked through the city streets. It was dark, and there were hundreds of students prowling the streets at night. The college really defined the city and brought it to life. I couldn't imagine what the city would be like without the universities at its epicenter. We passed college kids that looked familiar but didn't acknowledge us, and we noticed some of the homeless people that lurked the streets, dragging shopping baskets filled with everything they would ever own and hanging around burning barrels giving off heat. The smoke and heat raised up into the city's cold night sky. I watched the smoke rising and fading away, up and up and up, until I couldn't see anything anymore.

Walking up that hill to Alexa's house at night was a royal pain in the fucking ass. It was like climbing a fucking mountain, because the roads were so goddamn steep. It didn't make sense to me, but I knew I shouldn't complain. Before I knew it, we would be inside in the warmth of Alexa's house, surrounded by strangers and acquaintances, friends and enemies, people and more people. We would be drinking and drinking more. Our insides would heat up faster than our exteriors that had been abused by the nighttime's cold. The season was slowly withering into the next one as the temperatures began to plummet, and the world began to get colder and colder.

Up the stairs to Alexa's house and in through the front door, we were greeted not by Alexa but by one of our mutual friends, Callie. Callie told us that Alexa was upstairs with some of her friends from high school who were in town to visit, and she informed us that the alcohol was across the living room and around the bend in the kitchen area. We knew the drill.

Sam and I headed for the kitchen, and we said hello to the people hanging out in the kitchen around all the booze. They said the one customary word to us and then pretended we never existed by returning to their conversations. I filled up a red plastic cup with straight whiskey and dropped in a few ice cubes, while Sam poured vodka and orange juice into a blue plastic cup. I took a deep swig from my cup, and the strong taste made my body cringe and convulse slightly.

I had decided that I wanted to go check out the basement, regardless if anyone was down there or not. Sam didn't give a shit about most things, and he had the heart of an adventurer, so he naturally had no reason not to follow me in my exploration of Alexa's house. Plus, we didn't know anyone upstairs, and I was wondering where Lewis was. I had been in her house once or twice before, but it wasn't for an actual party, more rather it was just a small gathering, and we would sit around, talking and drinking casually. As I opened the door to her basement, light from below began to pour up the staircase and into the upstairs hall. People must be down there, I thought. I started down the stairs, and they were old wooden basement stairs, so they howled and creaked with each pound of pressure I put on them. At the foot of the stairs, I looked around and there I saw Lewis with a group of people. They were all sitting around, silently listening to music and passing a bag back and forth.

"Lewis, what the fuck are you guys up to?" I said, staring at the bunch, who all looked like the most conspicuous group of druggies. They all had long hair, bandanas, rough worn out jeans or dirty khaki pants, worn converse shoes. They looked more like a group of wandering gypsies than college students.

Lewis sat there zoned out, not saying a word for a while but then finally started to speak, saying, "Psilocybin jam."

For a while the words meant absolutely nothing to me, until Sam started smiling and lifted up a little baggie with tiny, dried-up mushrooms inside of it.

Sam opened up the baggie and ate a large handful of caps, and then he washed them down with his screwdriver.

"The journey shall commence!" Sam declared, smiling and turning to head back upstairs with his one arm raised in the air as he carried his imaginary staff or flag. Ginsberg with his sunflower scepter.

"We are going to Schenley Park to roam through the woods, if you guys want to come," Lewis said as he was standing up, and the band of wandering gypsies mimicked his movement in unison. The sheep that ate the shrooms and obeyed their shepherd.

"Maybe later. I want to at least see Alexa first," I said.

"Okay. You really should come, though. We can discuss metaphysics and peer into the depths of the cosmos. It's supposed to be a really clear night tonight, so we should be able to see some of the stars through the trees and smog of the city," Lewis said, smiling ear-to-ear like a maniacal cheshire cat, perched in a tree gazing through the looking-glass.

"Yeah, I'm sure Sam and I will meet up with you guys later. Have a good *trip*," I said, laughing at my pun, but most of them were too stoned to get the joke, either that or it just wasn't funny, which was probably the harsh reality of it all. Not being able to make people laugh that were high.

I went back upstairs with Sam; and he quickly began to get more and more distant and eventually went to sit down on the couch in the corner. I had finished my whiskey, so I went and got more and then sat down next to Sam on the couch, partially examining the people of the room that I had never seen before and partially inspecting the external signs of the drug's progression on Sam. I didn't know if he had ever taken shrooms before. I hadn't, but I was intrigued by its prospect. He would stare off into what I could only imagine to be a totally different world, contained inside the one that always surrounds us. I figured that the drug lifted some of the oppressive reality sensors in the human brain and allowed the person to experience things that were not necessarily unreal but were instead meta-real, because they existed only in an imaginary world unlocked by the psychoactive components of the mushrooms that were beyond or higher than the world seen in a state of normalcy.

    I was almost zoned out in a euphoric drug-like state of my own, until I heard a knock at Alexa's front door. That knock altered my life more than any psychedelic drugs could ever aspire to. I sat on the sofa next to Sam and was almost half-tempted to get up and answer the door myself, but I was in some contained form of paralysis, where I was a divided entity, separated from my own body, a mere floating husk of my soul, watching objectively; however, in a matter of seconds, Callie was coming down the stairs and the door was opening and walking through the rectangular frame was Lilly. I couldn't believe my eyes. It was actually her. I thought that I had accidentally been slipped the drugs and my mind was delving into realms of my subconscious and projecting her imagine into an imaginary world that swam and sang and paraded around before my very deluded eyes. But I was wrong. She was there, and it was more real than anything I could have ever known.

    Callie shut the door behind her, and they stood in the entranceway talking. Lilly was bundled up in her winter peacoat, but I could see that she was still shivering there by the door. The cold had certainly gotten to her. The snow had finally begun to fall in the city, and I couldn't helping staring and admiring her as she stepped through the doorframe, gently brushing the snowflakes from her dark hair. She looked more beautiful than anyone or anything I had ever seen. She shouldn't have had to walk in the cold night by herself. I wished that I could have been by her side, walking through the nighttime, my arm wrapped around her keeping her warm. I wanted badly to go over to her at that moment and take her in my arms and warm her body all over. It was obvious from watching the movement of their lips and the gestures of their bodies that Callie was giving Lilly the same introductory speech she had given Sam and I when we came, and sure enough, Lilly was walking towards the kitchen to get herself a drink. I chugged my whiskey that was still almost half-filled, cringed almost violently, and asked Sam if he wanted anything else to drink. He simply moaned or mumbled but said no human words, so I just determined that to be a distinct enough "no" from him, and I hopped up and walked towards Alexa's kitchen.

Inside the kitchen, the same fools were gathered by the booze, still talking their nonsense, but I didn't notice them, nor did I care to notice them. Lilly stood, slightly bent over looking in the refrigerator for something to drink, maybe a chaser or mixer. I stood in the doorway to the kitchen, ignoring all the other people, gazing at the curve her body made as she was leaning over. She had left her coat on the rack by the door, and now she only had on a tight-fitting t-shirt that conformed to the beautiful form of her beautiful body. Her back was mildly exposed, and I couldn't help admiring her gorgeous skin on the small of her back. It was a pure and exotic color that looked like it would be heaven to touch. I thought of all the other places of her body and the curves of her body and how that delicate, pure skin was stretched out across her bones. I couldn't even fathom how soft and smooth and comforting it would be to touch her all over with my hands. I longed to be hers and for her to be mine.

She shut the fridge door and was holding a bottle of juice. She poured the juice into a glass with some vodka and shook it around. I knew I had been standing in the doorway long enough, looking like a crazy person, so I walked over towards the countertop and reached for the whiskey bottle. That was when she finally noticed me.

"Owen! What are you doing here?"

"Oh hey, Lilly. Uh, I'm friends with Alexa. We have philosophy together. What about you?"

"Alexa and I had almost the same schedule last semester, so we became pretty good friends."

"Ha, awesome. So how are you?"

"Ah, I'm doing great. I can't complain."

She took a sip from her drink and didn't make a face.

"Good, good. I'm glad to hear that. It's so great to see you again. I looked for you in psychology," I tried to say nonchalantly, while I was finishing pouring the whiskey into my glass and dropping a couple of icebergs into it. I watched them floating, half-submerged and half-exposed, and thought of Hemingway and his characters hopelessly drifting through a vast sea of frozen waters.

"Yeah, sorry I didn't make it. I forgot that I had a test, so I had to sit in the library cramming," she said, half-smiling and shrugging her shoulders.

"Aw, that sucks. What test did you have to study for?"

"My lit course. I remember the material perfectly, but I get thrown off by an overload of important dates and obscure theorists."

It would be an insult to compare her to an angel or say her smile was heavenly. She was beyond that realm. She was entirely unique in herself and beyond the capabilities of comparisons or definitions. To me, she was simply on a higher level than anything I've ever experienced. I had seen plenty of beautiful women that had captured my attention or captivated me, but there was something so much more than that about her. Something that was simply higher or beyond that. She was her, and that was all there was to it and all there ever would be. There seemed to be some captivating, unknown force that was pulling everything about myself towards her. Some shift in the magnetic poles or the gravitational field. But everything was attempting to align. And I couldn't really put it into words, and it was futile to try. I would merely try to admire her, and maybe, just maybe, some sort of light, radiating from her, would shine deep into all the darkness of the world and of my existence and illuminate a universe I never knew existed.

"I've had that course and remember most of it, if you are ever looking for a study companion. I wish I would've stopped by the library and saw you."

After I said these words, I knew that the last sentence probably revealed too much about me. I worried what her reaction might be.

"I wish you would've too! It would've been nice to have a little break, and I'm sure you would've been able to help me. Sorry, I missed you in psychology. I was looking forward to our secret rendezvous," she said, slightly laughing to herself, looking like she was hoping I would smile.

"We shall have plenty of trysts in the future. In fact, if you get bored at this party, you are more than welcome to show up knocking at my apartment door," I said this in a comical, seductive tone, and she began laughing instantly.

"I've been dying for you to ask me, and I've just been looking for an excuse to leave this party at once," Lilly said, tilting her head slightly to the left as she imitated her own version of the tone of seduction.

We both started laughing and began to take a sip from our drinks at the same time, which in turn made us laugh more. We were both nerds, and nothing else in the world mattered. When we stopped laughing, there was a moment. One of those moments that people talk about, or some fortunate people have experienced first-hand. We just stopped everything, and it felt like the world halted. We gazed deep into one another's eyes, but we were examining more than just the pupils and corneas and retinas and lenses. Deep down behind that eye, we were peering through it like a window into one another's minds. Some say the soul, others say the heart, while others still simply say the mind. Whatever it was, at that exact moment in time, we recognized and acknowledge it in one another. We were two counterparts in life that completely connected in that one moment of all time, of nothing and infinity, and it was a moment that would be immortalized in our hearts or souls or minds for a long time.

The moment itself was fleeting but the thought was forever. The experience passed, and I regained my composure and sense of reality.

"Uh, but seriously, if you want to stop over tonight or whenever, you can, you're more than welcome. I could give you that book, and we could hang out for a little. Or if you wanted to, we could go somewhere to hang out."

"Yeah, that sounds awesome. I was going to hang out with Alexa for a while, because she wanted me to meet her friends from high school. But definitely afterwards. Where do you live?"

I told her where Sam and I lived, how to get into the building, and then I gave her my phone number, so she could get ahold of me.

"Okay, great. I'll see you later then. I'm going to go upstairs to see Alexa and talk all kinds of girly nonsense."

"Oh lovely. Have fun. I'm depressed I can't join."

"Haha, I bet you are. Bye, Owen."

"Bye, Lilly."

Lilly smiled and walked out of the kitchen, and I watched her as she went. I watched every single movement her body made as she walked out of that room. From her feet, up her legs past her knees up her thighs over her hip bones and across her beautiful curves and stomach continuing over rib after rib over her breasts sliding up her neck her chin her lips her cheeks her forehead and all over her incredible hair, as she turned, and I could see her profile briefly before she passed through the door frame and was gone. She was a comely creature that left me not knowing what in the fuck to do with myself. I couldn't figure out why she even wasted her breath talking to me. She was all the unexplainable things in life.

    I finished my whiskey and tossed my cup into Alexa's recycling bin, then found my way back into the living where I saw Sam was still sitting, completely zoned out, on the sofa where I had left him who knows how long ago. I ambled over to Sam and told him I was going back to the apartment and that he should come with me. He nodded but still didn't say a word and just stood up. He may have mumbled some words but they were either inaudible or didn't make sense to me. I wasn't drunk but I was buzzed. I could feel the alcohol coursing through my veins, but I could control my speech and thoughts and actions and movements. I told Sam he could go into the Schenley park woods if he wanted to with Lewis and his gang of wandering gypsies, but he didn't say a word. His eyes were wide and he seemed to marvel at everything.

    We grabbed our coats and left Alexa's house, out into the cold black night, wandering across the city back towards our apartment. The walk back seemed to be much faster than the walk over. I didn't know if it was because it was later or because I was buzzed or because Sam was stoned off shrooms. Either way, the journey back was much quicker, and I was thankful. Sam did not say one fucking word, and he didn't even mumble or make primitive sounds. Through those crags of the giant buildings, on those city streets, there was a bitter cold breeze that blew against our faces and stung our skin. As the cold made my eyes begin to water a little, I looked up between the buildings towards the sky and noticed that there were delicate snowflakes forming in the sky and falling down towards the ground. However, they weren't quite making it to the ground. The air closer to the ground between the buildings must have still been too warm from the day, because I was watching the snow from far up, sparsely falling, then melting and evaporating before it got too close to the ground.

It felt like we had teleported across the city streets, then we were through the door and up the stairs, down the hallway and through another door, and we stood in the confines of our reclusive, exclusive a-part-mental suite.

I shut the door behind me and watched Sam disappear down the hall and into his room. Moments later, music began to rise and fall in crescendos and decrescendos. The music grew louder and louder, and it was absolutely the only sound that filled the apartment and perhaps the city. I recognized the sound of the song immediately: dun, dun...dun, dun, dun, dun. High hats on the drum set kicked into the song, and it picked up but in a naturally mellow fashion; Airbag, the first song on Radiohead's *OK Computer*. I knew Sam was intending to play the entire album all the way through, because no one randomly starts with that song. Despite how good it is, people tend to sift through and pick a different tune. No, Sam intended to be sprawled out across his bed, on top of his covers, enjoying the tunes of OK Computer as he rode out his trip as magnificently as he possibly could.

I listened to the psychedelic melody and the tone of the song shifting and evolving as the songs progressed and the tracks changed. I sat on the soft couch with my eyes closed, letting the music fill my ears, thinking about the bright green cover of that book, the black ink against the silver refracting CD inside the book, and her beautiful, flowing hair coming through my door into my arms and into my dreams, lips outstretched longing to embrace me and her body pressed passionately against mine.

~~~

I had fallen asleep on the couch and woke up with my eyes a little bleary still from the alcohol, and I had trouble adjusting my vision. At first, I had no idea where I was, but then as I began to wake up more, I understood that I had fallen asleep, alone on the couch. The apartment was now relatively quiet, except the faint hum coming from Sam's room. I looked at my watch, and it said it was past four in the morning. I was stunned. I completely passed out on the couch like a drunkard, like a moron, and I wasn't even that drunk. I fell asleep on the couch like a seventy-year old man watching television would have.

I stood up and rubbed my eyes a little bit, I didn't want to let myself wake up too much, afraid that by the time I finally made it to my soft, beautiful, comfortable bed that I would be wide awake and pissed off, so I forced myself to yawn and kept my eyes slightly squinted as I shuffled down the hallway.

At Sam's room, I stopped and peered in to find Sam sitting upright, cross-legged on the floor with his computer on the floor in front of him. He was listening to Sigur Rós and watching a Mandelbrot set zoom sequence video on his computer. I recognized it immediately even though I was exhausted.

He turned around and looked at me, then smiled and said, "Hey man, how's it going?"

He was still wide awake and, I assumed, still stoned from the shrooms. I didn't really want to talk, because I really just wanted to go back to sleep at that point, because my mind was starting to wake up more, and naturally it was beginning to remind me that I had been having a dream about Lilly, and it was simultaneously reminding me that she hadn't actually come over that night. So I was just trying to head to my bed with the high hopes of returning to the dream I was having of her and me.

"It's going alright. Fell asleep on the couch. Gonna pass out in bed now." I noticed how my speech began to deliberately get weaker, removing the subject of the sentences and even reducing forms of verbs. Lazy talk, tired talk, linguistic elimination. But Sam was wide awake and still having a very solid trip.

"That's just great, man. Isn't this music incredible? There's really something to it. It seems so simple, but yet so multi-layered and complex. And music in general is some phenomenon that has such a powerful control over human beings and our mind. It really, honestly alters levels in our brains and evokes such intense emotions, and it's especially prominent and potent since I'm stoned. You gotta try em sometime. They heighten and amplify your senses, thoughts, and emotions to such a beautiful level." "Okay, Sam. We will talk in the morning. Enjoy it, man. I'm going to make it to the bed, before I am on the floor here snoring. Night, dude."

"Alright. G'Night."

And I walked through my door way, leaving the door open, partly because I wanted to hear the music coming from Sam's room, because it would help me sleep, and partly because I was literally so exhausted that I didn't have the energy or motivation to close it. I hit the bed and the pillows, and I was out in less than a minute. The melodic, ambient sounds of Sigur Rós slithering down the hallway and into my room, up and into my ears and mind, and I quickly slipped off, back into the dream I was having.

•

I ended up taking a two hour walk in the snow. I entered the trail, and it was total darkness. The pure white snow appeared to be calm and the bare boughs of the dead tree branches lurked and arched over the pathway that led farther and farther into the woods. It looked like the path stretched on into eternity. I walked and treaded through the snow. It was about 5 inches deep, and it swallowed my feet entirely and part of my jeans. I walked relatively steadily, delicately losing my balance every once in a while. I realized how difficult it was to tell depths and curvatures in the snow, whether there was a hill or a dip. In the darkness, all the snow just looked smooth and flat and endless. I kept walking, my cheekbones and eyes were the only exposed parts of my body, so they took the most beating from the cold. It had to be about fifteen degrees Fahrenheit, plus wind. I trudged on, pulling the strings on my hooded sweatshirt, so it closed in on me and cut off some of the wind from hitting my ears. Then I adjusted my scarf and made sure it was pulled tight and covering my mouth and nose, so when I breathed it was mostly just recycled air, but it was warm. At first, it felt like I was barely covering any ground whatsoever; it felt like I had been walking for fifteen minutes, but it had only been about two in actuality. It felt like I was crawling. I was used to being spoiled and traveling in automobiles, trains, or airplanes. It had been a long time since our species relied on walking long distances to get where we needed to be.

I embraced the cold, but she still seemed to be a little hostile to have me in her environment. Surprisingly, to me at least, my legs and thighs were the most cold. I tried to walk military style, lifting my legs high into the air and kicking them, hoping that more blood would rush through them and they would warm up. I didn't want to have to fucking run, that was for sure. Next time, I would have to bring thermal pants, I thought, because that thin denim didn't quite do the job in those temperatures. Eventually, my body started to simply ignore my cold legs, and I just kept walking.

I came up on a metal scrapyard to the right, and they had lights that must have stayed on all the time. They were those whiteish security lights, and they cast specters and shadows across the pure delicate snow, and, for the first time, I could see the other track marks on the pathway: a human's tracks, and they must have been walking their dog; however, it looked like those marks were left at least a day ago, before the snow started falling. In the light, I could also see that it was actually still snowing, not heavily, but delicate little snowflakes were slowly finding their way to the earth's cold ground. I stopped to watch them floating through the beam of light, falling from the sky and slowly drifting through the air and to the ground. I continued walking and was surprised that I was not heaving from exhaustion, instead I felt completely invigorated and alive. I wanted nothing more but to keep walking and walking. I recognized the sound of the stream flowing next to me, moving too fast to freeze. I must do the same, I thought. Keep moving. Don't stop.

The lights were now against my back, casting my shadow and other shadows in front of my eyes on the pathway. I noticed that the human and dog tracks along the pathway were no longer present. It was only the smooth, glistening top of the snow as the white light reflected on the top of the delicate surface, and my feet that treaded through it, leaving a trail from where I came from and where I presently was, and I could see that trail stretch into my future.

The light faded out completely, and I was back to the open snow-covered path, through the tunnel of bare trees in the dark; however, there was a slight light coming from the moon that had revealed itself finally from behind the clouded night sky. The stream also seemed much louder than it had before. I wasn't closer, but it was definitely moving faster. I walked and walked and walked on. The snow flattening and sliding underneath my feet and soaking into my shoes and caking onto my pant legs. I started to notice a slight ache in my lower back. I realized that I had been holding my head downward as I walked through the snow to keep my face covered with my scarf and avoid the wind. Fuck it, I thought. I lifted my head and embraced the cold that immediately seemed treacherous, because my face was warm and had been sweating slightly, so once the freezing air hit my face, it was a painful shock. But it quickly passed, and then it felt incredible. I realized that I was completely neglecting looking around and taking everything in. I wanted this walk to be spiritual in some sense. Where I connected with the universe. Perhaps or something.

I closed my eyes. Then I continued walking, feeling the cold air blowing against my exposed face, the snowflakes gently clinging to my flesh and melting almost immediately, leaving little water spots that would tear and cascade down my face, until they froze or evaporated. It was too hard to tell which occurred first. I slowly started to feel the pressures of my mind release and all of my consuming thoughts shake themselves free and become more clear as I walked farther down the path into the woods with my eyes closed and the cold and snow embracing me and swallowing me. At first, I felt a little nervous and disoriented, thinking that I might just fall with my eyes closed or walk over the edge of the path into the running stream below. There would be no one to find me or help me. I blocked that out and kept walking. Relatively quickly, almost immediately after the initial paranoia passed, my mind slowly began to enter a new realm of itself. I could sense how small and irrelevant and unimportant my existence was in the whole of the universe. I was nothing. And I felt it. Merely a small particle that had no major effect on the workings or continuation of the universe. And all of the insignificant events that people constantly let ruin their happiness on a day to day basis were all meaningless.

  I could feel the snow on my face. It was beginning to fall more quickly and in thicker flakes. The trail my feet had stomped into the snow was even beginning to slowly be covered up as I continued to walk. By morning, there would be no trace left, as if I were never here on this trail, as if I had never existed, as if these thoughts had never actually been a part of anything.

  I opened my eyes and in the distance of the darkness of the path, I could see lights burning through the nighttime and the snowflakes that scattered and danced about their luminescence. Walking closer towards the light, the snow that I walked on began to light up more and more, and I realized that my tracks were not alone. There were several weird slithering tracks that looked as if a giant python were slithering along the pathway, but I knew that was impossible and it were probably just from the wind. Then I noticed deer tracks, maybe about three or four deer, casually strolling down the pathway in the same manner that I was. I looked to the right up into the woods, squinting: nothing. To the left by the stream and across it: nothing. Up ahead towards the lights and the opening field to the left: nothing. They were long gone, and I was alone, but their tracks remained, marking their journey and their existence, even if I would be the only one to recognize and perceive it.

The lights were coming from the various streetlights that were surrounding a plant of some sort, perhaps public water and sewage. It always typically had a scent, but I think it was too cold to travel through the air that night. I walked on and passed it, intersecting with the road that ran through the path. There were no cars and all was silent and serene. I crossed the road and walked across the bridge, slipping and sliding every few steps. Apparently bridges do freeze before roads.

That part of the path was more narrowly closed in, but I had been walking for over a mile and my pace had begun to speed up, so I was covering more ground and before a short time, I was already out of the corridor-esque pathway and into a much more open area.

I walked across the field to where there was a bridge. I didn't notice that there was a hill, until I was already in the process of descending and carefully navigating, attempting to not fall hard on my ass or face. I made it successfully down the hill and across the small landing, up to the bridge, but for some reason the bridge was fenced off and chained. I shrugged, because it really wasn't that big of a deal, so I looked across it for a while and admired the water that was rushing quickly beneath it, then I looked over to my left and noticed a series of large rocks, piled in echelon fashion, so I walked back down the walkway away from the bridge and then cut across the snow-covered grass towards the rocks, finding a nice rock that wasn't completely covered with snow and had another rock below that I could rest my feet on.

I sat down, crossed my legs, and closed my eyes. I thought about lying down, but I didn't want my back to be covered with snow, because I had a mile in a half walk back. So instead, I just sat there, upright, with my eyes closed taking in the sounds of the rushing water....

~~~

    The incline was steadily climbing higher and higher above the city as Lilly and I sat huddled close together in the car. The cold had driven our bodies close together. I sat with my hands in the pockets of my jacket, my eyes catching glances of Lilly out of my peripheries. I couldn't help ignoring the beautiful sight of the city at night for glimpses of her profile. Those clear cut, smooth cheekbones, beautifully illuminated in the dim light of the car as she peered out the window, down over all of the city. There was still a gap that separated us that I could perceptibly see and feel.

    At the top, we exited the cable car and walked towards the overlook. My wool scarf kept me warm but made my neck itch. It was one of the coldest nights of the winter in the city, but I couldn't avoid taking her to one of my favorite views on such a beautiful night. I would constantly go there to think and ground myself, but I hadn't been able to go for a while, and now I wanted to take her there and show her the city. She looked gorgeous in her thick, long peacoat, the snow coating her jacket and her cap that covered her hair.

    We walked up towards the railing of the overlook, that delicate cement slab that seemed to lurch dangerously over such a steep drop-off. With her beside me, it felt strangely safe. It felt okay.

    As the entirety of the city came into view, I couldn't help being slightly taken aback. As many times as I had seen that view in the past, there was something about it that seemed new, changed, enhanced, more beautiful. The stark, black of the sky filled my eyes, and I felt that I could almost see a few stars glimmering through the polluted air, as I watched all of those delicate, gleaming flakes of snow falling so perfectly, so beautifully from that black sky down upon all those buildings, those lighted up buildings, down upon all of those streets and down upon all of those people, and I saw all those snowflakes plummeting down upon the water of the river, partially frozen but still streaming, covering all of the earth in a beautiful white blanket, a pure coating of the most beautiful white anyone could ever see. Something so pure from such a dark, intimidating sky, falling down upon such a cold, bleak world. But it seemed so beautiful and perfect. In the brief flight, those fleeting snowflakes were the most beautiful thing I had ever seen.

Then I turned to my side and saw the beautiful form of Lilly, she looked incredible and she seemed to be closer to me than ever. I felt so happy and so alive. My heart began to stir and all of the thoughts inside my head began to move so quickly through my mind that I couldn't possibly follow them or even begin to understand them. We stood there for some time, silent and overlooking the city, admiring that incredible view, but I was now stuck looking in a completely new direction.

"Truly amazing, isn't it?"

"Yes. It's absolutely beautiful. I've never been up here. I never imagined that the city could look this incredible in the winter."

"It's surprising to find so much beauty in such a harsh environment."

Lilly laughed at me, which I was beginning to realize was quite a common event, but I was okay with it, and the more that it happened, the more I heard her laugh, the happier I became and the more I enjoyed it.

We walked off of the overlook and sat down on one of the benches, again huddled close together, our legs and bodies pressed side by side, aching to keep warm.

"Have you ever felt like everything you have been doing with your life is entirely meaningless?"

Lilly laughed a little, continued to look towards the railing that cut the city into even fragments through the bars of the guardrail, then she responded to my nonsense.

"Quite frequently. Sometimes I don't know what I am doing or why I am doing it in the first place. I work so hard towards some things, but then I wonder why."

"Exactly. I had spent so much time wondering why I tried so hard or why I thought so much about so many things..."

I trailed off and tried to figure out where I was going with this, because it seemed like I just started talking for no apparent reason and that I were just rambling again.

"...but, I don't know. I became so disillusioned so quickly before that I completely lost faith in everything. I refused to believe there was any meaning in anything that happened in the world. That everything was completely arbitrary. That none of it had any bearing or significance, that we just futilely attempted to attach or prescribe meaning to so many meaningless events. In a way, I still believe that...but...now, well, now I believe that we can make meaning in our lives. If that makes any sense. I still believe we live in a meaningless world, but we have the ability to attach meaning to our individual worlds, our individual lives, and all of those lives that are intertwined with ours, through friends, loved ones, and family; I believe that we are able to pursue the things we love with our entire being and we are able to love all that we revere with our entire being, and to me, that creates meaning, personal meaning, no grand or universal meaning, but a very beautiful, unique, and maybe even delusional, meaning, but it still is what keeps us living and loving and keeps us happy for such a brief life that we are all so lucky to possess."

Lilly now turned her gaze towards me and was locked onto me, and I couldn't help but feel stupid, like I had said way too much, that I had embarrassed myself again. But she spoke to me in such a calming voice.

"I've come to a pretty similar revelation myself. I have been trying to fill my life with the things I love and the people I love, in order to have a purpose to my individual life, not so much life in general."

"It may be absurdism, but I believe that we can't live wholly meaningless lives. Our lives are meaningless in the grand scheme, or to other people that have no connection with us, but subjective meaning is the ideal goal, or something like that, I suppose. That's what I believe in and attempt to achieve now."

Now I was glancing at the bright lights that were coruscating from the buildings, and I suddenly felt her hand on my leg. I closed my eyes just to enjoy the sensation. The reassurance of her touch, the connection. Her warm, gloved hand touching my cold leg in the frozen weather, warming it as she touched it, and I couldn't help thinking that it had some significance, whether it did or not, it meant so much to me.

Some time passed, and we just sat in silence. We were both consumed with our own individual thoughts.

Lilly said, "Have you ever had some surreal moment, where your mind disconnects you from reality, and you aren't sure whether you are some insane person or if the world is just that crazy and you might be the only person aware of it?"

I wasn't quite sure what she meant, so I asked her to elaborate while I chuckled.

"Well, I've had these moments where I am so sure of something, but then my mind slips into this dark corner of objectivity, and it seems to make things seem like it wouldn't be that strange if I had completely imagined everything. That is one of my biggest fears."

"What is?"

"Being crazy, but not being aware of it, I suppose."

The snow continued to fall.

"I feel the same way all the time. Well, not all the time, but it has happened a good bit. Our brains are mostly insane, I think, and I feel like sometimes that they make connections that don't actually exist in reality. Plus, I think so fucking much that I'm not sure half the time where the difference lays or what's the division between some thought I've had or some scenario I've imagined in my head versus what has actually unfolded. And then on top of that, I have lucid moments where I'll remember a dream, but I'm not sure whether it was a dream or something that has slipped deep into my memory and just so happened to be awakened by a peculiar phrase or sight or smell or something."

"So Proustian, you are."

I just laughed and looked back at Lilly.

"Yes, I dip my madeleine into my tea, and then I marvel at how my entire world crumbles before my eyes into a heap of dust upon the ground, and time and everything else falls into just concepts that are no longer even the slightest bit believable."

Lilly turned her head and began to look at me intently, deep into my eyes. A delicate honesty. An honest revealing. A purity unattainable with words.

The snow began to fall more heavily, and the wind blew against our thickly-clothed bodies. The wind raged on the top of the mountain there. But the view was beautiful, and I was no longer that cold. It was initially a little bit of a struggle to talk without my teeth chattering, but I had adapted.

"Have you ever read *The Bell Jar*?" Lilly asked me.

"Yeah, it's one of my favorite books."

"I sometimes think of Esther and how Plath chronicles her persistent struggle against the norm and deals with her feelings of complete, utter inadequacy. So much of it was based off of Sylvia Plath's actual life, and as much as she was persistently being labeled as the crazy person, I felt like she was the only person in the book that appeared to be actually normal. Do you know what I mean?"

"Absolutely. She was the only person that seemed to be grounded in, or at least understood, reality. She had fallen into the role of the iconoclast, the one exiled from society. They cast a cold eye on her, and she felt inept, but in my opinion, she was the only person in the book that was honest. Honest and real and beautiful. Everyone else seemed false and bitter. I am so glad that she wrote that book, but I am saddened that she didn't quite make it out as she had Esther. I am glad that Esther escaped, but it showed the strength that Sylvia didn't quite have, but I suppose, wished she did or hoped that others would have."

"I agree. It was one of the most beautiful pieces of writing by her, and possibly, of all time. Which I know sounds vague and cliché, but it's one really great book. The book was also extremely empowering, especially in its bold attempt to defy and break from those norms of her era of writing. Sadly, some or most of those ideals are still present today, but they are masked instead of being out in the open."

"I couldn't agree more. I have always had an affinity for those people or those characters. The ones who are clearly outside of the spectrum of society or normalcy. Because those terms and ideas or concepts to me are complete bullshit. Those people that slip into those roles of life seem to just be, sadly, automatons in a way, like they are just actors playing those parts because they don't know any better. And then they get so good at being the actors or actresses that they are that they forever lose themselves, their individuality, their true essence of being."

"Sometimes it's so hard to continue to fight against that vacuous whirlpool. It's like a current in the sea that is perpetually attempting to pull you towards the rocks and obliterate the most beautiful, unique and true characteristics of every single one of us. And all of us get swept up every once and a while, but the strongest willed of us will continuously fight against that. And I think you and I are both the same in that aspect."

There was a pause and silence filled the cold air around us. Lilly stood looking into the dark night sky, at all of the city lights that illuminated everything.

Then, as she sat there looking out across the vast city, she said, "If we all were to learn to become better students of literature, perhaps we would not struggle so much to become members of humanity."

I turned to look at Lilly, and our eyes aligned in the most simple but perfect of ways, and I just looked deep into those eyes, smiled and recognized something that I had been searching for for such a long time.

"But I'm getting quite cold. Would you like to head back?"

"Absolutely," I said.

We stood up, and I had the boldness to wrap my arm around her and pull her close to warm her up, because it felt both natural and instinctive. We walked back to the incline in that particular fashion, and on our descent in the car, as those gleaming lights were reflecting off her beautiful eyes, she slipped her ungloved hand into mine, and I squeezed it gently as we were lowered back into the light and the life of the city.

~~~

...there was a loud soaring noise of a plane passing overhead. I didn't even bother to look up, but I couldn't help noticing the lights from the plane as they flashed on and off, they reflected and appeared on the surface of the water. There, then gone. There, then gone. And because of the light from the airplane, I noticed something moving in the water. Then another, then another. At first, I thought they were fish, just because they were in the water and moving, but then it dawned on me as I looked closer and analyzed them that they must've been the remaining leaves of the season that had fallen onto the water and were being swirled back and forth from the cascading current of the stream. I could see about twenty of them, making their way back upstream and then getting caught in the current and being pulled back down the stream. I thought about how they looked like butterfly wings against the rippling surface of the water as I closed my eyes and listened to the sound of the stream.

I sat there for about thirty minutes before the cold began to invade my body. My legs never really warmed up, but they just got colder. So I stood up and buried my hands deep into my jacket's pockets, then turned around. I noticed a large light pole that was casting a shadow from its base, and I followed it through the snow and realized that it met right at the end of my feet. I had no idea where the light was coming from that was making it cast its shadow in my direction, but I didn't want to think about it; instead, I just walked in that direction, following the shadow back onto the path and heading back the way I came.

When I came back to the water place, I stopped to admire the snow falling in the light of the twenty or so streetlights. It looked absolutely magnificent and beautiful. I couldn't help but smile, knowing that I had been searching for some transcendence for a long time, but I knew that it was a gradual process. When every living thing dies, they return to the ground and become one with the earth and one with the universe again. The universe has given me the chemical components that make me a living whole, and all things must come to an end, so when I die I will return those parts of me. It's that simple, just like returning a book to the library. Those twenty-one grams will leave my body when I am dead, and they will no longer belong to me, they will belong to the earth. Perhaps they always have and always will. No one really recognizes or realizes how connected we all actually are. We share both similarities and identical qualities biologically with other members of our species and other animals also. And to our earth, we are connected through the chemical compounds that make us up and every other living organism and the compounds that hold the earth together and make life possible. And all these atoms and particles stretch out of us from the depths of all our hearts out into the great, potentially infinite, expanse of the universe through the dark sky of space amongst all the bright, burning stars.

I started to walk backwards down the path, so I could continue to watch the snow falling against the light of the street lamps, then when I realized that the darkness was around me and I was no longer standing in the shade of the light, I turned around and began to jog down the pathway, farther and farther, for some unknowable reason. Finally, I was heaving and struggling for breath, but I kept jogging, covering my mouth with my scarf, incapable of preventing myself from smiling and singing "I'd Rather Dance With You" by Kings of Convenience. I started to dance back and forth, not giving a fuck if the whole world were watching me at that exact moment, laughing, mocking. I started skipping back and forth, still jogging down the pathway through the cold and darkness, my feet trudging through the snow, each and every step, me on the verge of slipping and falling badly, but I did not give a damn. I just continued on, heaving and singing, dancing through the night with a huge smile on my face.

The snow covered my face and clothes. I was alone but content and no longer terrified. And all I could think was that even on your most lonesome nights, when insomnia replaces the comfort you should have nestled inside of you, remember, and never forget, that there is a love that is winding down the roads of your future, waiting to wrap you up and snuggle you in its warm arms until you fall fast asleep.

•

A couple weeks had passed, and I hadn't really seen or heard much from Lilly. The winter had ended after its last, triumphant cold front that always leaves everyone feeling depressed, thinking that spring is on the horizon and then stealthily the cold swoops back in for one more final freeze. But the snow had ceased to fall, and now it was typical early spring weather in Pittsburgh: rain, rain, and more fucking endless rain.

    The whole city was drenched; Schenley Park's beautiful lawn was soaked and saturated, mostly looking like a mud land, and parts of the city by the river had flooded, leaving roads closed, cars submerged, which felt more and more like normalcy as it continued to occur. It was the early season of having the feeling like being constantly assaulted by rain, or the feeling that we were all perpetually under water. And the truly sad thing was that I didn't mind the rain all that much. The bleak, gray skies that typically ruined peoples' days. I was perfectly okay with it. The sun was nowhere to be seen on most days, and the rain continued to fall in torrents, but a day was a day was a day to me. Rain or snow or sleet or shine. It didn't have much of an effect on me. I preferred beautiful, sunny summer days just like everyone else, but I didn't let the lack of vitamin D from the sun on a rainy day or in the winter get me depressed like it had in the past.

Not to say that I wasn't feeling a little blue those past couple weeks. I had still been thinking about Lilly a lot, but as the time passed, I was able to push the thoughts farther away or dissect them or distract myself more efficiently. It is sometimes silly how time works. It hadn't diminished the strength of my feelings in any way, but I became better at controlling them and making sense of them. In a way, I think that it was a good thing, like my feelings were secretly lurking and growing stronger. The farther the gap of time that separated when I either saw Lilly or spoke to her, the easier it was to carry on my life without being weighed down by the thoughts of what she was doing, when I would get to see her next, etc. etc. etc. But those moments when I would look at my phone and notice I had a message from her, or heaven forbid I'd pass her in the street or see her at the library with a group of people, my heart would rage and all of the strong emotions would return as they had all originally been, being awakened from their subconscious hibernation. I would see that sparkle in her eyes as they looked into mine and that smile on her face as she first caught sight of me from far away or across the room, and my heart would quickly begin to flutter and beat like crazy. All kinds of endorphins would be released throughout my brain and body, and the feeling left me feeling completely overwhelmed every single time. Lilly was my sun shine that shone like a radiating orb through the rainy darkness of all my existence and all of the world. Besides, there is nothing else that can compare to the beauty of the present or the beautiful potential of the future.

It seemed terribly difficult for our lives to actually, finally align; we were both very busy and overwhelmed from a lot of different aspects of our lives. It seemed like two parallel lines spanning across a massive grid that I felt subconsciously, deep down would align and converge and become one beautiful, eternal trajectory. Lilly's school work load became almost ten times as demanding as it had been at the beginning of the semester, as had mine. Plus she had a lot of stuff going on with friends and family, events, et cetera, and as for me, I was working on a lot of different writing projects that I had wanted to do for some time, and I was finally playing guitar again. Also, Sam and I were hanging out a lot, smoking a lot less, and really coming up with some great ideas for various endeavors.

Time had become a consolation for me, because I had learned through my years of observation the incredible power of time. As depressing as time is by its effects on all of us, slowly breaking us down until there is nothing left, it also helps us cope with what makes us want to break down more quickly and rapidly. Every bad thing that happens will pass in time. It will always be destined for the past. And with time, the pain and the sadness or the anger and the hurt will slowly dissipate and diminish over time. It might not entirely disappear because our memories have ways of reminding us of things both good and bad. However, there are some things that we remember and there are others that we quickly and easily forget.

Since I had met Lilly though, I had not only begun to dream more, but I also began to feel much more content and happy with life and everything, despite the anxious and clueless feelings that having deep and quickly developing feelings for someone can and will do to a person. I had always wondered how everything about love seems like pure insanity, like it's the most absurd, craziest feelings or ideas any person could ever come up with, but yet, there's a small element of it, no matter how minuscule and insignificantly small, that seems right, that seems okay, that seems perfect, that seems rational even, that seems sane. But every time I had met someone that I was strongly attracted to, physically and mentally, I couldn't help feeling like a complete lunatic, attempting to analyze or make sense of my feelings or my thoughts. And with

Lilly, in a way, it was even worse. I was more attracted to her, to her beauty and personality, than anyone I had ever met. But I realized that there were overwhelming forces at work that I wasn't fully aware of that were making love grow inside of me. The seeds had been planted and sown. I could feel the roots spreading all throughout every last inch of my body, building and creating a sturdy, impenetrable foundation that could never be uprooted or stopped.

All of the madness presented itself before me and persuaded me to simply believe in its logical reason, its consistency, and its natural beauty. And that's what I did.

And I realized that love is something that none of us may ever be able to truly understand, for it works in such sly and mysterious ways; however, for better or worse, it is something we all perpetually strive for, regardless of everything else. We don't have control over it once it takes hold of us, and even more frighteningly, we don't have control over whom love deems we devote all our affections to. We are the impotent puppets that play and put on shows for some sort of gods out there, as we entertain with all our foolish banter and the stupid things we say and do while we are in love, and we realize we are doing them but we still cannot stop ourselves from playing the part of the fools in love. We all are, and always will be, forever fools in love. But we are forever at peace and content with our lot.

●

For spring break from classes, I really needed a break and I really needed to get away from everything to be left completely alone with just my thoughts and attempt to try to figure things out. So I decided that I would drive northwest to Michigan for some seclusion in the woods, near the beach on Lake Michigan. Plus, I decided to finally take Sam's advice and try shrooms. I figured camping in the woods, near the beach and the lake would be the ideal setting for seclusion, my thoughts, and the trip. I packed up all the necessary things that I would need, including a baggie of dried mushrooms stashed in my backpack, and tossed everything in the car and set out on my expedition.

The weather was beautiful and the sun was raging hot. It felt like summer already as the sun's rays beat down on my face and neck during the drive out there, and once I was finally there, the heat didn't let up at all, but it was still beautiful and perfect.

I set up camp and pretty much just hung out in the woods for a week, walking through the sandy trails through the woods over the dunes to the beach, reading and eating baked beans from a can. The water of Lake

Michigan was so cold despite how warm the air and sun were. I had dipped my arms and legs in briefly, but I had no intentions of going all the way in or swimming. This was only partially a vacation, but I wasn't looking to treat this trip like a beach vacation. This wasn't the ocean, but it was just as or even more beautiful.

The first two days I spent walking through the trails in the woods during the day, reading as I walked and allowing my mind to wander aimlessly, then in the evenings I would return to my campsite to cut wood and start a fire just before nightfall. At night, I would sit in my chair by the fire, listening to music and sitting their contemplatively, staring vaguely off into the darkness of the woods that surrounded me or staring deep into the burning, raging flames of the fire, and I thought about everything, and I thought about myself. I thought about life and love and happiness and what holds all those things together, what makes all of those things important and worth having and fighting for, and what gives all those things meaning.

My third day there, I drove and ventured through the small town and surrounding areas that were nearest to where I was camping. I explored and walked around the trails, through the sand, over dunes, and through the woods, making mental notes and taking everything in, one sponge, one massive act of osmosis, attempting to swallow the entire world or imprint all those beautiful sights and sounds and thoughts into my mind forever. Most of the area was deserted during that time of the year, so it seemed as if I were on a deserted island. Or as if I were shipwrecked, with only a few other people. We were the survivors, exploring and living off the land in a pseudo-way. Perhaps, it was crowded during different times of the year, but while I was there it was a ghost town.

That night, I went into the small town there, near the upper peninsula on Lake Michigan, looking for a good meal. I stopped at a small diner that was in the town. I walked in around dinner time, expecting to see a decent amount of people inside having their supper: families, friends, loners like myself in a similar situation. But I walked in and realized that I was the only person in there, except two men that sat at the bar watching a hockey game. I stood in the doorway, waiting to be seated, and looked down at my watch, but realized that it was six-thirty and there should've been a dinner crowd but there wasn't. The woman behind the bar told me I could sit anywhere, so I sat at a table near the bar with a decent view of the television, so it could keep my mind semi-occupied while I enjoyed my dinner.

The waitress had dirty blonde hair, a compassionate, gentle face, and came up to my table smiling. She was probably in her late twenties, and she seemed content. She asked me what I would like to drink and handed me a menu. I told her I wanted a Guinness and a few moments to look the menu over, then I returned her smile, and she went back behind the bar to get a bottle for me. She asked the two gentlemen at the bar if they needed another drink, and they both ordered another. Rum and coke, whiskey and coke.

The two men at the bar were both drinking quite seriously. One was a younger guy in his late twenties like the waitress, but the other man was probably later thirties, early forties. They sat there drinking like old friends, watching the hockey game, making jokes, overtly hitting on the waitress as the alcohol began to alter them. They were both already clearly drunk. They finished their drinks as the new ones came, and they talked with the waitress about fishing.

"But I don't like to keep the fish once I catch them. I usually just catch and release."

"Well that defeats the purpose. We will go out fishin' next weekend, then head back with our catch and cook em' over the fire at my house," they both seemed to say, agree, and alternately chime in.

"We've been talking about going fishing for weeks now, but it hasn't happened yet."

"Well, it's always up to you. You're off this weekend, so it will happen."

"Yes, I am off this weekend, thank God. I'll have to borrow one of your extra reels if you have one, because Derek's taken mine."

"That's fine. I got plenty of extra reels and lines in the back of my truck. And plenty of supplies in my tackle box for you too. Lousia will be glad to have you back over at the house, so she can talk that woman shit with you again," the older man said.

"That will be nice, I haven't seen Lousia in a while. How's she doing?" the waitress asked, as she rounded the bar, walking towards me with a bottle of Guinness in her hand.

"She's fine. She's fine. Pain in the ass, like always. That woman is always talking nonsense."

The younger man started laughing, then took a sip from his drink but never stopped looking up directly at the hockey game on the television.

"Here you go, hon. Did you know what you wanted to order yet?"

I ordered the rodeo burger with sweet potato french fries then smiled and thanked her, and then watched her walk away, back around the bar, give the order to the cook, then back into her conversation with the two men at the bar.

"Yeah, well you just wait till her and I get together and team up against you two bastards."

They continued to talk a little bit more back and forth, jokingly bickering and then back on the discussion about going fishing. The younger guy was barely saying anything, and it was obvious that he had a thing for the waitress. It was also obvious that he was very drunk. I could tell I made him uncomfortable for some reason, just by the strange glances I got from both of the men when I walked in, and the looks every once in a while from the younger man when the waitress would come back to my table to check on me, and she would smile and have small talk with me. I was a foreign animal in their territory. When she'd return behind the bar, the older man would be talking on about the hockey game and fishing, but the young man would speak in a softer voice to her whenever she came over to them, to lean her back against the bar and look up to check the score of the hockey game.

I finished my meal and paid my bill and was leaving, and the waitress said thanks and that she wished I would come back again. I said maybe, and she retorted with hopefully, then I heard mumbling and a more audible voice from the younger man, asking what she meant by hopefully, as I was pushing the glass doors open and they were closing swiftly behind me. There had been no one else in that restaurant, and it was the only restaurant in the entire town. The place really was deserted. So I got back in the car and headed back to my camp to sleep soundly from the three Guinnesses I had. In the car ride back, it started to rain, changing from a light drizzle to a heavy downpour. Then back at the camp, I ran from the car in the rain and lay down in my tent to sleep.

My last day there, I decided to experiment with the shrooms, because after a night of rain and very strong winds, Michigan had returned to its naturally beautiful state. The rain had caused the heat to break, so it was a more comfortable temperature, and the violent winds that had shaken the tent all throughout the night previously had stopped.

In the late afternoon, I took out the baggie of shrooms and laid them down on my copy of the *Upanishads*, split them in half and ate half of them, chewing up their squishy, styrofoam-like consistency, and then I washed them down with orange juice and gatorade. I wanted to wait a while to see if they would kick in, so I sat cross-legged in the tent, with the light pouring through the openings of the screen, and I began to read the beginning of the *Upanishads*. I read the first few sections and wasn't feeling much different, then looked at my watch and it had been almost a half-hour, so I decided to take out the bag and eat half of what remained. I washed them down with the orange juice then went back to reading. The book was talking about mystics, consciousness, the eternal spirits, and the creator of all things. "O life-giving sun, off-spring of the Lord of creation, solitary seer of heaven! Spread thy light and withdraw thy blinding splendour that I may behold thy radiant form; that Spirit far away within thee is my own inmost Spirit." I thought about all this while I was reading it, and I was thinking about the shrooms slowly beginning to kick in. I didn't feel drunk or high, but I merely felt a calming feeling washing over my entire body and mind, and my senses were becoming much more keen, and my emotions and feelings much more acute. I continued to read. "He is known in the ecstasy of an awakening which opens the door of life eternal. By the Self we obtain power, and by vision we obtain Eternity." I was laughing to myself, as I read this, not because it was humorous, but it seemed like these ancient Hindu writers had to have been experimenting with shrooms.

The sun continued to pour through the tent openings and illuminate the inside with light as I continued reading, and I still felt my senses rising and becoming stronger. "He is seen in Nature in the wonder of a flash of lighting. He comes to the soul in the wonder of a flash of vision. His name is Tadvanam, which translated means 'the End of love-longing.' As Tadvanam he should have adoration. All beings will love such a lover of the lord. You asked me to explain the *Upanishads,* the sacred wisdom."

It seemed as if these words, as I read them, were hitting on a perfect chord, pressing the fingers down upon the keys, and the melodic notes were ringing out deep within my soul, and it was fulfilling my longing and my questions and, not so much providing answers, but soothing them and evoking a feeling of overwhelming acceptance within me.

I then reached the parable of Nachiketas meeting with Yama, the god of death. As Nachiketas sits inside the cave of death, he waits for three days without food or drink, and then death appears and grants him three wishes. For one of Nachiketas' three wishes, he desires for Death to explain life and death to him, so he shall understand it. N. says, "When a man dies, this doubt arises: some say 'he is' and some say 'he is not.' Teach me the truth." However, Yama attempts to persuade N. to ask for something else, but N. is resilient. Yama finally concedes and tells N. that there are two paths. One path attains the good, while the other attains the End. The first series of paths are between joy and pleasure. For it is best to reject pleasure and pursue joy, as it is also best to pursue wisdom and reject ignorance in the second series of paths. Death says, "If the slayer thinks that he kills, and if the slain thinks that he dies, neither knows the ways of truth. The Eternal in man cannot kill: the Eternal in man cannot die." Then he continues saying that "concealed in the heart of all beings is the Atman, the Spirit, the Self; smaller than the smallest atom, greater than the vast spaces. When the wise realize the omnipresent Spirit, who rests invisible in the visible and permanent in the impermanent, then they go beyond sorrow." Then Death says to N., "Not even through deep knowledge can the Atman be reached, unless evil ways are abandoned, and there is rest in the senses, concentration in the mind and peace in one's heart."

I sat the book down and couldn't help but think about how everything I had been reading pertained perfectly with all that I had been contemplating on recently. Between death and love, life and meaning, etc. I was stunned, and even more so because it seemed to have such an inadvertent significance with the language being written seemingly skewed towards hallucinogenic use. The great Soma, they say. Some believed it was the *amanita muscaria* magic mushroom, the beautiful little red-capped mushroom with the white dots that you see in Super Mario Brothers or that you see gnomes sitting atop.

But whatever it was, it was something that enabled them to connect in some metaphysical way with the world and the living, and I suppose, even the dead or not-living. I decided that I needed to get out of the tent and walk around instead of just sitting inside the tent, relaxing and reading.

Taking a drink from the gatorade and putting my tennis shoes on, I exited the tent and zipped it closed, then walked down the pathway away from my tent and into the woods towards the beach with my hands in the pockets of my shorts, my right hand holding the baggie with the remaining mushrooms in it. As I walked up the hillside trail through the woods, and the ground underneath me changed from dirt and gravel to sand, I removed the bag from my pocket and stuffed the rest of the mushrooms in my mouth as I continued to walk along the trail, heading towards the beach. I wasn't feeling that much different. It had been an hour since I had eaten the first half of the bag, and I knew that sometimes it could take up to an hour to kick in, but I felt like they would have at least started to kick in. I was hoping that the walk and moving would help them circulate through my body more quickly.

I walked the mile to the beach, came up over the sandy dunes, standing atop the mass of hilly sand, looking out over the vast beautiful beach, with a view of strands of green vegetation sprouting out through the sand, random and rare flowers also sprouting from the desert sands, and then cliffs, mountains, sand dunes, all etched into the earth from millions of years ago, and the deep blue of the waters of Lake Michigan. The sight was absolutely stunning, and I just stood there for several minutes admiring all of its beauty and grandeur.

Finally, I continued down over the hill of sand to the beach where it leveled out, and then I sat down in the sand near the water, and I just sat there gazing out across the water, watching and listening to the waves come crashing in against the sand, admiring the seagulls that lay out on the water, swaying and bobbing back and forth with the waves, and the others flying high up into the air and swooping down, skimming the water, then shooting back up into the sky, navigating and screeching and cutting through the air and gliding on their outstretched wings. I lay there and closed my eyes and let the sounds and smells of the sand and water carry me away to a beautiful place. I could finally start to feel an infinitesimal disconnect from normal reality. The shrooms provided me with a heightening of my thought process, my senses, my perceptions, and most prominently my emotions. I had not eaten a large enough dose for visual or auditory hallucinations, but there was an indescribable, indefinable calmness, connectedness, and purity that ran through my whole body and mind. The levels of chemicals in my brain were altered for the best. My serotonin had been a jigsaw piece that was snapped perfectly into a snug-fitting position.

~~~

As I passed the time on the beach, sitting and eventually standing and walking, thoughts began to flood my mind, and I couldn't help but think about love and the importance of love. The feelings of belonging and finding oneself.

The most poignant element of the whole experience was this stark, infinite feeling of sadness that took complete control over my entire body, and it made me swoon and long for a complete and pure human connection, to reach out and touch that part of the human soul that had revealed itself to me, to connect to that in another human being. I longed to build a relationship that would entirely nourish that major component of the human condition, and all life, that seemed to feel lost or missing.

I concluded that love is the only true heaven, nirvana, the only OM that exists in this universe. It is all that we strive for, it is everything holy that we desire. But we don't understand it. No, we certainly think we have it all figured out, just like god and life and the meaning of everything, but we do not. We don't know anything. We are striving to understand it, to make sense of it. It is the one ultimate goal we are evolving towards, but we must try and try diligently to progress towards that goal if we ever have any true hopes of attaining it.

And I also thought of lonesomeness and what it means to be truly alone, while I walked along the shores of Lake Michigan. The winds raged and blew the sands West and East, farther and farther, collecting amongst all the trees and dunes, and the waves perpetually crashed along the shore. They may never cease. They may always continue for all eternity, unchanged. I couldn't help feeling caught in the middle of something, with the waters to my right, the woods to my left, the sky above, and the sands and earth below. Everything appeared desperately to be wanting to belong, to be a part of something, whatever that something was. They all strove to feel whole, to be a whole.

And then I noticed an old, deciduous tree stump, rising out of the sand, immediately at the water's edge, and I couldn't understand how it had gotten there. So far from its home and so close to the water. It was so far from the woods, yet it made it to the water. And when I saw the waves coming in and crashing down, on and around it, I knew that it was much more alive than I had thought. It had broken away from the forest to dig its feet and roots deep in the sands to remain where it felt most content.

The birds chirping in the trees, the crickets singing in the tall dune grass amongst the wildflowers, and the calming sounds of the wind and water along the shore: I gazed at the massive sand dunes up and down the beach and marveled at how they seemed mountainous. All the arcs and lines of the shoreline carved out along all this sand by ancient glaciers. Everything here is built on sand. And the skies open up and accept everything for its true form. And everything is one. And everything is pure, and true, and honest, and whole.

~~~

As I was heading back towards the woods, the shrooms had definitely taken control of me, or much rather, had taken their effect. But they did not have control over me at all. I was still me, and I was still more than capable of doing everything I could sober, perhaps even better. The rest of my cognitive function and motor abilities were left completely alone and intact. My perceptions, emotions, and thoughts were merely enhanced.

I walked back up the sand dunes away from the beach, hearing the sounds of the waves crashing down on the sand and the roar of the wind against the water top diminishing as I walked farther up the hill and into the woods. And as I entered the woods, I realized how at peace and at one with everything I honestly and finally felt. There was an indefinable connectedness with everything in nature that poured through my body. Everything felt alive, and not in the sense that I saw talking caterpillars, smiling cheshire cats, and walking trees. No, it seemed like everything had a pulse. That everything was one organic whole. And it was more than the hippie talk of everything being groovy and fine and alive and whatnot. I understood what the *Upanishads* were saying even more so than before. There is something eternal and living in all things, from humans to trees to caterpillars to sand. Whether it's life or a spirit or the self or Atman or god, we don't know. That is our futile and desperate attempt to define the indefinable. We have all named it something different, those who have witnessed it or seen it or felt it or heard about it or simply have faith and believe in it. It is the unknowable. And there was something in those woods as I walked through the sand, looking up at the giant pine trees, that revealed a glimpse of it to me. I always had a strong connection and belief in pantheism, believing that god is in all things. I always believed more so that Nature was god. But as I stood in those woods then, it seemed much more complicated than that, much more unexplainable, but there was also a beautiful, reassurance that came with that realization and understanding. It was okay that we didn't know and never would. In death, perhaps, we will have our answer. But everything in those woods appeared to be alive and eternal, and it all felt like it was a part of me and I were a part of it. And as we are all made up of atoms and chemical compounds and everything else on earth is made up of the same organic matter and atoms and chemical compounds that comprise us, it doesn't seem that insane or hippieish of a conclusion to reach.

As I was coming out of the woods, it was slowly beginning to get dark, so I returned to my tent and grabbed my iPod to play some music, while I waited for nightfall. The music was the most incredible music I had ever listened to. I listened to all the songs that I normally loved and all the songs that had emotional significance to me or at least evoked emotions within me, and those songs were so emotionally overwhelming. I lay in the tent, listening to Bon Iver, Sigur Rós, Sufjan Stevens, Kings of Convenience, and Jónsi, and in so many ways, the music was life-changing. I had experienced almost all emotions, happiness, sadness, anxiousness and borderline fear to their most extreme and acute abilities. Mostly sadness and happiness. They fluctuated back and forth. Borderline fear came with sadness as I meditated on death and couldn't help being overwhelmed by the thought of dying one day, but I attempted to reassure myself with the connectedness I felt with everything at that moment and all the words that I had read in the *Upanishads* that helped reinforce the ideas and beliefs I already partially held.

Once the sun had gone down and all I could see was darkness through the tent, I climbed out of my sleeping bag, put my tennis shoes back on, and exited the tent, walking down the pathway towards the parking lot and my car to sit on the hood and look up at the night sky.

When I got out from underneath the awning of trees and could actually see the sky fully, I was completely stunned. I had never seen anything so stunning and so beautifully amazing in my entire life. The night sky looked like the darkest black quilt woven neatly, elegantly with all of the world's most luxurious diamonds and gems, and I stood there, neck tilted back, eyes locked onto the sky, staring and marveling at all of the beauty of the sky, the world, space, and the universe. It seemed so surreal, so unreal. It looked fake almost, like I was peering through the Hubble telescope with my own eyes. I was watching the constellations twinkling and burning brightly against that dark background. I felt the quick weight and release of my minor role in it all. I, a mere speck of matter, my delicate, fleeting existence like a tear thrown into the vast ocean.

And I could notice some of those stars slowly moving across the sky and burning out before my eyes. Stars dying right before my eyes. Others continuing to thrive and burn fuel. And then the most miraculous and unbelievable thing happened. A shooting star leapt and lurched across the sky right for me to see. I almost didn't believe it, but then I knew that my eyes did not deceive me. I had never seen the sky or stars like that before in my life. And shooting stars in a sky view like that had to be relatively common. I continued to stare at the stars, and the only thing I could feel was the purest joy and happiness, and all I could think was how I wished Lilly could've been there with me, beside me, right by my side, our backs on the ground and our heads to the sky, her in my arms, head on my arm and chest, and a blanket wrapping both of us up perfectly snug. All I wanted in my life was to see those stars shining and jumping and refracting light off her eyes as I couldn't help but look deeply into them, ignoring all of the sights that I was staring at, because I knew, as marvelous as it all was, it was nothing without her. All I could think was, "If you could only see these Michigan stars, dark eyes, then you would know how much I love you."

•

I woke up and rolled over in bed, not wanting to pull the sheets off of my head, not wanting to get out of bed. I reached through the covers with my hand towards my nightstand to grab my phone and check the time. As I pulled the phone under my covers and just cracked my eyelids the bare minimum to read the time, my eyes opened wildly and stared at the screen, then I sat up completely in bed, began to rub my eyes, and then I looked back down at my phone.

There was a text message from Lilly from about thirty-five minutes previously, asking me if I would be free to grab some coffee. I looked at the actual time and it was eleven-thirty, which was still pretty early for me, because I was going to sleep typically after the birds had already begun to chirp and the sun had already rose.

I quickly got out of bed, sent her a text, telling her that all I had to do was get ready if she still wanted to get some coffee, and that I could meet her wherever she wanted to meet in about fifteen to twenty minutes. As I was waiting for a reply from her, I already had all my clothes laid out, or more rather just thrown onto my bed, which I didn't even understand why I was doing, because I never laid clothes out. I think I was just trying to cut back on time, waiting for a reply before I jumped in the shower and actually started to get ready. Surprisingly, it actually worked. I got all my shit together and grabbed my towel to get in the shower when I heard my phone beep. She still wanted to meet up and in twenty minutes at the coffee shop down by the museum. I told her I'd see her soon, and then I jumped in the shower and got ready so quickly and excitedly and idiotically like a mental patient finally being released from the sanitarium.

In Kiva Han, we sat there chatting for quite some time. She had nowhere to be that day, and neither did I. And I couldn't take my eyes off of her. I sat there staring deep into her brown eyes, then slowly admiring the curvatures of her beautiful face, the outline of her lips and the gleaming of her beautiful white teeth. She probably thought I was a psycho the way I looked at her, with that uncontrollable, unavoidable smile that covered my entire face. My face gave everything away. I looked down and saw all my cards lying on the table. She had to know. She had to know everything about me. And for the first time, I really didn't care.

After finishing our coffee, we decided to walk around the city for a little bit. It was such a beautiful day outside. The sun was shining; the sky was a clear, beautiful, oceanic-looking blue, and puffy white clouds that looked like various recognizable shapes floated delicately through the air. She made a comment about one of the clouds looking like her favorite flower, and I turned my head sideways, looking at her as she looked up into the sky with a smile on her face, and I wanted to take her in my arms and kiss her so badly.

We had made a loop around the buildings and Schenley park and were now crossing through the green that spread out and welcomed students to lie and sunbath or read upon its grass across from the library. As we walked underneath the awning of the pavilion back towards the coffee shop, I asked her if she would want to go to the art museum. I hadn't been there in years, and I was dying to go see the exhibit they had. She thought it was a great idea, so we crossed the street and headed towards the museum, her hand slipping into mine, our fingers entwining beautifully, as we stepped off the curb in complete synchrony, across the street and through the little, intervening walkway that had wildflowers blossoming about as the smell of lavender filled the air.

Inside the museum, we began to walk separately but very closely together, occasionally brushing up against one another as our eyes were deliberate and fixed upon the art that hung along the walls. The exhibit was showing "In Pursuit of Beauty," the art work of Russian painter Andrey Avinoff. Her hand slid into mine as we entered into the main room and walked down through the hallways that had gorgeous paintings of butterflies and flowers juxtaposed against such harsh city and architectural landscapes and structures. I noticed that a significant portion of the paintings were left incomplete. I thought of so many great works of literature that were never completed, and I felt that they seemed to sing a beautiful tune of their own. Some stories are never quite finished.

The paintings and drawings that hung along the walls were captivating, but I seemed overwhelmingly distracted, unable to pay complete attention to Andrey's masterpieces. I tried to stare at *Iridescence* that hung on the wall right in front of my eyes, but I kept sneaking glances of the beauty I found radiating from Lilly, who stood beside me, eyes focused upon the painting.

"Those colors are so vibrant and beautiful."

"Yeah, I know. The bubbles are almost surreal. They're insane. It looks like there's several paintings all combined"

"I can't believe he traced a lot of these first. They are incredible."

"Yeah, I enjoy seeing the incomplete ones. It's almost like peering into his thought process, how he made that progression towards the beautiful."

We continued looking through the corridor of paintings and drawings and came across an amazing sketch that looked unreal, like it could not have ever been drawn by hand. I wondered where that type of talent comes from and where it had gone when it seemed to have left this world.

I have always been intrigued and have found beauty in the simplest things. I enjoyed the Avinoff exhibit, because he seemed to feel the same way. The complex simplicity and beauty of a butterfly or an orchid. I marveled at his incredible ability to capture that simplistic beauty in his art, and I admired him for how he truly did pursue that beautiful life, catching butterflies in his spare time and drawing the intricacies of those flowers.

As I walked through those hallways of the art exhibit, I began to come to a startling revelation about love and beauty. I believe that the ultimate love springs from true beauty, but beauty can often be deceptive, because there are elements of beauty that often quickly catch our eyes. We must strive to avoid falling in love with beauty. Instead, there is a beautiful, honest love that recognizes beauty in all that we love. It is visible from the surface, but we must have a keen eye for it. It hides behind the beauty of the surface, but it's calling out from the depths. For I have been fooled into falling in love with something that overtly presents itself as beautiful. That is a false love. When we have fallen unexplainably in love, and we find all its aspects beautiful, as well as everything that you look upon. The true love leaves us utterly surrounded by beauty.

In that art exhibit, I was overwhelmed by a beauty I saw radiating from all of Lilly's aspects, inside and outside. I thought of Byron. "She walks in beauty, like the night/ Of cloudless climes and starry skies;/ And all that's best of dark and bright/ Meet in her aspect and her eyes." That was the beauty and the love I now recognized. The holy melody that the true lovers and poets of the world sang and continue to sing. I saw it looking back at me through Lilly's eyes.

Lilly and I left the Avinoff exhibit and passed through the Ancient Eastern art section, then on into the modern art hallways. The section where the Monet's, Rothko's, Warhol's, and Klimt's hung all there beauty on those bare, white walls. My mind was beginning to get an exhausted feeling. There was a bench that was in the area where we were, so I decided to sit down.

Lilly sat down beside me and asked, "Art-overload?"

"Yes. An over-abundance of visual stimuli."

We both laughed, but it was entirely true. There was so much art and so much going on that it was indeed an overload. I looked out across the gallery that opened through a doorway and expanded with all of the great artists' paintings hanging on the walls. I shifted in my seat to turn my head and look around at the painting that hung on the wall directly behind us. The simplistic, Pop Art painting by Robert Indiana loomed over both Lilly and I as we sat on the bench.

"This is so overwhelming" was all I could say.

"You write, paint, or draw with your hands, but it's always the heart that sings."

I looked over towards Lilly and her eyes were locked intensely onto mine. Something changed, and all of my fears and anxieties completely dissipated. I was almost unaware of what I was doing, then I realized that I was holding her face in my hands and pushing my lips up against hers, and she was hugging me closely, her arms wrapped around my back, pulling me tighter and closer. The instant I connected with her lips, the entire world melted away, and the only thing I was aware of was her and myself. I continued to kiss her because nothing else existed to me and nothing else really mattered.

Slowly, reality reacquainted itself with the two of us. But the world had changed the way it looked through our eyes, and we both knew it. I kissed her and stood up, offering her my hand as I stood. She took my hand, and we explored the rest of the art gallery, but both of our minds were elsewhere.

The museum was getting close to closing time, so we decided to move quickly through the remainder of the gallery and then head downstairs.

I've had love a few times in my life, but I realized there were all different types of love, and I knew that I had finally found the kind of love I had always been in pursuit of. The kind of love that takes two similar, longing souls and aligns them only to find out that they fit so perfectly together that it's almost unfathomable. And I don't mean merging our individual selves. Aligning closer than anything can come before touching, before losing its selfhood, to complement one another. I had thought that movies and novels and stories propagated that love is like a game and everyone must know all of the tricks and ways of playing. But I had met Lilly, and I was nothing more than myself with her, and all seemed to unfold in a natural, beautiful course. It may be extremely rare, but our two souls aligned, and there was a bond that became formed. One must be honest with what they want from life and from love and be honest with oneself if they ever have any hopes of finding love and meaning in their life. Disregard all external influences, and instead follow the mind and heart. For they may make mistakes along the way also, but they will eventually lead you to where you aspire to be, if you only lay trust within them.

We must learn how to be honest with ourselves and the world around us. If you always strive to be honest, with yourself and everything you do, for if that's how you spend your life, then you have truly found what the alchemist vainly sought: you will be able to turn everything base and cheap into gold.

With love, one cannot be delusional and believe in the idea of perfection as it is told and preached. Perfection exists in different and subjective forms. All things, including ourselves and our lovers, have flaws. But perfection is the act of loving those flaws. Perfection is the act of recognizing how those flaws fit within ourselves like snug puzzle pieces. We are all a little rough around the edges, until we find the perfect fit. Perfection is loving entirely and unconditionally. There is never, and never will be, an ideal of beauty. Beauty lies in what we love, and it springs forth and blossoms beauty throughout our whole lives.

I had fallen so deeply in love with Lilly. It had been building deep within me, but it finally crystalized and came to the surface of my heart and mind. The lotus rising slowly over time through the murky darkness, springing forth out of the waters and into the sunlight. Everything raised up within my mind and heart, and I realized that I was completely unaware of how thoroughly she had burrowed herself into my life and thoughts. Images of her hung in the deepest corridors of my mind, whether I was day dreaming or just walking down the street; they hung there like the world's greatest and most beautiful paintings stretched across the walls of an art gallery.

•

I fell asleep on the couch but awoke to the sound of the rain falling down in torrents, against the windowpanes, the windowsill, the walls, the earth, the city, and all those stoned kids that hung out in the woods in the park. My eyes felt heavier than usual. I hadn't been sleeping that great for the past couple weeks. I would go through phases of sleeping only three or four hours every single night and feeling perfectly fine, and then all of a sudden I would be passed out and sleeping for almost twelve hours each night and feeling thoroughly exhausted like I hadn't slept at all.

I was also beginning to have very vivid and bizarre dreams. I had been hoping for dreams of my own for a long time, and they were finally here. Vivid. Almost real. They really felt fucking real. Some were recurring; others were entirely unique and only lasted the night.

The walls in the room looked old, like it needed a new paint job, but the paint wasn't quite peeling yet. The room was somewhat dim. It was light outside, but the blinds were closed, and the curtains were pulled shut, so only a miniscule amount of light was capable of pervading through the barriers. There was no bed, only a dresser and bookshelves, and I lay on the floor against one of the walls with a composition book in my hand drawing. The clarity of the pages in my dream was incredible, but the image was blurry. I sat there drawing and sketching, but the image remained unclear. I had no idea what it meant to me in my dream or in life.

The rain continued to fall from the sky. Pat, Pat, Pitter-pat, pat, pat. Little drum beats mixed with Morse code. Everything was a symbol to somebody. Everything meant something to everybody. Meta-metaphors.

That blurred drawing haunted my dreams, but I couldn't even began to fathom what it might mean. Maybe it was some horrible omen or premonition. Or maybe that image would become vivid, and I would perceive it in the real world somewhere, and everything would start to make sense. Yes, I thought it would be a prophesied, déjà-vu-like dream that in some bizarre, magical way would predict my future. Dreams that you remember vividly, and then they unfold before your eyes while you are awake at a later point in time, either the next day or a week or a month later. They would come. It would be there all over again, replaying and reliving itself right before your eyes. Perhaps it meant something. Or perhaps it meant nothing at all. Maybe in death the answers would be revealed or maybe they would be sealed up and gone forever.

But now the dream seemed different. There was a bright white light pouring through my blinds despite them being closed and despite the rain that continued to fall. The light became so bright and illuminating that it filled the room, and I couldn't see anything, and I had a strange feeling like I no longer cared about the picture on the page.

Kuhn, Kuh. The rain seemed louder, almost like it was hailing. Kuhn, Kuh. What the fuck was that? Was it hailing? Was Sam knocking shit over or hitting stuff in his room? Kuhn, Kuhn, Kuh. Shit. It was the fucking door, dumbass.

I jumped up from the couch, rattling myself free from my thoughts of dreams and the falling rain. I caught sight of the clock hanging on the opposite wall: 12:34 a.m. I wondered who would be knocking this late and that was when my heart began to race with anxiousness.

Opening the door, my heart almost flat-lined. Lilly stood there in my doorway, her hair was soaking wet and dripping water from the tips. She was soaked. She was shivering. I made her come in and sit down on the couch, while I ran into my bedroom to grab my spare blanket and a cardigan to wrap her up in and try to keep her warm. As I was walking back into the living room, she was taking off her wet jacket and shoes. She was sitting down on the sofa, and I walked over to bring her the cardigan and blanket and sit next to her.

I handed her the cardigan, and she quickly swung it around her back, putting one arm through and then the next. Her teeth looked so white in the dark room, but they were chattering from her being so damned cold. I sat down on the sofa with her and put the blanket around her. We sat there, perfectly content, not saying a single word. I watched her body tremble and shake, and I took her in my arms and held her tight. I would've given her all of my warmth if I had too. I would've given her everything.

I didn't realize how dark the room was before she came, but it didn't really matter. I wanted to say something to her so badly. I wanted to ask her what she had been doing or what she was thinking. But it felt so right to hold her tightly in my arms, to have my arms completely wrapped around her entire body, holding her close to me. I was there to protect her and keep her safe. She felt so cold but soft, like I could squeeze her forever. She stared off in the direction of the turned off television, and I held her tight with my face resting against her neck and shoulder. I didn't want to let go. I didn't want to ever let go. Her body was beginning to become warmer, and I felt her chest rising and falling, and I moved with it perfectly. I closed my eyes hoping it would last forever.

Faint music was pouring out of Sam's room and into the living room onto the couch, where we sat. I had completely ignored it, but now I heard it coming in waves that crashed against our delicate bodies as we embraced. I couldn't make out a melody or any words for that matter. It was mostly a choppy mash of some notes that would reach us and others that wouldn't, but it really didn't matter. All that matter was there was music, and we were there.

Something compelled me to let go of her body. She had stopped trembling from the cold and was obviously warmed up. But I just let her go and walked quickly back towards my room, not really knowing what I was doing. I grabbed my iPod and a lighter and came back out into the living room. While I was still in the hallway, I caught my first glimpse of her beautiful face in that dark room, and my heart began to flutter. It happened. I felt it. My pulse was rising. I put my iPod into the speakers that were sitting on the end table next to the sofa, and I picked a playlist I had made that had a lot of mellow, acoustic music. I lit the candles that I had bought before for the coffee table, at the time not knowing why, but now knowing perfectly.

The flames on the wick flickered up quickly on all the candles, and little beams of light began to burst into the dark room. I watched the reflection of the flame in her eyes, flickering and jumping about her irises, and I admired the new form of light that illuminated her gorgeous face. I had a strong desire to kiss her, to make her mine, to make her love me. She evoked an immense passion inside me that I never knew existed.

I set my zippo on the coffee table and rested back down on the sofa next to her. Staring into the flames and watching them move, I felt like it was unreal how close she was to me now. She had been a part of my mind, a part of my dreams, but now she was sitting on the couch in my apartment right next to me. I closed my eyes, and a vast sea opened up and began to flood all my other senses. I could feel the world rotating and the forces all shifting, pulling the two of us closer together and closer still. I felt a touch. Her thigh made contact against my thigh. Then her hand touched my arm. I could still see the flame dancing around on the inside of my eyelids, and then I opened my eyes.

Turning towards her and wrapping my arms back around her, pulling her close, her eyes met mine in the dark room, and I saw the flames burning and jumping in both her eyes. I felt her fingertips slide up the back of my neck, through my hair, and she gently squeezed my head and hair in her hand. Then the world dropped its guard and showed me all of her secrets.

Lilly's hand grabbed my hair, and my hands, the right on her left hip and the left on the small of her back, pulled her body closer to mine, maybe even on top. Her soft, moist lips made contact with mine. She kissed passionately with just the right amount of pressure, my bottom lip below hers and my top in between hers. I kissed her hard and held my lips against hers, pulling her closer to me and holding her tight in my arms. Then our lips unlocked but were like magnets that were sucked back together regardless of how hard they tried to keep themselves apart. We kissed and kissed and kissed more. Her lips parted delicately and perfectly, and I slipped my tongue deep into her mouth. I could taste her. I could feel all the flawless grooves of her mouth and ridges of her tongue. My tongue moved across her tongue and across her teeth and in and out of her mouth. Our lips met then parted then separated then were reunited then parted then locked perfectly together like a perfect match or a hidden clue to a long-unsolved mystery. The world around me became enlightened. It was the type of kiss you can only imagine in dreams.

She pushed me back against the arm of the couch, and I lay there as she climbed on top of my body and we continued to kiss. An atom bomb could've been falling outside my window, and it would not have had any effect on the two of us at all. I rubbed my hand against her cheek gently while we kissed, and I ran my fingers through her hair. It felt so smooth. I wanted to feel it between my fingers more and more. I put my palm around the back of her head and slowly slid it down to the back of her neck as we continued kissing, and I softly pulled her face in closer to mine and pulled her lips tighter against mine and held that kiss. We held that kiss to make it last. She moved on top of my body, and I felt my heart racing all over my body. I was so turned on. She was so damn beautiful and sexy, and I had never felt a love so pure before in my entire life.

  The music played softly from the speakers beside the couch, and the candles continued to flicker through the darkness of the room. The rain fell and fell, pattering and tapping on the glass and on the roof, but nothing seemed to exist beyond us and our two bodies. I caught a glimpse of her darkened eyes in that dark room, filled with music and burning candles, and I imagined those eyes always in my mind and in my life. I imagined those dark eyes, waking up in the morning beside me and consoling me and telling me everything would be okay and flirting with me and making me feel alive. I was in love with her as our lips continued to meet in that dark room.

●

"Yeah," said Sam. "Yeah."

"You are full of shit."

"I am not. I am dead fucking serious."

"I don't believe you. That is hysterical."

"What? Why?"

"You actually used to do that?"

"Yeah. I know it was a little weird, but like, I don't know. It seemed normal enough at the time. You know what I mean. At that age, at least," Sam said, slightly defensive.

"Yeah, I got that. But why? Just explain that," I said, wanting to know the answers.

"I don't know. I can't really think of a reason. I didn't really like comic books all that much, but for some reason, I always wanted to be, or thought I was, a superhero. I don't know where it came from."

"Ha ha ha. Okay, so explain it to me."

A couple walked into the coffee shop on Forbes Ave as Sam and I sat inside drinking coffee and talking. I watched the couple come in from the cold and walk up to the counter, the guy with his arm over the girl's shoulder.

I watched them with my eyes, but I didn't break from my head facing Sam, waiting for him to explicate his story.

"Well," he said, pausing and sighing then continuing, "The one year for Halloween, I had my mom sew me a superhero costume that I designed myself. I would sit in my classes, not really able to concentrate. Mind you, this is like the third grade. So anyways, I would sit in class with my plastic lunchbox full of crayons and pencils and shit, and I would draw these costumes with my crayons."

"Ha ha ha. You don't really seem like much of an artist."

"I'm not. That's the sad thing. But anyways. So, I would draw this shit, and that Halloween I showed my mom and she smiled and responded all motherly and sewed me the costume as close to my drawings as possible."

"So what did this superhero costume look like, exactly?"

"Well, I don't really know why, but I made it such awful fucking colors and my mom didn't even say anything about it. It was dark hunter green with yellowish gold stripes and black, with a black cape. On the front was a diamond shaped emblem kinda like superman but inside it was a big 'I.' Then I wore these..."

"Wait wait wait. What was the 'I' supposed to stand for?"

"Oh god, you really want to know? You're really going to make me tell you?"

"Well, yes, naturally."

"Fine. The 'I' stood for my character, my superhero personae."

"Which was...," I said, trailing off, waiting for Sam's answer, because I knew it would be great.

"Aaaahhh," Sam let out a long sigh, then said, "the 'I' stood for 'Invisiboy.' My special superhero ability was the ability to become invisible at any time," Sam said, sounding utterly defeated and ashamed.

I just laughed saying, "Well, Invisiboy, you couldn't think of a more creative super power? The name is in some ways unique. At least for a third grader, but why invisibility?"

"I don't know. Sometimes when I was little I just wished I could vanish and disappear and cease to be seen or bothered by people."

"Yeah, if it were only that easy. Okay, but you still didn't say how this carried on?"

"Oh...yeah, well. Uh, so I dunno. After that Halloween, I just kinda continued to wear the costume. At first my mom thought it was really weird. I would wear it all the time. All day, every day. I wore it to school underneath my normal school clothes."

"Ha ha ha. That's fucking great. That's the best part of the whole story. I can't believe you wore it underneath your school clothes."

"Yep, I wore it until the middle of the 5th grade."

I just sat there laughing, imaging youthful 5th grade Sam, walking into school and through the hallways, wearing his normal school clothes but seeing weird bulges in them. I couldn't believe no one said anything.

"And no one said anything? Not any teachers or kids?"

Sam sat there silently for a while. I knew that he had heard me but was pretending that he didn't.

"What? ha ha ha, what is it?"

"It was in 5th grade in the middle of math class when Denny Lumis noticed. He sat one seat over and one seat back from me. I guess when I sat down, the shirt I was wearing got stuck on the chair and pulled up, and Denny saw enough. He saw the cape, the bizarre colors, probably the stitching on the side of my top that said 'Invisiboy.'"

"Oh man. No fucking shit? Then what happened?"

"Well at first, he didn't say anything, but then Mr Fennel asked if anyone knew how to solve the problem he had written on the board, and that's when little dicksucker Denny shouted 'I bet Invisiboy knows the answer, Mr. Fennel.' Well fuck me, but I about shit my pants, and it felt like my heart was going to stop, when I heard those words. So after that, Mr. Fennel all inquisitive asks who said that and what were they talking about. Denny raised his hand and said, 'Sam, sir, thinks he is a superhero or something. He is wearing a cape and costume that says Invisiboy.' So Mr. Fennel immediately says, 'What's all this nonsense, Sam? Is this true? Get up here right now.' So I had to go up in front of the room, and that old worthless bastard made me take off the shirt I had on top of my costume in front of the entire class. I took off my shirt and dropped it to the floor in shame and embarrassment, standing there with the top of my superhero costume exposed to the entire class, my entire hidden identity exposed. It was awful, man. But it is kind of laughable now."

    Except neither of us laughed.

    I didn't know what to say to Sam. He just sat there, staring off at something or nothing, his eyes looking glazed over like there was nothing but emptiness behind them. He was reliving that day in his mind as I sat there looking at him. He was that child in front of that room again, becoming a martyr all over again. I felt awful for him, not knowing what I should say.

    "That's just awful, Sam. That teacher should've been castrated, putting you on display for open embarrassment."

    "Yeah, probably. I dunno." His voice trailed off slightly, then he continued, "I walked home from school that day, three miles in the rain, and when I got home, I went straight to my room and took off all my costume clothes and buried them in an old box at the bottom of my closet. I've never opened that box up or even touched it since that day. My mom never asked about it or said anything. I guess she just figured I grew out of it. I dunno...."

I took a sip from my black coffee, and it was a little bit more bitter than usual. It tasted very potently smoky, almost like cigarette ash. I thought about mortified fifth-grade Sam and his humiliation. I couldn't imagine how traumatizing that would be for a kid, to be that embarrassed in front of his entire class, while they all mocked him, his teacher mocking him too. Some people are just fucking assholes. The kid was clearly afraid of something, and all he wanted was some comfort in knowing that in some imaginative, alternate world of his he could control things, he had power, he could become invisible, and in his real world, he could hide from all the things that frightened him. Everyone can relate to that.

I felt bad for Sam, so I wanted to try to change the subject, that way he wouldn't go too far back to that time in his life.

"What the fuck are we becoming with our lives?" I said, not making eye contact with Sam but kind of staring blankly out the window.

"What do you mean? Has this become an existential Seinfeld episode?"

"I don't know, maybe. Sometimes it seems like that more and more. But I mean what are we doing with our lives?"

"Uh...I don't know. What is anyone doing with their lives?"

"Good point. But I don't want our lives to just waste away into nothingness. I want to make something of them. I don't want to meet death, looking back at my miserable life, feeling completely defeated."

"Neither do I, but what can any of us really do?"

"I just don't want to....I don't know. I feel like the path we are heading down leads us into pure bitterness. I can see you and I becoming balding philosophy professors that are dejected and morose as fuck. I just don't want that."

I actually hadn't been happier in years, but I wanted to cheer Sam up a little, and we always jested in a similar manner.

"I often feel that we're going to become überly cantankerous. In fact, fuck, I think we're almost there."

Sam let out a deep sigh of desperation and took a long sip from his coffee.

"That is exactly what I'm talking about. We are so fucking cynical already. What on earth does the future hold for us? We are either going to die in a few years, because we've aged mentally way too fast, or we are going to be so bitter that everything we touch is going to turn to decrepit ash."

"Ha ha ha. Yeah, it's certainly going to be interesting. We both have to try to stay alive, though, and not lose touch with one another, just so we can see what has become of each other."

"I don't want that for either of us. The world shouldn't have turned us so cold already. We need to dig down deep and find more beauty and faith in humanity. I want more from life. I want to travel and see the world. I want to spend my life with a beautiful woman who's into the arts and has dominant genetic traits. I want to love her so spiritually that it would instill fear into everyone's god. And, I never thought I'd say this, but I want to have a beautiful baby with that woman. I can't live my life in the other scenario."

"I think that the cards have already been dealt to us, Earl Russell. We've gotten the shitty hand: intellect. We have the pleasure of understanding the world for what it really is. It is more of a curse than anything else. In fact, I honestly think intelligence is some form of mental illness. In fifty fucking years or something, I guarantee that it's right up there with schizophrenia and dissociative disorders. I mean, didn't half of the world's most brilliant people have some form of one or another?"

I started laughing and drank some of my black coffee down. I was glad to have Sam as a friend, because he realized that I was beginning to reveal too much of myself, so he tried to guide the conversation elsewhere. He was a good friend, but I didn't like the concept of being an ignorant guppy persuaded into taking the bait. For some reason, I just wasn't afraid to put myself out there, to just throw my emotional thoughts on the table and see what they looked like in the light. And if a crowd happened to gather, then sure, I'd be fine with or without that.

"I seriously wouldn't doubt it. I absolutely over-think everything, from love to religion to literature to changing my goddamned socks. It is a fucking curse. I am plagued with all of this futile knowledge that isn't applicable to my life. Or is it all too applicable? I mean, all the literature I have read has allowed me to travel into the plausible lives of millions of people, and even understand the world in a way, but it leaves me with as many questions as answers. Right now, in life, I just want fucking answers. I am trying to convince myself that some things are unexplainable and will remain that way, but it is so hard convincing ourselves of that in the society we've grown up in. Everything is based on doubt, so I doubt the sanctity of everything that is precious now. I want alleviated from this ailment. I need a cure. If only full frontal lobotomies didn't ruin peoples' lives and shock therapy didn't lead to Hemingway's final breakdown and suicide, I would try to find salvation in them."

"What do you suppose we do then?"

"I have no idea. Drink, perhaps. What do you want to do?"

"I only aim to have a grand library. For, books are the only way to humbly brag. They are the trophies of the intellectuals."

I laughed at Sam's natural ability to mix truth with jest, but my mind was elsewhere, so I continued.

"I am just beginning to realize for the first time that this is pure madness and not in a good way. I want to chase life into a corner and not reach death knowing that I never lived..."

"Like Thoreau."

"Exactly. But I don't want to be heartbroken, living in solitude near the pond forever. That lifestyle can only suit one for so long. I feel that I've been living that life already but without the illumination. I feel a change deep in the marrow of my bitter bones."

Sam just laughed at me, because I had never really spoken this way with him before. At least not too frequently or at length. I didn't blame him. He probably felt partially uncomfortable but partially relieved, because I thought I saw deep down in his eyes that he felt the same as me. I have become convinced that everyone has the same deep, lurking secrets and emotions and thoughts at the core of their being, because it is human, and we are all humans; however, some people are so petrified to talk about all of it or mention it or even allude to it, but I don't want to be afraid anymore, and I want to mine for it in my soul and lay everything I find out in the light for everyone to see, so when they recognize it they will say, 'that looks vaguely familiar.' His look of desolation masked by good humor enabled me to continue my exuding of thought congealed with emotion.

"Everyone needs love in their life, eventually. There is only so long of a period of time where we can exist without it, I think. I used to think for a while that love was only a counterpart or unnecessary, complicated complement to life. It's often just such a treacherous thing. I used to align it with the uncertainties and dangers of navigating an old sailing vessel through rough, icy waters in the nighttime. But now, I am beginning to reconsider. There is a reason why love is largely unexplainable: it's because it is supposed to be the ultimate majesty of life."

"So you believe in what Plato wrote and that old Latin phrase?"

"I used to be in disbelief, but now I can't help but feeling differently. Reduced to a mere biological standpoint, our only motives are to reproduce. Therefore, we search for a mate who appears to embody good genes, and then our body releases chemicals and madness throughout our brain, and the love emotion is evoked. Although, I can't help but feeling that there is more to it than that. I have just been thinking that I can live my life perfectly okay without having to believe in the existence of god, but I can't do it knowing that there's no such thing as love. In fact, I believe that they can often contradict one another in a lot of ways. Regardless if there is a god or not, it is worthless trying to change how I feel in order to accommodate the creator that *may* be there. However, I can't see love, but I can see its results, its consequences, its proofs. And even more importantly, I can feel it. And besides, who would want to believe in a heaven or god at all in a world where there exists not love?"

Sam had been silent for the entire time I was talking, but I saw an expression in his face that I had never seen before. It was entirely, soberly rapt in attention at what I was saying. I could see his face contorting and the sadness in his eyes finding a secret affinity in the words I spoke, and his silent response comforted my mind and soul.

"I think it is absolutely ridiculous to believe in an eternal soul of the body that survives death, but I must admit it is a pleasant consolation that I would like to toy around with. But I know, I fucking *know*, that there is something spiritual in life, embedded inside every person. If people want to refer to that as the soul, then fine, but I think it is something more. There is an aspect of all life that goes beyond the body and intellect, and I think that's the spiritual realm. As you mentioned, it's in *Phaedrus,* where Socrates says that 'the madness of love is the greatest of heaven's blessings.' Love is completely and utterly irrational and if we ever attempt to rationalize it, it becomes rubble amongst the ruins. In the beginning stages of love, it is pure madness. The lover is incapable of everything except the thought of the beloved, and they will be able to go days without eating or scale a rough cliff edge with their bare hands. Eventually that madness begins to settle into a calming contentment, but that spiritual madness, in all true love, like an eternal flame never ceases to fully wane into nothing but a steam of rising smoke. No, the true and eternal love burns deep and long and flickers but refuses to fade."

"But what about the idea that there's billions and billions of people in the world, and in our lifetimes, chances are we will actually only encounter the most infinitesimal fraction of them. How are we to ever know the *true* love of our lives, as people say? It just sounds like a cruel fairy tale to me?"

"I used to think that way for a while and gave it a lot of thought for a long time without reaching any positive end. But then, I thought about it differently. I found it hard to refute that statement, because mathematically and statistically, believing that there is a one and only true love is like believing that the end of a rainbow exists and at the end there is a unicorn who is in actuality just god. It is pure nonsense and completely implausible, but then I turned the question sideways in my mind. People continually say that they just *know* when they find the right person, just like they believe they *know* there is a god or any other obviously *unknown* fact that they claim to entirely know. At first, I dismissed that argument, because it is completely illogical, but then I decided to think more about it, and I realized something that was so vital to it all: the feeling of *knowing* that all of these people clearly and explicitly cite delves deeper into the topic. *Knowing* is an internal harmony. When each person feels that eternal, spiritual burning love and *know* that searching the earth's ends for a better match would be useless, then, at that moment, that is when it becomes true love. Of course, there is no way of ever knowing anything, but when the lover believes that no one, even world's away, could rival their beloved, that is when the flames burn the brightest and refuse to wane into that painful smoke rising into the heavens."

"You are becoming the epitome of my 'intelligence is simply just madness' hypothesis," said Sam, smiling behind his coffee mug.

It was beginning to get dark outside, and throughout our conversation, there were less and less people crossing the streets, roaming the city. I continued thinking but tried my best to relax my mind and turn it off. Sam and I had been in the coffee shop for hours now, and my eyes were starting to react negatively to the light. I felt as if I were entering into a delirious realm of my own mind, and the coffee was burrowing deep into my blood vessels. The caffeine was making my body start to have gentle spasms, and I realized that I hadn't eaten anything. My appetite had been changing, and my sleep patterns were also altered. I felt the madness gripping me, and I could only think of Lilly, coming to me from the cold, dark, wet city streets into my bedroom to wrap her soft arms around my body, refusing to ever let go, refusing to wane into a cloud of smoke.

~~~

Sam's story had reminded me of my freshman year at the university. It was a typical, chilly autumn day in mid-September of my freshman year, and I had spent most of the day outside, attempting to enjoy the remnants of the beautiful weather before the world would become buried in the snow and the cold. Those days I wasn't very "inspired," we will say, about my classes, so I often felt it much more important to do the most futile and mundane in opposition to my actual coursework. In fact, I missed more classes that first semester than I could have ever had the hope of attending. Regardless, I spent one of the remaining days of that season of that year outside reading leisurely. I found myself admiring the sound of the wind blowing through all those stiffened, brittle leaves, hopelessly hanging onto those boughs in sheer desperation, and I listened to the songbirds that refused to migrate, their songs pouring out of their delicate vocal chords out into that cold autumn air. Most of the time, I just preferred to take life slow and enjoy those small feats of nature's miraculous beauty. I would sit at the base of the trees, my back against them, lying perfectly still underneath their outstretched arms, and I would just watch the branches shake in the wind and the leaves as they slowly became dislodged and floated gently, delicately, divinely, poetically towards the earth.

I recommend the experience to anyone at least once in their life, because there was nothing quite like it. The leaves descending from the tree onto the earth, like dead rain drops waiting to be consumed by the dirt.

As I sat underneath a tree, I read my book and enjoyed looking up occasionally to people-watch, gazing at all the different people walking to and from their classes. For some reason, people-watching became a major entity in my life, where I felt the need to do it, or more rather I couldn't help not doing it. It wasn't something that I did in a creepy manner, but it was merely an inquisitive aspect of my nature. I enjoyed analyzing and watching things from afar, objectively, not necessarily judging anything or anyone but simply admiring. I found people and the human condition immensely interesting, and I just felt I'd be a foolish person to ignore it and not relish in it as much as possible.

Therefore, I would read and watch, then read and watch some more, and that pretty much consumed a large portion of most of my days.

I tend to remember a specific day from my freshman year, because I had actually gone to one of my classes that day. Now as startling and impressive as that may have appeared, that was only the beginning of this day being seared into my memory center.

I had my humanities class at two in the afternoon, and since it was a nice day and I had spent most of it outside already, I didn't think that going to class for an hour would be too detrimental in depriving me of a beautiful day. I figured I would go to class, sit there, listening occasionally, staring at the bland, bleak walls, imagining myself elsewhere, allowing my mind to wander into the most abstruse regions of thought, and, before I knew it, the class would be over. Well, that was the plan, but I ended up getting there quite early, so I didn't see any reason why I shouldn't continue to read my book, while I was waiting for my classmates and teacher to arrive and for class to officially begin.

I sat in the back right corner of the room, right from my perspective of looking from the back of the room towards the front and towards the door, and I may have been slouched slightly in my seat with my hood pulled up, since it was cold out. I just read, enraptured by the, quite frankly, appalling and horrifying detail of the story, ignoring the other students pouring into the open doorway like viscous corpses searching for their seats. I hadn't noticed my teacher enter the room, but I knew there was still plenty of time before our class would actually begin, so I just continued to ignore the external world and read. Well, I don't know how long it was before she noticed me reading, but apparently it caught her attention, and when she noticed the book I was reading, I am guessing that is when her attitude drastically changed for the worse.

Her eyes must have caught the glimpse of the relatively blasé but slightly disconcerting glare from the face on the cover of my copy of *American Psycho*, because as much as everyone crowding into the room was incapable of disturbing my concentration, a shrieking voice began to raise into the air and collided with my ears. I held the novel out in front of me, slightly resting it upon the edge of my desk, so my arms didn't get too tired, and, at the sound of the noise, I sat up a little, and my eyes lifted from the page towards the source of the noise: my humanities teacher as she stood in the front of the room, looking across the half-deserted desks straight at me.

"What is that *abomination* you are reading? Put that away right now! I don't want any such repulsive nonsense in my classroom," she spoke these words with deliberate vindictiveness and condescension.

I sat there stunned, incapable of an actual response, just holding my book, staring back at my teacher and feeling dozens of eyes incredulously glaring at me for my obviously extreme opprobrium. Did she actually say *abomination*? I wasn't so shocked at being accosted or the way she ousted me in the class, but I couldn't see how she could possibly be so absolutely deluded and narrow-minded and be a teacher in the humanities discipline. Apparently, I had set inaccurate standards for too large of a group of people.

There was an awkwardness that filled the air of the room for the remainder of the class, and I sat there the entire time, mulling over the scene that unfolded in my mind, vainly attempting to make sense of it. It just didn't make any sense. It was so stupid. It was one of the most ignorant encounters I've ever had. When the class was finally over, even though no one turned around to look at me in the back corner, I felt cold eyes on me like I was some heinous villain or a plague-carrier. My teacher refused to make eye contact with me as I slowly packed up the rest of my books and threw my bag on my back and slowly made my exit from the room. This *is* an exit, and thank fuck, because I needed to get the fuck out of that room, away from that class and that teacher, and all those other arrogant classmates that developed a superior complex towards me that day. I laughed once I pushed the doors open and walked outside into that beautiful autumn day, laughing for a good twenty minutes, thinking how they would've all reacted if I were Bret Easton Ellis, or even better, if I were the American Psycho, Patrick Bateman.

~~~

  That book was definitely notorious and would probably be inappropriate to assign for a class reading, at least at that level, but I don't think she had any right to judge me in my reading or personal decisions outside of the classroom or in life in general. In fact, some parts of the book were so detailed and graphic that I had to skip over them, and I think that was the ultimate intention of the book: to provide a portrait of how demented and insane an actual "psychopath" could be, an introspection into the potentialities of that psychology. Wasn't it the writer's duty to try to pursue unexplored regions?
  I figured a teacher in the humanities field would understand more than others the facetious labels that are attached to books, their authors, and their reading audiences. She was just as judgmental as all the other foolish, ignorant people in the world. She was the type of person that disgraced the freedom of speech amendment. She was the type of person that banned or burned great works of literature, because they had "dangerous" ideas. She had tried to ban *Ulysses. Howl.* She was the type of person that went on witch hunts. She was the type of person on the jury that put hemlock in the cup of Socrates. Yet, I was the prosecuted, the martyred, burned at the stake in the name of conventionality and all human ignorance and fear.
  I never said anything to her, because I knew it would not be worth it, but regardless, neither she nor anyone else in the class looked at me the same; or more rather, they actually refused to make eye contact with me. The utterly humorous side was that chances were not one person in that classroom actually *knew* anything about what I was reading nor did they care to find out. But they knew how to baaahh and walk the straight line when the shepherd gave a command.
  I could not get over the ironical humor that that liberal arts professor was condemning someone for a

radical book, that really isn't all that radical. The entire purpose of a liberal education is *liber*ating, freeing, the mind from the confines and bondage of conventional thinking and allowing the student to think critically for themselves, creating ideas of their own. Now, this teacher obviously didn't represent the whole of the university, but instead she was a rarity among her whole profession, and in my opinion, a complete hypocrite. To me, it was the equivalent as having the Pope perusing the streets of Rome and giving speeches of Shelley's "The Necessity of Atheism." Thankfully, the rest of my teachers that would follow epitomized the essence of education: empowering the learner opposed to a.) bludgeoning them with programmed answers, b.) stuffing them into an oblong box, and c.) throwing them into the dark cave of delusion.

Enough harping and bitching and complaining. The past is a worthless corpse that exists only in the mind, but I was altered from that point on for quite some time in my education because of that horrible experience. Not that I was traumatized, but it just went against everything that education should be, and I can't really blame her all that much, because she may have been having a horrible day, or that book may remind her of something unpleasant in her own life. She just could've handled the situation a lot better, but every human throughout their lives can envision hundreds of instances where they could've handle things a fuck-load better. At least, that's how I am. Maybe it's just me. Maybe I'm just a fuck-up. But I don't think I am that much more of a drastic fuck-up than many others. The beauty of me that I enjoy applauding is that I am completely unabashed to admit it. Flaws are as protuberant in our physical appearances as in our personality, rationality, et cetera. We are just all a bunch of fools in capes of flesh, trying to do the best we possibly can. I am really not all that different from you, nor you from me. That is just how it goes and always will. I admire all people capable of admitting their flaws.

~~~

  I had been having conversations and performing various scenarios in my mind, and they all seem to involve Lilly in some way or another. I could envision her walking by my side throughout the city or through the park. Or I could see her in my apartment, sitting with me on the couch or in my bedroom, cuddling with me on my bed. Or we would be inside the bookstore again or in the library studying or inside the coffee shop, studying or talking or leaning over the table to kiss each other and smiling with my hand underneath the table touching her knee.

  She was always on my mind and always in my thoughts. All day, every day. I couldn't get her out of my head, and even more, is that I didn't want to, even if I could. But I needed to get out of my apartment, because I had been cooped up all day inside, and my head was beginning to reel with borderline insanity. Something about the artificial light, or sun light deprivation, just really gets to me one way or another. I can spend the entire day inside, as long as I go outside to get some fresh air and light for at least a small amount of the day.

  I left the apartment and didn't really know where I wanted to go or where I was actually heading, but I had my typical spot where I enjoyed relaxing and entertaining my thoughts. For some reason, I didn't feel like cutting through the buildings, which is substantially shorter, heading to the park from Bouquet, but I decided to head out onto the main street. Maybe I wanted to see life to make sure it was still there in the world. So I headed up Bouquet and turned right on Forbes, walking down past the shops and college living with the Hillman library on my right. I decided that I would continue and cross the next street instead of turning down it, heading towards the Carnegie Music Hall. I crossed the other street, the Cathedral of Learning leering like an antiquated monster as the darkness that night brings was slowly beginning to descend upon the city. I walked slowly passed the bus stop in front of the Music Hall and stopped, so I could look up and admire the building's sphinxes that guarded the entranceway: Shakespeare and Bach. Two madmen. Two brilliant fucking madmen. Maybe Sam was right in corresponding madness to brilliance. Most geniuses were entirely insane, but then again, not all of the mentally insane are geniuses. The fallacy unfolds the argument when turned upside down.

And I was quickly beginning to realize that we need to have balance in our lives. More than likely, that persistent pursuit of knowledge *drove* those brilliant minds insane. It becomes like an unstoppable force, an eternal loop that is hard to break free from. To enter the dark room, the farther we go, snooping around, the farther we distance ourselves from that door that leads back out into the light, into the world of the living. But I had learned that that pursuit was a form of bondage too, and to pursue it and break free from it, then we were truly free beings. The pursuit of thought, education, and philosophy can consume our lives, allowing darkness to pervade all the beauty around us, by narrowing our visions on such a bleak, lonesome quest. Blinding us in so many ways that we are incapable of seeing the love that is the foundation of our entire beings. Leading us into a solitude that may never be possible to return from. We forget how beautiful and wise it is to simply not know. To wonder.

I pushed my hands harder into my jacket pockets, because the nighttime air was chilled that evening, and turned around to make a left and walk over towards the Carnegie Library end of the massive ancient building. The building in its entirety looked like a huge goddamned megalithic structure. I passed the loading docks for the library, the bike racks out front, the statue on the right, "Free to the People" above the entranceway of the library, and the two return boxes: one for books, the other for everything else. I turned left and walked up the sidewalk, thinking about Lilly, her image floating through my mind and the feelings that began to captivate my body felt so entirely real, as if she were in front of me, holding me and kissing me, in reality. She recreated my life. She came in and took me by surprise, and I knew I would never be the same.

Crossing the bridge, the nighttime sky had completely conquered the only remaining light. There was no one around anymore in this area of the city; perhaps that's why I tended to prefer it when in deep contemplation. I walked across the bridge, looking to the left at the industrial sites and machinery of the night, raging in all of its glory. But what really caught my attention was the art that covered the fencing that prevented all of the depressed city dwellers from walking off the edge of the bridge. In the fencing holes, yarn, or some sort of string, was tied around and around in various shapes and in all different colors, and it looked beautiful. It was so simple but so beautiful. Yarn-art. It was brilliant. The symbols the yarn made looked like old Native American paintings or symbols, and it was incredible. From the tops of the fence, there were also papier-mâché works of art that were hanging down, and I watched them blowing in the wind as I walked passed them, peering at the yarn and through the holes in the fence across the vast abyss that sunk beneath the bridge and at all the buildings that lit up in the night.

Across the bridge, I continued to walk towards Schenley Park, which was getting closer and closer and was on the left. The trees that arched across the walkway had finally regained all of their foliage, those delicate yellow leaves that had descended onto the cold pavement created their own works of art. The leaves looked beautiful, and I saw stains that their yellow-fading-to-brown colored compatriots made on the surface of the cement sidewalk, and it looked beautiful with all the stenciled outlines of leaves. It was another perfection of nature. I knew I was getting close to my Zen place, because the vast field to the left opened up and there were three trees in the middle of the field in the distance, lights glowing in the distance behind and the buildings of CMU glowing farther to the left. Then behind all that and to the right and farther back, there were trees and trees.

The walkway continued to wind down the road and farther into the park and the woods, but I headed up the stone stairs on the left, continuing to trudge up the cement walkway that climbs slightly uphill underneath the shade and protection of huge trees. Walking farther up, I climbed more stone stairs, and there was a bench that faced the road and city and overlooked all that I had just conquered, so I sat down, my chest heaving a little and the sight before my eyes overwhelming any concern of anything. Directly ahead was the Phipps Conservatory. I admired how beautiful the city was at night, with the yellowish-orange street lamps burning in the night, against the trees. A few cars passed, some going farther into Oakland, others leaving. A woman jogged down the pathway I just travelled, across the bridge, passing the artwork without noticing, then disappearing past the libraries into the dark city night.

My breathing eventually slowed down, but I still sat there admiring the sight before my eyes. There was something so simplistic yet so captivating about it and about everything. I closed my eyes for a while to rest them and tried to let my other senses increase in their receptiveness. My sense of smell grew stronger as I breathed in the fresh, spring, nighttime air.

With my eyes still closed, my hearing became amplified, as I listened to twigs snapping and cracking farther into the darkness, over in the wooded area of trees. I thought of what animals it could possibly have been: squirrels, raccoons, not many deer in the actual city, but you'd be surprised. It had just become dark, but the birds in the trees overhead were still making some noise, fluttering from here to there, the mother chirping out speech to her babies and the male crooning a bedtime melody.

My eyes opened back up, and I spotted a bicycler rounding the bend and riding towards the bridge and into the city. He looked a little like Sam.

Then my thoughts returned to Lilly, and I stopped feeling so cold inside. She soared through my mind, and I never wanted her to leave. I couldn't figure out how or why I couldn't stop thinking about it. She had this power over me, and it's not that I wanted to break it or take it away from her, but I wanted to understand it better and admire it and admire her more and enjoy it for all of its greatness. My life had been so full of rationality that I almost forgot what being irrational was like, or more rather, how beautiful it was to be completely irrational and spontaneous. I felt as if the glass shell that had been closing me in for years was slowly beginning to crack, and as the light of irrationality began to shine from within me, it reflected and refracted off those cracked pieces of the glass in such a kaleidoscopic grandeur. And deep down, I knew those cracks were slowly going to spread and splinter and that light was going to have to break through those narrow openings and radiate out from my entire inner being out into the wild world. Just the thought of that happening put my mind immediately at ease and brought a huge smile upon my face. The bell jar shattering.

I crossed my right leg across onto my left knee and sat there on the bench in Schenley park, overlooking the intersection by Phipps, enjoying every second of it. I sat in utter silence, except for the sporadic snapping of branches and the rustling of tree leaves as the wind blew through the city like a calming ocean breeze. I emptied my mind of thoughts and just enjoyed being alive, sitting there in the city on that bench. I was thankful for everything at that instant. I felt so fortunate to be alive and be alive in the era that I was born. I was grateful for everything in my life and for being appreciative enough to recognize the most beautiful, exciting, and pleasure-bringing elements of life in the most simple things. I had always been a little depressed for a while in the past, but that eventually subsided, and I vowed to never take anything for granted again, and I began to develop the most incredible happiness from the common, the ordinary, and the everyday. The leaves blowing in the wind overhead. A couple walking down the street hand-in-hand or lying in the park together. The birds in the morning and all throughout the day, singing beautiful melodies and songs and wooing their loved ones in the most pure way. Walking over one of the many bridges in this city and looking down at the river, flowing on and on and on and on. The giant buildings and their bright lights, glowing magnificently in the night. The people that smile back at you on the streets or at least make eye contact and silently acknowledge your existence. The incredible taste of fresh coffee in the morning or a hot cup of tea, morning, midday, evening, before bed. Tea's great at any hour during the day. The enthralling feeling of being completely rapt and absorbed in a story in a book or in a movie. The feeling you get when you're walking leisurely with nowhere to go and nowhere to be or the feeling when you're walking quickly and your blood's flowing faster and your heart's beginning to race more. Hearing a song that you absolutely love on the radio or in the coffee shop or at a party or in the bar or in an elevator or at the grocery store or inside your own head. These are all the things that matter the most. Lying down at the end of the day, realizing that you made it and it was worth it and it's worth doing it all over again, regardless of how mundane your day actually was. I realized that all of the simplest things that I derived joy from only got better with my love for Lilly. Her being in my life, and the love that she filled me with, it made everything so much better. I think that's one of the reasons I carried her with me all day in my thoughts. That way she was always there, even when she wasn't physically able to be there. She illuminated every aspect of my day, and I only wanted to be able to lie with her at the end of every day, with her head resting on my chest, her eyelashes tickling my sternum as she blinks. Her words, telling me all about her day, rising up and into my ears. Me kissing her forehead. Her arms wrapped around my waist, squeezing me tighter and tighter. Then slowly, slowly, us together drifting off to a perfect, beautiful sleep.

    The days end, but the world keeps going, and love like that is the most incredible thing any living thing can ever hope to encounter in their entire existence. The world's most simple pleasures and the most beautiful forms of love are the ultimate reasons for living.

•

I believe that it was Socrates who said that the unexamined life is not worth living. As simple as that seems, it is one of the greatest philosophical axioms ever expressed, because all other new ideas and philosophies spring and have sprung from the wells of the human heart that Socrates and the early philosophers had dug deeply into the core of the mind and intelligence. I have learned in my life that it is best to live by such a simple and beautiful idea. To live our lives simply, but beautifully. Continuing to question aspects of life and aspects of ourselves is the only possible way to strive towards progressing, or at least bettering ourselves in an attempt to reshape the world around us. It has enraptured my life, my being, and, I believe, has changed me ultimately for the best. Regardless of what a person's beliefs or ideals may be, we are better and stronger people if we question the beliefs and philosophies that we hold for ourselves and others, and if we also wonder if there are any new ways of viewing the world and ourselves through our same old, tired and withered eyes. New ways of perceiving a wider and more objective and, hopefully, truer vista of the world. Whether you lay your faith in humanity or a god or nature or nothing, we must all continue to persevere and live our lives harmoniously and holistically by accepting and loving. This may be one of our most difficult tasks, but it would be shameful to view ourselves as being humans in the entire grand cosmos without trying diligently to improve ourselves constantly. Of all the most tragic and deterring events, mentally, physically and emotionally, that have occurred throughout my lifetime and that occur in the world, I have always had a generally unwavering, unshakeable faith in love. As painful as some of the experiences I have had had been, or that I have read about or seen, I have been unable to be shaken down by the philosophers and gurus and common cynics of the world or disbelievers in love or true love. They make plenty of valid points, and statistics and even basic observation tends to support and reinforce their theories rather decently. However, I would have to add to the debate that as humans we have not learned or mastered how to truly love yet as a whole. Some have far surpassed the rest of us and achieved it, but the general lot of people are flailing about and attempting and failing miserably. As depressing as the truth and reality may sting the heart and mind, there is a greater hope that consumes that sadness. The majority of us are resilient and refuse to give up. Some do give up, but most continue on regardless, whether out of being stoic or out of pure stupidity. I tend to believe more in the former. Love is the one thing that most people refuse to let slip away from their lives, despite how many times they have been let down or turned into emotional ruin from the collapse of the hopes and expectations they have had of love. And it is indeed heart-wrenching and heartbreaking and mentally debilitating even to a certain degree that we have put human beings on the moon; or that we have hypothesized string-theory that could potentially explain the creation of our world and universe; or that by cuddling with a loved one or even a favorite animal, that it is medically beneficial because of the release of oxytocin throughout our bodies; or that regardless of our age, gender, sexual preference, ethnicity or any other external, idiosyncratic component of every human being, that underneath all of our skin, that may have been battered and damaged and has seen the world or has loved or has given birth or has helped another person, underneath it all, we are the same. The blood flows through all our veins and arteries in the same manner. Our heart, a massive, mechanistic organ keeping us alive. The air in the atmosphere being consumed by our lungs and oxidized throughout our bodies to continue on living. In all of us, humans and other animals, or plants and organisms and some of the most simplistic bacteria or forms of life, there is all a common thread between us all, and we are all similar and in sync and in tune in such a staggeringly wonderful and beautiful way.

      In philosophy, Occam's razor dictates that by cutting away the excess from something and finding the simplest answer or explanation is generally or often the best resolution, and for most cases, that is certainly the situation. And the reason why I mention all of this and these ideas through my ramblings is not to become another didactic dictator whose sole aim is the persuasion and education of other people. It is to present a viewpoint, whether seen as valid, solid, or even worthy of attention, and allow every person to analyze it from their own solidified point in space-time, as objectively as they possibly can. And not so much my views, but analyze what they believe in and who they are. And Occam's razor may potentially work for a general starting point of cutting out the bullshit and nonsense of normal living and culture and other external forces working to influence us, or even what I am saying, and then penetrating to the core of our beings, and being unabashed in criticizing ourselves and not being petrified of asking ourselves who are we, what do we truly and honestly want, what do we believe in, and if life is the only gift that is ever given to us then how do we want to spend our lives? What will make us happy? What will make our heads and hearts swell overwhelmingly with a powerful love, and how can we aim to achieve the things we believe in and hold dearly and inspire those around us that we love and admire dearly? And how can we love another person if we do not truly love ourselves? And how can we hope for the best in another person if we do not strive for the best in ourselves? And even more importantly, and in a pragmatic sense, how can we ever attempt to connect and understand another person and/or the person we love deeply, if we do not attempt to first understand ourselves?

It is certainly much easier to be frightened or weak or willing to just give up, opposed to the alternative of standing up, facing things head on and refusing resiliently to surrender to the overwhelming travesties and atrocities that will eventually plague all of our lives. Very few people have privileged enough lives to live their entire existence without having anything tragic happen to them or around them. Often it is easier to just lie in bed all day and hide yourself away from the world instead of rising like an intellectual warrior to challenge everything that is frightening. It is terrifying to ask questions that you may not want the answers to, but it is better if you do. The shock wears off quickly and we evolve, we adapt. Because we are human, we are capable of all these things. We feel enlightened, and we feel like stronger, more intelligent, and generally better people. Wisdom tends to reign supreme over intelligence. So perhaps, wisdom is trying and failing and not being afraid to try again. Perhaps, wisdom is facing your greatest fears and staring them down, even if you run away like a child at first, but then return to conquer them. Perhaps, wisdom is living through experience, viewing the world in a new way or striving to make sense of it. Perhaps, wisdom is making a wrong decision but being a strong enough person to admit it an' attempting to make it right. Perhaps, wisdom is ·o of the past and living for the present and the 'erhaps, wisdom is the Sartrean idea of *mauvaise* ware of your ultimate freedom and refusing to let arbitrary, illusory conventions determine your choices, or even worse, your ultimate happiness. Perhaps, just maybe, the most-wise thing of all is to refuse to lie down and let your life pass by, instead of facing it head on and living it and doing what makes you happy and taking justifiable risks and loving the people and things you love with your whole being. Perhaps, none of this really matters and perhaps it will all be disproved in a matter of months or years, but it is all about doing something. Live the life you have been given, and as Thoreau has said, live it deliberately. We may never truly understand anything. We will probably never know or have proof of whether a god or creator or supreme being exists, and everything that we believe we know may all crumble once we learn more about ourselves and the external world; however, at least we are striving and continuing the process towards these objects instead of surrendering ourselves to ignorance. We strive for change and happiness and contentment. Some of us may have been born with it, but I tend to doubt that to an extreme degree, believing that most of us are an undeniably perplexed group who are confused and scared shitless about just about everything in life, yet we have evolved such a miraculous capacity to push these thoughts and ideas to a region of the mind, so we either forget about them entirely, or they creep up in the dark lonesome nights, or they reveal themselves to us in a staggeringly profound dream that we awaken from in sweats and tremors, but incredibly, we quickly forget. For instance, we all die. All living things die. There is no way around this. Whether we go on living in some form or another or in another hidden realm or hidden reality is a whole different philosophical inquiry. The main point is that we die. Our deaths are unavoidable, and the person who we are now and as we perceive ourselves, at this exact moment, as you are currently reading this, at the moment of death, we will entirely cease to be who we are now. Think about that. Focus on it. It is frightening, but it is a major component of *life* that is woven into all of existence, but we have become so capable and powerful at removing that concept and thought from such a large portion of our entire lives. An utter disavowal. Mostly, because it is not beneficial to constantly have our thoughts consumed by the idea of *death*, because it inhibits our ability to *live*. And that is merely only one of many, many different thoughts that we are so great at removing from our psyche. And, as I have said, for very good, beneficial reasons. But we must not entirely disengage ourselves from thought and critical analysis of these thoughts, because like with all things there must be a beautiful and harmonious balance between everything. Whether you believe those concepts to be karma or physics or just common sense, things must be generally in some form of a balanced harmony, in the world in general and in our personal, internalized worlds.

People often believe that life is determined by some predetermined series of events, whether it be fate or destiny. But I believe life is much different. I believe that our lives have the potential of an infinite amount of potential scenarios or courses; however, we may only be able to recognize or see only an infinitesimal few. It's almost like Gaussian points stretched out across a free field, a giant net spanning out like a lattice over time. There are many courses to take, some parallel, most being completely arbitrary. But that is the view of life I have adopted, and it has enabled me to believe that I have the ability to take control of the reins and make the choice of sending my life along the general course I think seems fit. Capricious events on both cosmic and insignificant scales are perpetually occurring, so it makes it hard to be delusional enough to believe in entire control. However, we have the ability to do what we want to do, most of the time at least, and surround ourselves with the things we love dearly and find meaning in, and, to me, I believe that that is more than enough. Despite the whirlwind of misery and boredom and discontent that circulates around our lives and often gesticulates to beckon us into oblivion, I can control my internal cosmos and a small portion of the external world that gets flooded with the light of my inner being. And from that, I have found utter contentment, love, and happiness.

But even I can only believe this to a certain extent. It seems to me that there is so much that is part of our world, our universe that is massively unexplainable, and I believe it will always stay that way. We have produced hypotheses to answer the questions of 'how?' But we are often too afraid to admit that we will often never know the most important answer of 'why?' The grand question, the unfathomable answer. To even the most realistic, rational mind, one has to admit the possibility of there being more, something much more powerful and beyond ourselves. The why.

And as I have stressed, I do not attempt to persuade or didactically teach. I am no teacher or educator. I am merely an observer and a listener and a learner. I only hope for people to become aware of their own internal abilities to think, and to question and to live. For truly, what else is there. Because when we learn to become fearless intellectual and emotional giants, what is there in life that could ever deter us from living. Nor am I suggesting that we live our entire lives as some sort of revolutionary or philosopher or anything else. Do not accept titles or roles that govern and bind; instead, accept yourself for exactly yourself. And at a certain point, a contentment begins to flow through the blood that reaches the heart and mind and all the appendages that is soothing and calming, but that soul of fire and courage and curiosity and intelligence will never fizzle out or fade away. It will remain and begin to guide your life automatically and yield beautiful results.

For me, my pilgrimage was not across expanses of vast oceans or lands or deserts. It was an excursion and journey through the plains and fields of myself, my mind, my being, and all of those things combined that influence the view flooding in through my eyes from the world around me. And with any journey, there were patches where I had to travel through the darkest of nights, and some of the most painful and deterring aspects, ideas and objects revealed themselves to me and made me not want to continue on, but nonetheless I continued on and I still continue on. Because I also found fields of the most beautiful wildflowers and orchards of the most delicious apples, and I have had revelatory moments of love and connections with some of the most incredible people and souls that have ever blessed this beautiful world. And of all the bad that can ever happen or exist, the good will perpetually outweigh it all. It will rise about and up and grow wildly against everything forever and always. And for those reasons, I will continue to live and continue to love with my entire being for my entire existence.

And the same events and time of my life that I was sure were going to push me over the edge of a precipice into having a complete and utter mental breakdown were actually the most transformational and enlightening moments of my existence, because to explore the dark and the depths of life and the self and then rise up from it all back into the light is one of the most incredible experiences that can ever be had. And for it to happen to the soul of such a simple and common person like myself, I believe that it has the capabilities of changing and transforming others and altering the world and humanity for the better, if only their souls were courageous enough to believe and hope and love and, ultimately, live.

As much as I have stressed the solipsistic lifestyle, it can only be fulfilling and rewarding for such a brief period of time. The self is a beautiful thing that must be nourished and delicately taken care of; however, it is something that often feels barren or filled with holes or hollow or empty when surrounded only by itself. As social creatures, we must be surrounded with friends and loved ones. And deep in the soul of all of us, we desperately desire throughout our entire lives the connection and support and acceptance and love of another soul. And in our entire lives, above all the other achievements and incredible experiences, the most astounding, rewarding thing to ever happen to a person is to have their soul align perfectly with another person's soul. In both ideas and beliefs, and in that unspoken, indefinable component of love that only lovers know and understand, everything aligns as beautifully as the symmetrical aura of a flower, like a Fibonacci sequence in nature. Astounding. And I had found that and experienced that in my life, and I couldn't have been more content and happy. When love fills your soul and your entire being, regardless of the highs and lows, you continue to soar above everything in reality and you continue to overflow with complete courage and beauty.

Besides, when we reach the end of our lives, we only vaguely remember some of our greatest accomplishments. More importantly, we remember the lives we lived, the lives we shared with our true love. The one we loved enough to let into our life in the first place. The one we loved enough to share our brief, beautiful existence.

At the end of *Origin of Species,* Darwin concludes that "there is grandeur in this view of life, with its several powers, having been originally breathed by the Creator into a few forms or into one; and that, whilst this planet has gone circling on according to the fixed law of gravity, from so simple a beginning endless forms most beautiful and most wonderful have been, and are being, evolved." And it is beautiful in its own right that one person's unique, visionary view of the world can alter all of humanity's view of the world. And I have no use in what I am saying now for the context in which Darwin was speaking of evolution, even though, I believe he was also broadly speaking of the world and humanity. I apply it to a newer context of the broader sense. That hidden from our view, all the things that our eyes are incapable of seeing or perceiving, there are miraculous things happening. We should not aim to live our lives blindly, but there is also so much we can never have any hopes of seeing or understanding. Hidden from the view of our eyes can be also the most beautiful and wonderful roots of love, anchoring themselves deeply into tough soil and sprouting and spreading out in the world and in the hearts and souls of everyone. And it is in that way that most of the world works, out of our sight or viewing capabilities and far beyond our ability to understand. And as strongly as I believe in questioning most things, some things are better to be simply appreciated for their existence at all. Hidden in another realm or dimension, the sown seeds of love are watered and nourished and grow rapidly and amazingly into and throughout our lives, leaving us mostly in awe in a world full of so much mystery and confusion, stretching its beautiful boughs out for all to see and believe in, and reminding us that there's always a reason to live.

~~~

We had crossed the borderline that separated the spring from the summer, and everything was now beautifully in full bloom. The birds flapped their wings and sang in the thick foliage of the trees, and the wind hummed as it blew across the sky above us.

Lilly and I lay in the grass of Schenley park, our backs against the prickly green, our heads towards the blue sky, watching the white, familiar shapes of clouds swimming past our eyes, and our hands tightly interlocked. I watched the orange sun slipping down upon the horizon. I felt so beautifully content for one of the first times in my life, regardless of being so uncertain about what the future could possibly hold. I had begun to just believe and accept all that would happen, believing that some of it was completely out of my power but some of the most important aspects were in my control.

Those past months with Lilly had been so beautiful and amazing and mostly unexplainable, and over the past year, so much of my life had been shaken into crumbled ruins, but I was able to build an even more beautiful structure out of those pieces and scraps.

I knew that since the semester was over, reality was quickly setting in. I had another year of school left, and I had no idea where it would take me or what I would possibly end up doing, and I knew deep down that it was entirely futile to try to plan or believe something so concrete would be what actually unfolded. Things just happened. With something that far in the future, I knew I would just go with the flow. There were some things that we simply cannot force. We just have to leave our hearts open and hope for the best, regardless of the fear of pain.

But I knew that Lilly was graduating and would not be coming back next semester. She would be moving back home to Massachusetts soon, staying there with her parents, while she looked for a job. I knew there would be a massive distance between us, but I believed that that couldn't corrupt the closeness, the connection that was between us spiritually. However, as uncertain as the future may be, I had faith and a belief in those fine threads of the world that connected everything, and I believed that everything would follow some seemingly arbitrary course. I knew that things wouldn't naturally unfold or follow some course, but I knew that whatever happened, we would adapt and make things work. Maybe there *were* secret, hidden forces at work that we will never understand. Synchronicity. The workings of some mechanistic universe.

The grass tickled my back, and I leaned over and locked my lips against Lilly's. I was caught up in the present, and that's where I wanted to remain. The future would eventually come, and I had no intentions of rushing it. I believed that all would remain steady, and in the moments where it changed or shook, I would grasp it and calm it or calm myself.

We hadn't talked much about the approaching situation, but it seemed that there was a general, mutual understanding about it, between us. Everything would be fine. Everything would be okay.

For now, I lurked in the present, both cautiously frightened of and eagerly in love with the future.

I just held her hand in mine, with her head on my chest, and I watched the clouds moving swiftly across the blue summer sky.